I0764413

Also by John Fraser
and published by
AESOP Modern Fiction:

Animal Tales
The Answer
Black Masks
Blue Light / Starting Over
The Case
Down from the Stars
Enterprising Women
Happy Always
Hard Places
An Illusion of Sun
The Magnificent Wurlitzer
Medusa
Military Roads
The Observatory
The Other Shore
The Red Bird
The Red Tank
Runners
'S'
Short Lives
Sisters
Soft Landing
The Storm
Thirty Years
Three Beauties
Tomorrow the Victory
Wayfaring

PEOPLE YOU W
NEVER MEET

PEOPLE YOU WILL NEVER MEET

John Fraser

AESOP Modern Fiction
Oxford

AESOP Modern Fiction
An imprint of AESOP Publications
Martin Noble Editorial / AESOP
28a Abberbury Road, Oxford OX4 4ES, UK
www.aesopbooks.com

First edition published by AESOP Publications
Copyright (c) 2019 John Fraser

www.johnfraserfiction.com

The right of John Fraser to be identified as the author of this work
has been asserted in accordance with sections 77 and 78
of the copyright designs and Patents Act 1988.

A catalogue record of this book is
available from the British Library.

First edition 2019, revised 2024

Condition of sale:
This book is sold subject to the condition that it shall not, by way of
trade or otherwise, be lent, sold or hired out or otherwise circulated
in any form of binding or cover other than that in which it is
published and without a similar condition including this condition
being imposed on the subsequent purchaser.

ISBN: 978-1-910301-53-1

CONTENTS

1	What You Are	7
2	My Country	67
3	More People You Will Never Meet, But Who Know Everything	115

1

WHAT YOU ARE

'THERE'S what you are. There's what you think you are. There's necessarily a context, a shell, holding those two together.'

'I know about psychology,' Adnan says. 'Don't try it out on me. Besides – a shell you leave behind. It's held you, mind and body, till your time is up. You're free then – watch out for the hawks.'

We perch, and amid the olive trees far off the olive figures do what they've been trained to do. He holds his rifle casual...

'It's not a rifle,' Adnan says. 'It's the stick I use to keep the dogs from off the sheep. A rifle – and they shoot you – a stick, you'll just be beat.'

'We know it's an injustice,' I say. 'Why bother with the words? "We were here first?", "God told us to", "We're pure and you are dirty foxes" – why not just say, "All true. Everyone's unjust. It's innate. Rights? More antique words. Be realistic. Treat everybody bad." So what? Where lies the difference?'

'That's what they say already. You're right,' he says. 'If everybody says "We are unjust" – what is the difference?'

Adnan's my friend, but on the other side there's sex and sitting down on chairs.

I'm on holiday – I can pass over to the other side.

*

When I've gone, Adnan tells his friend Bukayr, named after the dumb poet, al-Harith: 'I told my friend our tale. We're our grandfathers' unborn sons. Those over there – they're ghosts. Ghosts have to modernise of course, work the locks, make dumb calls on the phone, and push us down the stairs... Ghosts, Bukayr, malicious imps that multiply like roots that do not copulate – you split them: autogenesis. That's them defined, and what they all believe in too, that before the humans, there were ghosts – before the beginning, after the end. It's logical.'

'Experience,' Bukayr says. 'So long as no history creeps in – it's an ephemeral good or bad. When it's over, there's no hurt. It's lodged there for the telling.'

'I could get out,' Adnan says, 'If I was a rasta. Convert, be unlike anything dreaded – just wear the dreadlocks, then once out – become a renegade. Renounce it all: maybe you keep the rhythm and the songs.'

'You could be a troll,' says Bukayr. 'Sit and yawn beneath the tree of life, until it all goes down, the humans die, the sun – black rock... I think God sits and sculpts the little birds, with a watchmaker's glass screwed in His eye, screws in their eyes. Maybe He thinks of sex, spills a few stars. It's only important, sex, if you aren't getting it, and someone's locked its door.

'Birds – do they have free will, Adnan?' he asks. 'It seems it's moot. Once you wind up the humans, set them to scurry round – there's not much left for You to do. Birds too – each with its tune, its map, finding an empty shelf, interleaved between the other tiny tunes and appetites... How'll they do in snow? Without a drink? It must be fascinating, worth a million years of observation. Nothing more's required, no new models, colours ... the humans tag, compute them...'

'The best part, Bukayr,' Adnan says, 'is – they fly. Maybe there's a number on their leg, but from the ground, it is unreadable. No document, you fly along the coasts, the rivers – threaded together, a cape of beads ... going home. Going to your other home.'

'That's riches.' Bukayr says: 'Having palaces, Summer and Winter. We, though, are just God's Slaves – the birds don't have revolutionaries, nor cages. We Slaves – sit in the cellar and await the summons, that tolling bell. Maybe God has a bird – would He keep it in a cage? Dove or raven? If it flies – what explorations, in those unwatered interstellar spaces, unmeasured black! Bird of wisdom, bird of death?'

'We're bound to stay,' says Adnan. 'This is our place.'

*

Billions of jerked-off stars, thinks Bukayr: each with a wriggling coil of life that seeks a conjugation before it sputters out. If stars could mate – there'd be a billion gods and goddesses, creatures like in star maps – the lion and the giraffe – each one in space too wide for any voice or bellow to carry to another... Eternal isolation – each one alone and powerful, without a realm. Terrible creatures! Stuck up there in oceans of the dark. Can't get down. Or up. All points of flying spume, froth on a shoreless tide – away, away, 'I'll make new space for you, on, on!' Ask not why – pointless expansion, for ever, emptiness that fills the empty minds.

When there's tension, maybe there'll be war? A bigger war than now? What would you want – not to go backwards, that's for sure – there's going to be war! After? See if the war sorted things out? Maybe another war? – it's inevitable, there's been so many, it's never final. Maybe it's not the worst thing anyway...What is? Losing? A bad peace? Living in someone else's space? Deaths, expropriation – seeing the sheds burn and the animals inside? Just not surviving? That, you wouldn't know.

BELGIUM

'Here's resurrections', Adnan says. 'Anticipated, deferred. In the mass. Inflated angels, like old Michelin men, flying up to destinies anew, the land of dreams.'

'I've always had a soft spot for here,' says Bukayr. 'Belgium. Bruges la morte. You can live on *frites* and prosper. *Chiens chauds* too.'

'I always thought I'd drive the truck,' says Adnan. 'Maybe this is more class, lounging in the back. Off to pick cabbages. Here, we feel wanted, here we feel free. So few of us can run like us – either we're loyal to way back home, or else we mostly can't get out. It's both the same.

'Everybody here is strange, a stranger; we're the strangest. We're no threat, we ran. That's good – there's different faces everywhere, but there's resemblance – a dumbshow, apes expressionless. Us monkeys herded, stood on walls and jeered at: and here – look! there's ferris wheels. Resurrections, Bukayr – that is the speciality – and *frites*.'

'Cabbages,' says Bukayr, 'the hopalongs, the other leg blown off. Then peas. Peas in the north, cabbages down here – each with a non-communicating language. It's all like home – except the two states here are intertwined like vines, one black grape and one white. It's paradise, Adnan – two peoples going nowhere on one passport. Who imagined that with death, things would be so simple? You pass over, lift the curtain, die as what you were, and are reborn. In procession, into Ostend...'

'No offence, Bukayr,' says Adnan. 'But – go away! Separate! Two of us, young males: there'd be suspicion of our potency... To you – the peas. To me – the cabbages.

'View the locals through your poetry, in night vision, watching spectacles: fans red, purple, orange – waving their arms. When they don't speak, they're like my cabbages, your peas. Remember the song at the *Cigale*: "Fuck the pain away", she sang. That's good advice. She was Belgian too, I guess. Go do your act, Bukayr – make it a solo, wave your arms, and all the rest. Don't try puffing out poetry, not yours. See, out beyond your shaky light – the people. The dark unknown, for us, the new. Standing and shuffling, like crows or Girondins. Anything can happen, here or anywhere. My brother – farewell! Nevermore be seen together – our fetters separated, off we run again.'

And so – they part. So much for brotherhood. Adnan is right – two of you's a threat – away you go, Bukayr! Your dirty images – they'd better go off with you! All the worse for you, if they are sharp and true.

I

The Arab lands! The riches! I need to find the terra cotta cities. The ceramic towns – they're all in fragments. Passing through, a desert, then another one – then, something ran out. My document, the cash. It all became a desolation. I was lost.

I can always find my friend Adnan, of course. I prefer Bukayr. Adnan is hard. But there he'll be, intent, in the furrow, among the other cabbage-cutters brown and grey; doubled like a prisoner of war – the true soldier, impotent, bent over. His legs trudge in slow march, the eyes downcast have nothing but greenstuff in their sights. You're safe, a prisoner – if you go back, you're a deserter, naturally. The knife they give to cut – you hand it back at twilight, handle first, the point is broken off. It's pretty blunt.

Of course, Adnan is my friend, who I don't much like; Bukayr is Adnan's friend, not mine.

Don't exaggerate – there's no house of the dead, not where they are, not where they came from: no one's Lvov, no Babi Yar, not quite, not yet. Those cabbages – they live, give life! Freedom, dear freedom!

A house of the living dead – that's possible.

*

'I'm taking ship,' I tell Adnan. 'This is the world's most trafficked port. "Taking ship" means that while you're in it, it is yours. It would be the same with any floating thing – logs, or coracles.'

'Don't worry,' Adnan says. 'I'll say farewell, but ships – many return. And so will you. Don't be anxious – I have seen the world's end. It's nothing special. Where Bukayr killed his little brother – he tipped him, down the crevasse he went. You'd feel regret, of course, but without intent, you don't feel guilty, or responsible. Accidents – they're everywhere – drought, famine, massacres. No one set out to do them, probably. Part of the sadness of the world. As for the end – down there, they'd ploughed the earth – it was a porridge, maybe a cream caramel, ready for some stuff they'd build on it. That's what it will all look like, my friend. As I say – it's nothing special.'

'That's terrible,' I say. 'Bukayr. His little brother? He seems so creative. Maybe it's worse without intent. You don't know if it's what you want, or what you'll miss, or be happy for... The end of everything – it comes with ploughs, explosives too – the monochrome. The waiting, for it all to start again, from hovels on to happy families ... and back again.'

We're silent, probably thinking about far-off things. 'Maybe the end of the world is pinkish,' I say. 'Like the Greek stuff everybody eats...'

'No, you cretin,' Adnan says. 'It's not edible. Obviously. It's rubbish, primal mud.'

'I'll be back,' I say. 'I'm young, I'll spend all the money I was left, then I can start again – like you, Adnan.'

'No,' he says, 'nothing like. You're not holy. Ravens will feed me. Everyone's a prophet, but I'm the best. You, my friend, you're a blown egg, before you start to roll.'

'I'm going to Brazil,' I say. 'I expect. It's the closest place to anywhere – there's a huge lump of land, sticks out. It catches you, so you don't drift south into the ice. It's caught people down the centuries. Then I'll come back, and tell you what I think.'

'Yes,' Adnan says, 'you've the right turn – "take ship", "down the centuries". You're already finding the melodic path – go a step ahead today, they'll laugh at how quaint you are tomorrow.'

We look at an old cat in the street – it seems rheumatic, its back legs drag, like Groucho Marx walking in a silent piece: 'Identity,' says Adnan, 'religion – all a ploy. Don't get caught up – it's politics, by guys you wouldn't spend a moment talking to. Ignorant. Besides – identity, ID. You need it, but what's the D stand for?'

'You're right, Adnan,' I say. 'Being right, though – where'd you get with it?'

'That's right too,' he says. 'Bukayr rails against a god that defies belief. God rails against God – that stupid plan for impotence. As if He could do better if He tried! Politics? Nothing I might want – and once you have the taste for kicking naked men in cells – you won't desist. No, my friend,' he tells me. 'Cabbages. That's for me – the clean slice for now.'

'At least,' I say. 'The running's over.'

'No,' he says. 'It's never over. You must run. In the end, it's everybody, running. Maybe you'll come back, running still. Look in time for life that suits. Fraternity – it isn't in our nature. The sorority, at first, perhaps... Humans prefer to battle. Victory gives satisfaction, moving on. It's always best to win. You must be ready for a scamper.'

*

My ship – the captain's Slovak – we all eat with him – he doesn't dress.

You have to make some conversation: 'Travel,' I say. 'It should be free.'

'Nonsense,' he says. 'And are you crew or steerage?'

'Oh,' I say, 'I help around. No one's asked me yet to pay. But – think! Schools are free – you resist, learn as little as you can. Travel is different – you're a fish. You swim. You grow.'

'Rubbish!' he shouts. 'Someone must pay!'

'Who pays,' I ask. 'That there are rich and poor? Why – it's the poor who pay! It isn't right, it isn't logical.'

He sees a mutiny ahead. The matelots don't speak – maybe they don't understand our languages, but they are perking up.

'The sailors must be paid!' the captain says. 'You smartass tourists, swanning round! Who pays the crew?'

'The rich, the shorebound parasites,' I say.

'Well,' says the captain. 'Here you are! You have arrived. You get off here. This here is where the path begins.'

We're at a kind of spit. 'No, no,' I say, 'it's not Brazil!'

'Maybe not quite,' he says, pushing me off, into the small waves. 'Brazil started here. Free travel has no destination set and orderly. It is the thing in itself, you see.'

It's Senegal, and hot. My papers? – still on board, and off he goes. The trip is free, but perilous, and I speak Flemish, not a word of French.

The people are magnificent. My guide says there's 'abundance of cows, horses, asses' – production here of millet, too. For the market in canaries, surely – and the pilot takes me back, an old mail plane, teaches me to speak fine French as we go low, over squared-off camps, tracks confident and camels prospering...

*

'So,' says Adnan, 'your French is quite as good as mine. I see you've decided everything needs starting over – remember, though, the prohibition, Nansen passports, colonial levies ... mail planes precarious...'

'I'd not know where to begin a better route to where we are,' I say. 'Our pasts are never over, entwined in us, a dementia – howling in the night, incontinence to come. That is our destiny, Adnan – the species! That's our tool, our thumb, the face-paint that we have. Recognising brothers and not eating them...raising the cubs...'

'I don't do cabbages,' he says, irritated. 'No more. Now, I'm a packer. I put things in crates...'

'What things?' I ask.

'Wrong question,' Adnan says. 'It's the boxes that concern me. It is useful work...'

'I'm sure you'll leave it far behind,' I say, unsure. 'It's like my documents. Adnan – my identity is lost, somewhere sea-tossed or in a hold...'

'Oh,' Adnan says, 'for certain someone else will take it on. A photo with a different shade or colour, some religion scribbled on... Your sacrifice makes someone else's life anew. We should all do that ... and swap around. There – that's the message of hope. The philosopher says "every life that ends, ends as a failure". What will you do till yours?'

'Documents, Adnan,' I say.

'I don't know criminals,' he says, offended. 'Except for you.'

'It's normal,' I say. 'If you have forged papers, you'll join the outfit making them. Otherwise – they might tell on you...'

'Crimes that improve the world?' says Adnan. 'There's plenty – the claims are even more... I told you – you must prepare to run. The papers are all genuine – it's you that's not. Bukayr had his stolen – you won't be him, but nor will he.'

So, I'm now Bukayr, not him, not me, of course.

'You fit,' says Adnan. 'Your photo. That time in Senegal – your shade's much darker now. Of course, it's not the Bukayr that you know – it's just a nickname anyway. The dumb poet! Awkward scansions, before we were even born...'

'I remember – how apt!' I chant, *'sans mâts, ni fertiles îlots... Mais, o mon coeur, entends le chant des matelots*.' Of course, they couldn't sing – they had no common language, no words. Theirs was to keep the ship straight on. They said they'd seen and known enough. For them, the universe was waves, grey, unforgiving, endless. It's water's universal language, going 'a' and 'oh', undrinkable, waves like a drum, a heartbeat of some creature infinitely slow, and dumb. Even the universe has a buzz, a hum, no ears to hear it, but out goes the ground note, like ripples moving outwards from the oars.'

'We're modest subjects,' Adnan says. 'We two. But our sound – it's not as modest as all that.'

'Oh,' I say, laughing, 'I can be a spiritual – I was a spirit, flying from Dakar. But – these nations, looking for ideas that fire guys up: – religion... What's mine's never yours. God with us. No belief, except in their own selves. There's been so many injustices – what's a few more matter? That's what they think. They're going near the precipice, Adnan. They fear the void, but think they can fly, grapple, grab an enemy, glide safely down.'

'Well,' Adnan says, 'what will you do? They'll drag us with them – we're numbered, they know what we do and where we sit and watch them on our screens. It's history, my friend – we're old dead branches, dry and hard: – sharpen the saw! On from all sides – everyone is right. There's no other way. You need the heat, the crackle. You can't leave things as they are, and you can't go back and start again.'

'Cash, Adnan. Better they stick with that,' I say. 'As for me – "think rich, live poor" – that's how I live.'

'You've no money,' says Adnan. 'That's how – why it's the best. Now we must live like everybody else – precarious. My codes, the book of precepts – that's no help. It counsels resignation, trust. No word about the banks. What they call religion – all it says is – no booze, no partying, no dancing naked in your tent.' He sighs. 'I might write a book myself. I have the inspiration. What it needs is marketing.'

'That's shaky ground, Adnan,' I say. 'Your inspiration – does it come from God?'

'Where else?' he asks. 'From somewhere, that's for sure, outside. It's not there when I go to bed, and when I wake, it's there, shining like an eggplant, enfolded like a cabbage, intricate as broccoli.'

'I know,' I say. 'It's politics. Baking the bread and cutting up the goats – that comes in too, and dynamite, and doing maths. But – if it started off as poetry, romancing round the fire – it turns to politics. Squaddies, Adnan. I remember – that crusade: they killed the emperor's pet lion. They trashed his zoo, Adnan! What a crap idea! – and where's that lion's soul? What does it do all day, if somewhere it's around, seeking its lovely corpse, its tears like pearls...'

'I cannot help you there, my friend,' he says. 'Maybe my book will give you some idea.'

'Be very very prudent, Adnan. A guy's first book – it may be flawed, it might even be the last,' I say. 'Now – the truth. Where'd you stand on that?'

'It's a trick question,' Adnan says, put out. 'I'm not sure how big that one should figure in. In truth, in fact – it hadn't crossed my mind. As another emperor said – "*On s'engage, et puis...*"'

'Those emperors!' I say. 'When you're in Senegal – empire, republic – it all comes much the same. It's all been tried.'

'Go rent a suit,' he says to me. 'They'll take you in a bank.'

What do you suggest? New frontiers, hoping you'll end up where you want? Big powers deciding? A conference?

I worked the desk for Senegal. Adnan says – 'Those banks – they speculate. They are not clean. They bet.'

'I'll rent an apron, Adnan, and resign... There's a florist down the street,' I say. 'But – all the flowers are dead. They're bright – but all the plants ... their roots are boiled. Or else we'd have a garden in eternity...'

'Eternity is gestured to with wreaths,' says Adnan. 'Those flowers are dead as well ... maybe it's a comfort, or else – maybe that business isn't you, my friend.'

'The book, Adnan,' I say. 'In manuscript – maybe it's more secure. A secret history of everything, a blueprint for the rest...'

Christ in procession through Ostend – now, that's an afternoon you wouldn't want to miss. And Adnan – what's his stance on wings and horns, tails and pitchforks? 'I'd suggest,' I say, 'a kind of Totentanz, a joyful rumble – the deadly sins, the whore of Babylon, the flying donkey – strong men and shooting galleries, clowns, elephants...'

'No,' he says, 'you must have gravity. Throughout the universe, it's there, like aluminium or anthracite: – dig! – it's there. It holds it all together, stops the lot from float and fall. Even if – there's all the rest. The dark dense mass, cocking its invisible snook at all the straights...'

'That,' I say, 'is the drag. Everything is held in place – and yet … what we can see, it moves, there is a tide receding in the dark, that leaves the shores unlit, deserted, the lightships stand amidst the sand, grounded and peeling. We're styrofoam, packing, dead we lift and fall upon the pulse.'

'You,' he says, twisting my ear, 'you look for lightness – but it's kitsch: pictures in museums, shows, spectacles, tumbling, jousting, stuff forgotten as it trundles past...'

'A book is worse,' I say. 'It's all been doctored. A mirror with no image. It's false, Adnan, right from the start – it's writing, and the writer's trapped, a bald porcupine behind its single quill...'

'You're right,' he says, 'no book. No truth that's scribbles on a skin. The life that's lived, that alone has weight. Life constant in the flux, a salmon, or a shark, twisting, luxuriating. Eats. And disappears.'

We walk around – everywhere, it's ruins. The mines, tracks, bricks – all red and black and gone from use. Colossi, statues disarmed, denosed; the bones of lions fed to the dogs.

'It's a Senegal,' I say, 'where the slaves came from, where they waited to take ship: this is where the workers were. The class, we expected much from it – it's gone. Never accomplished anything—'

'Except its disappearance,' Adnan finishes. 'The communists – showing willing, trying to block the darkness out, failing, letting go the rock, into the waves... See what the books brought forth. What mattered instead was every kind of dead stuff: dead merchandise, dead labour, stored up in your bank.'

'They say those women wrote the Manifesto,' I say. 'But what to do against those empires? Senegal's was gone – but, Adnan, which is best, least worse, the Russian, built on sand and taiga, or the American, built on air?'

'It's a poor choice,' says Adnan. 'Maybe the Persians were the best. Though Bukayr – he would disagree. The Russian's more exotic – easier to shuffle bodies underneath the sand, raise no memorials to best and second best. No apologies – I think that's rather better.'

It's quite inconclusive. Maybe not worth the time. Take history out of everything – they say you're left with science. That means climbing in the tiny globe and have them light the fuse and blast you off – out, away from everything... Oh no! There's the goddam telephone, it rings, things you have to do, out there in nothing, but the voice insists. It's their mission you are on...

'You must die somewhere,' Adnan says, 'sometime. Better consider where. That's what we all must do. Perhaps the how. That religious stuff – it has no strategy for this. It's always politics, my friend, quite unpredictable. Prepare for what is next, what's unforeseeable.'

'What I need,' I say, 'is somewhere with a holy city, and, opposite, one profane, where I could feel at home.'

'Rome!' says Adnan. 'Up here, they're busy with their colonies, inside and out, the bodies that the wind uncovers, and they have to tamp them down, then up they rise again, like poisoned cabbages... Italians now, their sins are on a programme that they never watch. The people there – the ones you'll see, they all come from somewhere else and don't know where next they'll go.'

'You're right, Adnan,' I say. 'The other holy cities have been knocked down – now, the profane ones too. You're right, Adnan – it's only politics – and Rome is on the way to somewhere else, Africa, Asia. There's nowhere else for me. The originals, they went to America, founded new countries there, Argentina, Philadelphia – cities and states, that's where the old Italians went, and left the cities where they once lived empty, dust-blown, the golden statues depricked and stupid, gazing on their distance; the ostriches and cameleopards – too bulky for a paper suitcase, left wandering...'

I have some doubts. 'What shall I do there, Adnan, while I plan and contemplate my death?'

'You'll ask people to give you work,' he says. 'Cultured, regretful people. They'll turn you down, away. You must be humble.'

'The holy city?' I ask. 'That's a place of humility, for sure.'

'Your take is trite,' says Adnan. 'The holy city's not there to find you work. Belief? Obedience? Those wouldn't be your thing. Your disbelief in everything except sensation – it's no help. You need to have belief secured – then take your chances as a postulant. I know, I make it sound banal, the whole experience. Maybe you should try out somewhere else. Forget the holy city – as they say, unless you carry it with you in your heart – you will not find it: the roads lead outwards, and you'll find they don't return.'

'I'm a reindeer, Adnan,' I say. 'I like seeing people run – I know what to do. Join them and run. You're still yourself, even when you're in a herd. They don't stop if you fall down. That's good – they mustn't stop. But ... I wonder: in Rome's profane city, they don't speed – they crawl away. They don't look back – they curse as they inch on...'

'I've had all that,' says Adnan. 'Escaping from nothing, nowhere. Deserting from no army. But you still cry for what you've lost. It's good. It shows it's gone for ever, won't come back, and nor will you. Your city? All that's left behind is crooks and cripples – oh, and bones.'

'Yes,' I say. 'Bones. In holy city, they've collected them for years – there's undergrounds, alleys lined with little bunks, the skeletons grin out, they're comfy, death has come and left them with a richness: their ossatures, they must be worth like gold. They're livelier than live – for sure, by night they hop down, you could hear them with their click and clack, no! – it's not the roofbeams settling – doing some miracles, forcing the locks and taking worldly goods, polishing and swatting – no rust, no moths. They leave a smell of camphor and of kerosene. It's quite unique, Adnan, and holy too. But of course – they don't consume. They don't make work, and don't raise sheep, or anything. All that's left – it seems to me, it's being dumb, like Bukayr the original. Dumb poetry!'

'Russia'd be good for you,' says Adnan. 'They're all reindeer there; methane and meat – the animals are dead, long gone, but everybody has to run instead.'

*

Adnan, Bukayr and I – our problem is, we're moderates, we love ourselves. We'd like extreme results. It will not happen. More love. More disappointment. Others will suffer more, much more.

*

I write to Adnan. 'Rome's a bucket, Adnan,' I tell him. 'It's like that Russian spaceship in the movie, that's made its trip, and now it flakes and rusts, a husk. It's flown, and finished. A piece of universe, expanded fully, and inert.'

'Yes, yes,' he says, 'that's what they say, everyone.'

'And,' I go on, 'what if, beneath those mountains, the experiment they do, that makes the earthquakes – suppose they make another universe? A football. Silvery perhaps. Its first day. Heavy beyond scales with all its future, bursting to be free and on its way...?'

'You're right,' he says. 'There's no way we could make space for it!' He laughs. 'Those guys in casual clothes who set it up – they'd be Creators: a new universe whose properties are quite unknown, expanding like squids' ink in a black sea... Maybe some people sprout, grown out from spores, quite like us, same tin roofs on shacks, the debts, the fears. The faith... You're right, my friend – Rome would be torn apart. That birth, deep in the magma! Another bang, a bigger one! The national leg – quite lacerated, flayed. New world – a buboe. And oh! the shakes! That dragon's egg! Run, run away! Of course, there'd be new priests aboard ... the size of jujubes.'

'It makes one sad, Adnan, to talk to you,' I say. 'You know so much... I need my ignorance restored...'

'Those guys, Creators,' Adnan says, 'you'd think they'd wear white coats – but no – they wear some shabby stuff, like us. The point is – unlike Big God, you can know them, and the object they have made. The Other. The new universe. The leaden football. But – I think you can't know both, Creator and Creation. Because, my friend,' and we're both trembling with the insight, as he says, 'They don't know what it is, that they have made. And so, they can't know what they themselves might be.'

'Yes, of course,' I say, 'the commode, the vase ... the sax, parure ... the carburettor, tap... What are they, without a context, evolution? New inarticulate concoctions. The Makers – in their dark, they tap and chisel, make a wonder: then it's useless. Bits of stuff. Unsold at auction.'

'Something like those,' he says. 'The new universe. Like that. Like them.'

MARINA

I'm lost. 'Never, never ever, get in a stranger's car,' Marina says. 'They'll take you for a whirl, you won't come back, know where you've been or where you are.'

'I got into your car, Marina,' I say. 'I told you I was lost.'

'The car – it isn't mine,' she says. 'It doesn't count. I'm not taking you anywhere. I've maps, that's all.'

There's rows of glistening statues. 'They're shone up every day,' Marina says. 'They're brass. You take the patina off, they glow for hours: no one suspects where the gold has gone.'

There's not much in her room: a *kora* – 'I'm not supposed to play,' she says. 'I try, of course. I find it quite insipid.'

She has maps, though. 'Now, she says, 'Where'd you want to go?'

'Oh,' I say, 'away from here.'

'Then you just leave,' she says. 'You don't need maps.'

'You must have someone here,' I say, nosing around. 'A *griot*. Someone who can play, and stop the river's flow with melody...'

'Curiosity dressed as flattery,' she says – 'Those rags won't fit!'

'No flattery,' I say. 'Just you, playing bad.'

'I'd like to live for art – I suppose that means dying for it. At least, dying with it,' says Marina. 'They had a little civil war here, and the Romans wanted neither side to win – just both to go away. It sounds real civil, but it's pitiful as well.'

'You should have a garden, Marina,' I say, 'even if it isn't yours. Like the motorcar.'

'Oh,' she says, 'I have a garden – here in this room. It's all set out. I need the plants, some ground to lodge them in.'

'It may not satisfy,' I say, 'if you don't do it better than you do the *kora.*'

'Your trouble is,' she says, cross-legged on the tattered couch, 'You want an interesting life. The battles – they'll go on around. Not interesting, not at all. It won't be interesting, because you're not. Your life won't be at all interesting – the interesting stuff is all around. You won't join in, for fear you'll be blown up or starve.'

'That's not a trouble, Marina,' I tell her, 'it's maybe a limitation.. Everyone needs something to tell, and some technique to tell it with... I observe. You do nothing well, Marina: nothing that's definite, conclusive.'

'Nothing,' she shouts. 'No substance. Not you, not the music, not the garden.'

'You need to make distinctions,' I say – she's very angry now: 'You must reason better. There's all the flowers, and then there's what they mean to you – paradise, Eden, what comes in your head: or worms and grubs... Music's the same – what you want to hear, what sounds you really make.'

'Fuck you and your dualism,' she shouts. 'No Cartesians here – we are in Rome! We are. Forget the think! I'll show you if you're only thought, or if your body makes decisions for your brain...'

'You're losing me, Marina...' I say.

She has a machete, must be kept behind her on the chesterfield...

'You're all one, just one, my friend,' she says, 'and only you know – knew – what you were.'

She stands, and waves the machete, one, two, three sweeps – 'Look!' she screams, 'death! Look no further. Here I am!' – and I'm back in the street, I'm lost, I run, I'm still lost, it makes no difference to your speed. 'Never come back,' she shouts. 'You're finished!'

Marina is right – the interesting life means what she says: I am all one, brain, body, what I am and what I think I am.

It's true, of course – never get in a stranger's car.

If you come from afar, though, to study philosophy, or you find the holy city wanting – you can understand the threat. People from everywhere, losing patience ... patience lost all round, may the best civilisation carry all.

Things – take them seriously.

Better a short intense relationship that ends in blood, than one that drags and limps.

Adnan's suffered too – the philosophy; 'what you think you are'; the threats – it all makes one. A garden, a ripple on the *kora,* a stranger – it makes no difference. They're all in the same spectrum, the same band.

Does she want a death, or just to scare?

*

Adnan tells Bukayr – 'Our friend – there's nothing to hold him now. He thinks he's an attraction – but no, he's exasperating. He'll end up bad, in nowhere; he's tumbling in his void.'

'He's quite like us,' says Bukayr. 'When at last you get to fighting, of course – you don't want to stop. There's so much in your head. What price? What if you don't win? No one will pay to have you stop. Ask the highest price – why not?'

'Oh, our friend,' says Adnan. 'He won't fight. Eternal war, that ends in the Eternal Peace – it's not for him. It's not for us, Bukayr. The rest have principles, they say. We have crap jobs, and being wise.'

They think of playing tric-trac – but no – one of them must win, it's prejudicial. Where might it end – the luck, the canniness? Carries you away, like salmon, – the salt, the ocean, – carries you back, the reckoning will come, even if you don't consume, just sit.

'There's some of us,' Adnan says, 'Remember the campaign – the Collateral... Something like that, with cash, somehow...'

'Oh no!' says Bukayr. 'You'll end in jail, or on TV ... there's tax, and retribution. Forget it, Adnan.'

'It's the liberal dream,' says Adnan. 'A revolution in the revolution. You can't forget, Bukayr.'

'Forget, Adnan – there's virtue being last in things. Humans! They're the last – there must be a prize ... relax, and wait,' Bukayr says. 'Consolation must come. It's not justice – it's another wake. Good fellowship hugging together on the raft. That picture, "Skaters on the ice" – there they are, tying on skates, and falling through ... the dogs that fight, Adnan ... the life, gone, frozen utterly. You weep. It's gone, the life's stuck coloured on a board. There's no word, Adnan, not a hoarding, not a flag, nothing written on the walls. Everybody knows – the ice will melt, and down the skaters go. No need to tie on skates and pick up speed – we all know the jingle for the seasons' change.'

'You're right, Bukayr,' says Adnan. 'What people make is complex – much more than the makers are, and when I describe these images – it's trite... The most we could achieve with the Campaign – is documents. A big one, behind glass. Then offices, and guys, and sheds – full of the necessary stuff.'

The bus they're on – it isn't full: 'I want to see the Flemish stuff from Castile,' says Adnan. 'There's Mongolian too – wisdom and compassion, that's what they learnt, Bukayr, after winning half the world or more. Metalwork as well – the School of Zanabazar...'

'It isn't so,' says Bukayr, much excited. 'Their act was done, and they were gone. The wisdom – a myth. Like all the rest – those empires: are their children wise? Survivors – are they compassionate? My, Adnan, you're a skin of oil upon a board! Aren't you afraid your surface will skate off, you'll wake one day, naked, yourself behind a glass, flowing, an ant-farm, a formicular – your blood running obedient here and there, the liver gross, a clod, trip up to the brain, a muscle twitching here, hmm – a bit of sex? – the gut churning hot dogs out the arse...'

'You're the devil, Bukayr,' Adnan says. 'A spoiler. Just fuck off the bus – I paid your ticket, and your time is up; goodbye. No art for you today, no artefacts! Time is distance, light – and you have none of those...you have expired. Your poetry – it is the dirty side, the face we turn down to the soil.'

He pushes Bukayr out the bus door.

His trip alone is not enjoyable.

The best answer's justice – all around to everyone who's there. But...

RIYA

'I hope you're not too quarrelsome, Adnan,' says Riya.

'You must be accustomed,' says Adnan. 'There was my dear friend, the cretin Bukayr, dumb poet to boot, a scuffed and leaky one... He provoked. Most people, statistically, are mostly wrong. You must bear with it, the consequences, Riya.'

'It's a bad start, for a campaign of peace,' says Riya.

'Oh,' Adnan says, 'the campaign's more complex than just peace. Listen – there are two great trends in politics, our geo. First, take the nationals, the middling states: – reactionary, tribal. By global standards – small. Identity, Riya: they get off on that. There's no such thing – we are mosaics, every group and every person's made of rubble from a different ruin in a different broken town. *Tessere,* scrambled in a crate, we are: marble, gold, glass, asbestos, tin – what comes to hand. And the image that results at best is arabesques. Strong men? – another fiction. Tinpots, Riya.

'Then – there's the other, the global scene. The bourgeois puff blown stormy. One world, one system, all is guaranteed: respect and commerce. Crime, punishment, refugees, pipelines and camps – starvation, drought as well. Illusion, Riya. The one world – it's no toffee apple! Behind the scene – it's competition, the clanging spheres of phantom empires. Constellations smouldering, black powders ready to explode.

'Think: there are the tectonic plates – and then there's little geysers. The massive – and the smarting boil.

'Now – there's little points where tribes contest, they touch, inflamed... That's where we first can make our impact...'

'I've seen all that,' says Riya. 'But phantom empires – they touch too. The rivers, the Amur ... they kiss indifferently. And – peace, Adnan. Why? It's the root of conflict. Resolution – in the name of what? Survival? In a world of mortals, their clockwork running down, it's fantasy. It's all stale and vain, Adnan. The world dances to the strongest will. And we are small, we are confused, Adnan...'

'And quarrelsome, Riya,' says Adnan. 'You haven't grasped... Peace means you have to bring the big guys in. Repression, Rita – that's what peace entails. There must be something more. I'm after what comes next. If "victory" grates – "fulfilment": that could be the word. Peace after peace – eternal: I've heard about it, somewhere...'

'It seems – sort of familiar,' Riya says, playing along.

'Where there is fascism, Riya, you must be a communist,' Adnan says. 'Our friends – are Kurds, Afghans, Syrians and Kazakhs, Armenians, the Alawis, piled up together in new Istanbul: – the ghosts who do the work at dawn and twilight. Turks too, of course. And so it is in every place: we – they – are the uncounted, unnumbered, uncensed, unshriven – we are the disbelievers, those without a home who'll never go back to their home, where they were unregistered, invisible – grey workers of the world, too poor to own their chains, illiterate in every language but our own, our alphabet written only on the walls, our songs inaudible.'

'I understand you now,' says Riya. 'We are everywhere, we are the grass, the leaves, we are the wind that drives the liners, generators, icebergs, pizzerias, crematoria...'

'Yes,' says Adnan, 'all of that, and more.'

'So,' says Riya, apprehensively, 'I'm to go everywhere and help...'

'Riya,' says Adnan, irritated, 'you said "help". I said "friends". There's thousands helping people, all inadequate. Our friends are living global lives, that's all – they have no home, no state, and no identity ... fluid beliefs, and work at anything, take exploitation with a smile. Deny that you exist! And that is it! That's where we start our watch – the sore points, and the human spores... For your travel, we've no cash. We're a committee, Riya, not a charity.'

'We must have members,' Riya says: 'The cash...'

'Must be sufficient,' Adnan says, 'but I'm a witness, not a boss. I'll have to ask Bukayr, after all, to join. He's turned into a sour billy-goat. Then there's my friend – he attracts the feisty ones: – maybe there's a use for some of those. He's a broken compass – stay away from him. Sparring with Slovak women though – it sharpens up your game.'

'Why me, Adnan?' asks Riya. 'Because I stood next to you on the tram?'

'Oh, I can see you've class,' says Adnan, not caring either way, the yes, the no. 'You don't have to lead a bunch of guys, or speak some language, ingratiate: ours will be a centre for research. You need the eye, that's all. Someone will try to use us, pay us bribes, and then we'll need define ourselves. The aim is – to find a crack, a crevice in the rock, and heave and thrust until it opens up... Then in we creep – like soldier ants... Tectonic plates: – survey, insert yourself, and shape the continents!'

'They'll give us cash,' says Riya, 'The powers. But we might have to go to jail.'

'You can go to jail for looking like you're throwing stones,' says Adnan. 'Having a trial, charged with subverting something – that would be classy too. Besides, down below here, our room – there's a kind of *balera*. It's not a dancing school: nothing is taught. You pay to go, you drink and dance what you already know, maybe your grannie taught you – and all day there's music, a group, that plays the rounds and dances of the world, your hamlet too. Quite René Clair. That will finance us, we'll have a room above the frolicking... Remember Brueghel – *Peasants Dancing in the Snow*? That's the image that I want. My land is eaten, Riya – what is left is pictures, colours ... all the rest is silent words and doorless keys.'

That's his idea. The building rocks: and Adnan buys a table and more chairs.

*

'This business of the tram,' says Adnan, stroking Riya's arm, 'I know it's not a civilised remark – but you're taller than those people who don't rise up here, who've just washed in on the tides...'

'My father was a banker,' Riya says, pulling away. 'In Siberia. My mother – she came from the other side. He was cut down. I stayed just like I am.'

'My friend,' Adnan goes on, thinking of me: 'He is a flaky sort. I don't want him – his daredevil contacts, though, attract... And Bukayr – he's become a culverin, a fiery mouth, who tries to shrivel you...'

'In between those plates,' says Riya, 'you would get crushed.'

'It's just a metaphor,' says Adnan. 'If you don't find space, you must stay just as you were—'

'Crushed,' Riya finishes for him.

'You said it, Riya,' Adnan says, 'but I don't give in. That's another thing I don't believe in: sacrifice. I'll take another tramride – someone must be interested in the future of the world.'

Riya nods – she doesn't believe.

'I'm dross, of course,' says Adnan, 'I didn't plan it so, but there it is. I'm a free spirit, though, and I'll drag you along with me, till you make your answer. We'll be the future, however hot and short it is.'

'Lush places,' Riya says. 'With fronds and felines – those are dust. But cool and musty places – they will thaw, and grass will tower above me.'

'That's the idea,' says Adnan: 'But land...hmmm. Attracting the wrong sort; being dug up, planted willy-nilly...'

'Something that moves, yes,' Riya says. 'That attracts. My father was a thief – he lost his money. You say yours was a general, who lost his wars. Mine ended up with nothing. After the fall, a bullet. Yours had goats. If you don't move, you will get hit. But if you move, you'll throw it all away...'

'No, Riya,' Adnan says, 'you throw it in the ring. The banker in my game – she circulates. You lose – the bank does not. The guys – they die for territory – it all goes on a map. They don't get to plant a bean... Be money, Riya – eternal, circulating ... like the bank.'

'Well,' she says. 'I'm happy here with Belgium. Diamonds and coal, Indians buying gold napoleons, the best old age, best horsemeat steaks, parks with sculptures rusting through the plaster ... people from nowhere in the golden squares...'

'Yes, yes,' says Adnan. 'Everywhere's like that, except the Mississippi and Siberia.'

'That's what I mean,' she says.

'Your father,' Adnan says, 'must have been stupid, or imprudent, to get taken out – he could have been of use to us...'

'I'd not have met you on the tram,' she says. 'Besides, he hated guys like you, and every cause that hurt his interests – especially your ambitions, Adnan, if you could set them out.'

'Then, better as we go,' says Adnan. 'We'll only have your name, no lineage. It's not worth much of course; and remember, you're nothing if you turn your coat...'

It's true – it's easy to sound pretentious. Russians have changed, since they were three Sisters.

'Hey,' say Adnan, 'that sounds like salsa – let's go down.' And so they do.

'Don't ever do that again,' says Riya afterwards to Adnan. 'You bunny-hugged me! Moreover, neither of us is a sentimental type, that's clear.'

*

'You're the type with principles, Adnan,' Bukayr says. 'You travel and recruit, I'll sit and think.'

'I'm a herder,' Adnan says. 'Goats or people. Everybody follows green.'

'The idea is fine,' says Bukayr. 'These tanks, the ones that think. They're like intelligent armaments – that'll be my thing. It's how spies get in touch with spies. No one cares what you think or why – pretension is all. Confidence carries it all off. You can be left or right. You don't need pretend you like anyone. The guys that pay you – give you your cash and secrets, secret lies as well. As for the academic stuff – copy it off your screens!'

'That isn't what I want,' says Adnan. 'Though I agree, it's interesting. It's not enough. I love horsemeat. It revolts me. You run faster, but... It's à rebours. What's to do? Cry on your dinner...?

'Here, we're open books. I'm not the open book you have to memorise, that makes you recognise a sin, or cause a massacre, lots of death, prisons, all that. I'm honest as a pane of glass, Bukayr, keeping out the flies, letting light in...'

'You're confused, Adnan,' Bukayr says. 'A state for the stateless? Nothing! Your horse's tale – now, there's a real contradiction hidden there. Wanting what's rejected you, what will send you to the front. Yes, that's the root of love, true love. But you could end up catching air. I'll know the future...'

'Air, Bukayr, more air,' says Adnan. 'So, why waste time hating me, Bukayr?' he asks. 'I'm your best friend.'

'It's a farther shore of love,' says Bukayr, 'I dare say.'

IRMA

Irma's an academic type, out of a job. I recommend her to Bukayr. That work's too static for my taste.

'Adventure?' she says. 'I know about those. Sleeping with someone you don't like, bumping and humping in some VW van. It's a formula. In the end, the job's not yours. Maybe you write a little piece, "The taste of fruit – the Chola poetic re-examined". My! what a keyhole on the empire – the ragas and the rajas, the epics and the swags, the juices and the courtesans...'

'It's vain, I know,' I say. 'But it's *your* vanity written up. Even death, who steals the lot, can't steal your little article... It's your secret, you and the Cholas, if ever you meet up...'

'Oh,' she says, 'I shall, I should. Beautiful people – who else will rise and inherit the earth?'

'Adnan would love you,' I say. 'Keep on like that.'

'I hope not,' Irma says. 'Beauty and love don't mix. Read the books. Now, for me – no diving, no climbing, no sleeping in trees.'

'It's not a movie, Irma,' I say. 'It's thinking in the tank. You're beautiful, Irma, and so lithe ... not for me, I fear.'

'If I wasn't beautiful,' says Irma, 'I'd not have got to university and learnt to read.'

'I'm rubbish, Irma,' I tell her. 'The Madam of every idea, and everyone – I'm just Ganymede – drink every drink, taste every dish... A Tiresias: a grope from everyone...'

'Yes,' says Irma. 'You bastard! You've written for yourself the part that everybody wants.'

'My little compensation,' I say. 'For all the fun I'll miss.'

'Well,' says Irma. 'Bukayr sounds dull. Rooms with chairs, a table. Forget it! Libraries – that's even worse. I want a squad, a red wedge, a flying intervention. Thought without action – that's *frottage*!'

'You're grand, Irma,' I say. 'I like people with no secret life.'

'I can't wait to liberate some nation,' Irma says. 'It's easier than they say. Doing the politics, that is – then they have to go on working all their lives.'

'You'd get on well with Adnan,' I say. 'The inspiration's Adnan's, the derision's from Bukayr, and you serve him.'

'The bossy guys,' says Irma, 'these Westerners that bomb the rest – the trouble is, they're strangers to democracy. They killed the kings – then it was factions. And that's it! Parties! I know a party when I go to one – these don't compute, my dear. It's fraud. Bands and gangs, that's all that counts! I'll help your friends steer through all that, you bet!'

'I'm not in all this,' I say. 'Adnan is free, though – maybe he'll liberate the people who have no tyrant over them, no state, no country, who don't fight unless they're paid or terrorised or both... Start them off again with all these things they haven't got...'

'Oh no!' says Irma. 'That's not the kind of liberty I want at all. It's just being clueless. Still, I can be the ant that eats up all the plans and makes a shining tower, termite city of them. Paper and spit – the strongest glue there is.'

We hug. 'Goodbye, Tiresias,' she says. 'You're the story that they tell around the fire, lit in the desert night and visible far off, from our next life, where we'll make starfall...'

'Go to, dear Irma: follow the sound of dancing, then go up the stair...' I say. 'The door is reinforced, it's steel, you have to wait awhile.'

Later, Bukayr tells me – 'Irma is full of death, but not her own: Riya's replete with life, but not her own. Perfect. We plan grand strategy: for certain, we shall try to spare you, but don't forget to run!'

It's his big joke.

*

'You don't look half Chinese, Riya,' Irma says. 'Look – I'm your friend. We must wait till they corrupt Bukayr – until they buy him, find he can be trusted, they're suspicious. We could be anything. Be an informer – then you're safe! Once they know he will do anything, we can be honest. Copy stuff, and sell it back to them. I can give you love, Riya, it's what you need...'

'You can't be half anything, Irma,' Riya says. 'My parents gave me love – I don't need any more. You can be big or small, not fractional. My father was too big – he kept bets, and then they hid me. In a place so dark, I couldn't see.'

'To protect you?' Irma asks. 'Or kidnap?'

'Oh, if you go to jail,' says Riya, 'that combines them both, of course. This wasn't prison, though. It was so dark, I still can't see so well. I love the dawn – it doesn't last – you must get used to that. You're free, but what is there to see? There's no one round – yet there's everyone, they're all around, but it's like prison. There's too much humanity in jail, how you long for solitude, a lock upon the door, no love, no stories, no confidences. A bulb on all the time. A jailer, a dumb ape, who once a day, brings in your food. Oh Irma, I'd like to have a monkey. To keep it in a room, right next to ours. They say if you don't love them, they will die. Does it prefer the light? The dark? We'll slip our souls in him, and that will be a reason he'll live, we'll poke his food in once a day, and hear him – scampering and weeping, shouting out his prayers...'

'Don't con me, Riya,' Irma says. 'It doesn't strike a note. Be strong, resist! Monkeys aren't like that. Maybe you think you'll have a fling – maybe with Bukayr, be taken on. Monkeys are quite indifferent to who you are, so long as they get bread and water, and you lock them in their cage.'

That sounds like techno, coming from below.

'Don't hurt me, Irma,' Riya says, trying not to cry. 'I'm so terrible at judging people – I thought you were my friend, we'd take a trip, perhaps Irkutsk – there's booths where they sell sugar mice, or you can shoot, sex doesn't matter, not a bit. There's a wheel – like it fell off somebody's giant bike – going nowhere, except to heaven.'

'Don't be fanciful, Riya,' Irma says. 'You don't need it, not with me.'

'It isn't really what I want,' says Riya. 'I'd hoped to get a little deeper into things. It's dark here still, but everything is plain –

you get me, Irma? You can feel the shapes, even your own – touch, don't tell. Irma, I don't think we shall get on. You're quite superficial, in a bossy kind of way. You'll suit here, suit Bukayr...'

You have to run – it's tough, you're lucky to be in the fields, someone has to pick the peas. You're safe – no one else is, but still...

'Now now,' says Bukayr laughing, 'You monkeys – plotting? Waste of time. Planning?'

'It isn't what we want,' says Riya.

'Nothing ever is,' Bukayr says. 'Watch those apes! You may feel affinity – but they have a project. The human age. A chronicle. They can't write or talk, of course – so they have no reputation. No one deciphers what they record – the short and noisy history of mankind, as seen from up a tree. The monkeys have no friends, no heaven that awaits. As for hell – black flames? Here, in the waiting room, while the angels seek your documents – it's dry. Your eyeballs shrivel like pistaccios. Your gonads blanche like Spanish haricots: the ceiling – pecorino chunks fall on your head. Your gut is full of grit and tar – a tract! A track? The road, the journey? But you sit quiet: "better" says one door, "worse" says the other. You've no piss, so "gents" and "ladies" makes no sense. You don't see who goes in which door, or what they've done – you blink – the room is empty, then it's full again, new young guys – waiting for all those virgins, possibly – and then those in-laws, oh! the dowries, what a fuss! That's the "worse": "better"'s just the flames.

'All that's what the monkeys say, my dears! You'll never hear them, your past – it has no voice. Their history's one of suffering too – you'll only know, if you look into their eyes... There's wisdom there that humans...'

'Well?' Irma asks, annoyed. 'Don't humans have wisdom? Aren't you one of them, Bukayr?'

'Oh,' Bukayr says. 'I've gone beyond all that. Everybody's wise, if they just sit and wait. White time. It's the kind that has no space, no distance, and no curve. It's what you have inside your head – the stubs, padlocks, retorts, reports: a goodly boxful – you can tip it on the floor, then scoop it back for later. Another rainy afternoon...'

*

To Bukayr – the future. To Adnan – the wretched. Empty handfuls – worth a celebration, a theme...

*

'Butterflies!' Adnan shouts. 'That will be the theme. A party! Long live intelligence! No booze! Go sober where your wings will take you!'

'We could go downstairs,' says Riya. 'Not Bukayr, but the rest of us. Joy! The couples! Coupled. Couplets, Bukayr, hear them rhyme! I had one once, a mate, a soul – they did me wrong, and I imagined it. Imagination in power! Revenge! And punishment. Sure, they gave me that. Without punishment, what is life: life without justice? A romp, a ramp! I'm cured, all of you!' she starts to shout... 'Fear not – they gave me back my fear, I'm tamed. Listen, far below... hark! mazurkas! That's what you need for stately celebrations, since the bar is dry... Now, a verbunkos. Hussars recruiting – there goes Irma's flourish, that's for sure...'

'What have we become?' asks Irma. 'How are we transformed? These wings – they're huge – I can't walk in mine...'

'We've been informed,' says Bukayr. 'Briefed and paid by all the states. So – we're informers. State secrets – we filter them, enhance and purify, and all the rest. We're clean and flying. Trusted and bright.'

'The yellow and the purple – the peacock?' Riya asks, flapping. 'Or are we fritillaries? Cabbage whites?'

'No, Riya,' Bukayr says, 'we're red admirals. We sail our Soviet ships around the world, and at the edge – on, on! *davai*! ... and down they go...!'

'It's all been written down,' says Adnan. 'Demagogic plutocracy – that's the next cycle. How long will that go on? And next? Will there be a next?' He brightens. 'At last, at least, we have our wings. After a fashion, we can fly, have our own cycle, particular. Expect some metamorphoses – there's nets to watch for too! Remember, when we were those green and wriggly young expectant things – there were the hawks. As butterflies we're never taken seriously: on a radar screen, the butterfly's invisible, unless there's millions of them... Lots are no more – those cabbages ... farewell, unmourned: the end unnoticed. When you're settled in your plot, your tranquil garden, we are still precarious. We're creatures who can't steer straight, we waver, slip and slide from thought to nought...It's in our nature, we are blown all round ... and in the end we lay our eggs, making our offspring delicacies for hawks... And us? We disappear! Our dust dies with us, the colours, toxins, our alluring painted eyes – gone, gone utterly, corpses unseen, composted.'

It's true – there is no alcohol, no pills – and yet... The colours! And the camouflage! The nodding wires, antennas on every head, the stagger, waver, little flights from male to female, or to none.

'You idiots,' says Adnan, 'it was a metaphor, a flight of fancy...'

'Yes,' says Irma, 'and it's a party, and our flight is right. At dusk, we turn to moths, and at the dawn, you will not see us: moths fly to the moon, and it's at noon that they trek back, as butterflies, and so it goes, each day a change – of gender, and of politics – our flutter goes from left to right, ungoverned... We're unsteerable, Adnan...'

Irma, the great night peacock – and there's Bukayr, the owl-prometheus: Riya – a sphynx? bombyx? a blue morph? – something enigmatic...

Adnan folds out of the game, he should have been the monarch. Nothing. Instead, he's a dun shape, tight clasped as a cigar, a shadow on the chestnut door...

Sex and wisdom – that's Bukayr. He takes out a flask, nectar for Irma first, then Riya – the dance comes up, percolated through the floor – a chaconne? and all to bed they've gone, or – off, invisible, up to the moon?

*

'What a night!' says Irma. 'I can't remember everything – just my lovely chiffon wings, big eyes and tiny face, the rouge, the kohl, the patchouli: not walking straight ... who with who? And when and how? The cycles! Everybody pedalling. What comes next? – all of us, our round is done, we're adults so ... death and tatters, that's all that's left, the fatal mark tattooed – a deathshead, on our backs.'

'It's all a metaphor,' Adnan says again. 'You guys, you sicken me – you think only of your pleasures. Watch out for Bukayr – that flask, his bottle – kills. You innocents...'

But no one hears. The moment's one of victory, but Adnan plans another flight – from titter-totter on to action.

He's wrong – those capering butterflies – they're thinkers too, their skid from air to air is typical – those mates are quite professionals. They think, and so they scheme, they write their little articles, the poems metaphysical. Those antennas! They pick up everything – the fling, the strathspey, then the more demanding jigs, the crouching down, the gopak, Kurdish stomp, the conga and the jitterbug... They lead, they follow, they applaud, press their partners just a squeeze too close, a tongue slips in an ear that's cupped, a twirl turns to a caress – the boogy threatens to spill all, the foxtrots to its hole – the chickens lie disfeathered and disheartened in their cage: the mambo slips its fangs inside a jouncing petticoat...

*

'What have I done?' Adnan asks. 'What shall I have done? In whose service am I? Must every inspiration fire a massacre? Oh, my stone heart! Mister brain, that sends to kill the herds, poor cattle, driven over cliffs and buried in a dusty bowl... No pity. Anger, though. Inspiration turning into diced-up bones!'

'Come, Adnan,' Bukayr says. 'Either: "don't do it, don't touch any of it" – or forget this dreary Faustian stuff. It's what you want, Adnan: – your thinking tank: – of course, it's weaponised! It's mine, but it was your idea. It's what you wanted and you've got: don't apologise.'

'I know we are a filter,' Riya says. 'We don't decide, we pass: we're bright passeurs – but, I want order, order for me. Others – if they like, they can copy that.'

'Oh Riya,' Irma says. 'It's contradictory – you say you want, and then you say it isn't up to you. Me – I want anarchy, I'll find my way, and don't expect a thing from anybody else. I can manage, whoever comes, "Hi Yank!", "Khleb!Tovarishch!" It's all one world. The more you're valued – the less you're worth. That's my slogan, Riya – the more you are of use to someone else, the less you are to you yourself.'

'Arab nomads?' Bukayr laughs. 'Who wants them? You and I, Adnan, we're the ones who need the metamorphosis!'

'Bukayr, you don't attract,' says Adnan. 'It's your poetry – it went inside your soul, and festered. It's alive, alas. For you, there's no one else. You observe, you don't join the dance. Rage on, Bukayr!'

*

Who wants a nomad? If you are one – no one, you hope. That's the point, and that's why Adnan thinks he'll take the bus down at the depot, leaving Bukayr in full charge.

'I don't like Irma,' Riya tells Bukayr, 'but we're with you, both, all the way. Drive thinking and objectivity far – far and deep. Let's have us do exactly what we want.'

'There's something big, Bukayr,' says Adnan. 'While I'm away – can you be sure to handle it?'

'Oh yes,' says Bukayr.

'You know how these big seasoned cheeses work,' says Adnan. 'Every morning – apprehension: – and the will to make a score. Good news, they long for it, resolving something: that's their dream. Fame everlasting. I'll go around, show my face, ingratiate. We're clean, Bukayr, unknown, and so we're full of depth, authority... The perfect hand – that's what we're waiting for.'

'Of course,' says Bukayr, 'the big guys all have lucky numbers. We could be their luck. Something is unresolved – then three or four of them, their interests, they coincide. Together they can break the bank, they think: the bank will then belong to ... who can tell? We'll be in there, that's for sure, matching the bets. Our analysis? – we can get it off our screen. Some dossier from the past, just change the country's name. In doubt? – you get instructions from the biggest guy...'

'Yes, yes,' says Adnan: 'Nothing too outré, mind. A coup. A *coup de dès*. Remember – it's not the latest weapons that you watch – those are for cash and training. Follow the path of those they'll really use...'

'I know, I know,' Bukayr says. 'It's all up here,' and he slaps his head to show.

'Then – I'll be off,' says Adnan. 'I can't go on here. No, with you guys, I can't go on at all. The mechanism's stuck, as if there's treacle in the works.'

*

'I hear you had a party yesterday,' I tell Bukayr. 'Hope it was good. Oh, how I love a party, I'm its life, its soul you know...'

'Only us, and flighty ones from underneath,' Bukayr says. 'Quadrilles and such – it's not your scene.'

'I've found a lovely person for you – she is desperate,' I say, 'but well contained. "Loulou" she's called. Alas, we are just friends. She could be Berber – if she has tattoos, I didn't see them ... or she might be travelling back from somewhere else, carooming into me, and off again...'

*

'What are you?' Loulou asks, when I say she's got a job. 'Do you recruit?'

'No, no,' I say, 'I just want love and wisdom, like them all.'

'Excuse me if I ask,' she says. 'Which is more important – love, or wisdom – or to pass me on? You didn't try so hard with me – you didn't try for sex and knowledge, as your second best.'

'The job's exciting, Loulou: you're near the centre of it all...' I tell her.

'Is what they do just?' she asks. 'Or just wise? Your friends...'

'Something for nothing,' I say. 'That's what they do. Like what I've given you.'

'I need the job,' she says. 'It sounds corrupt.'

'Then,' I say, 'you can resign. The other things are always waiting, round the bend...'

'That would depend how far you've gone,' she says, 'if they are visible.'

'You're very sharp,' I say. 'You'll go far, and be unhappy.'

'You're pushy and ineffective,' Loulou says. 'Find a hook to hang on soon, don't leave it late – old guys like what you'll be – they're pitiful.'

'Nothing dishonest,' Loulou tells Bukayr. 'That creepy guy, recruiting me – was very vague. He picked me up – that bar ... we all were pissed...'

'You mean – you'll make things up? Is that dishonest?' Bukayr asks. 'It needn't be. You take your fact – polish it, then – what's germane, is where and when you drop it in the works. Those empires – Russia, China, Yankees – all reactionary. They'd love to stop competing, do a deal. Except – no one'd be happy then. Happy's the goal you never reach. You, Loulou – maybe you wanted something of the left – equality, clean governors, that stuff. Believe me – don't waste time in wait and seek! The world, you see, is hurrying to a grand finale, a last big bang with shamans' drums and trumpets, gongs, and all the rest. A new live subject? Fanfares for the common man, and woman and the rest? Resolve the past, on to a future quite incredible, and empty too? Gadgets that will scrub your brain and clean the floor? No, Loulou: I'm wise to all that stuff. We need to stage a duel – except there's four or five take part. Duelling empires – the decent guys aim at the kneecap, or the sky. Honour offended; vindicated – then the deal. The rough-house – then the handshake. You need a brittle place, with people tired of life and being sniped: there lies your pretext. First, your big guys wrassle, then concoct a peace ... it falls to bits, and then...'

'So, it's peace you want, Bukayr?' says Loulou, quite incredulous. 'It seems that once you're in diplomacy, and sending messages and finding pics upon your screen – you're getting people killed – lots of them.'

'In jungles,' Bukayr says, 'people get ate! That's what the trees are for – to hide the feasts. There's streams – to wash your neighbour down!'

'The liberation, then...' Loulou starts off.

'There's pictures of that too,' says Bukayr. 'How it will be. I want something else, something more...'

'The falling-out. The rupture, each against all... Danzig and Archduke... Peace and war, that's what they say. Everything just like it was before, but bigger, maybe...The evil purged, makes room for more...' Loulou says.

'Whoa! Rein back your horsemen, Loulou,' Bukayr laughs: 'Of course – that may be what comes about. It all depends on us.'

'If you're the boss, Bukayr, I don't want to see your interests resolved,' says Loulou, 'even if you say they're mine as well...'

'Oh, the books have got it wrong,' Bukayr says. 'It's not the enchanted ones who are the wanderers – it's all the rest, Arabs, Kurds, all kinds of Turk – and it's not the working men who're stateless, it is those! Either they've no state, or don't like the one they have...'

'Well...' Loulou begins...

'Enough!' shouts Bukayr. 'Don't go on, bring more and more hohums in – until you make what's wrong and right seem everywhere, in bits and pieces; a bland copout, a hugger-mugger – and quite meaningless...'

Loulou stares at him. 'Now,' Bukayr shouts on. 'Don't bring in contradictions – especially not mine. There's dialectics. Empires are inclusive, or they're not; they're built on cities and on sand, on documents, graffiti – surely you see my point, my scope.'

'We think, and matter moves,' says Loulou. 'To where we planned.'

'You need the cosmological eye,' Bukayr says. 'I'm just a poet, so, of course, sight is skewed and doubled, there's nature conjured up – cataracts and spectacles. Mistrust, enjoyment...'

*

'I'm not nostalgic,' Adnan says: 'I don't know this place – maybe it's not worth saving anything. I'd no idea it was so knocked about.'

'That was the Romans,' Mehmet says, sat beside Adnan as their bus sails on.

'You'd need to find some people,' Adnan says. 'New ones. To populate all this.'

'There's strong forces, though,' says Mehmet. 'You need to watch your back and front. This is the devil's land. You don't just need to put a brick on brick...'

*

'No one would come,' Bukayr tells Loulou. 'Adnan is wrong. It would not in any case be right: not just. Land always belongs to someone else. If you're not content with working it – you always want something different, further off. Everything must collapse, and everyone be set running up and down, before... What? Things may go back as they were before. That's not what I want, not what I want to make.'

'If you want justice,' Loulou says, 'it's not for what you did, it is for what you are. Only a few, perhaps the principals, get justice. As for punishment – that gets spread around – so far around there's not a scrap of justice in it, where it ripples out. You'd need to look in every case – it would take centuries. Anyway, we rarely see what comes down to punish us. It's like an influenza.'

'Well, obviously,' says Bukayr, irritated, 'that's not what I mean – you're talking of another kind of justice. By definition, if you see injustice – there must, hypothetically, be a justice waiting to be done. But – the just and the unjust – they must agree on terms, or else they're something else: revenge, big power, a compromise.'

'So,' says Loulou, 'you'll never get agreement. The unjust don't see it that way, defining terms. It's not as if there was a law. Besides, law doesn't punish, and it isn't justice...'

'Leave it, Loulou,' Bukayr says. 'No history'll get done, arguing like that.'

'At least,' says Loulou, 'have them turn the music off. Don't those guys sleep? The drumming...'

'If they stop,' says Bukayr, 'down the whole ship goes. Your heart will seize, your legs – like deathbed posts. They are our turbines, Loulou – guys who pound the floor like they were making flour – it's life, Loulou!'

'Life comes helter-skelter,' Loulou says. 'What if you end it all, when you provoke the crash?'

'It is the only way of changing things, Loulou. Otherwise – you forever take the bus, you are a crab who looks for a deserted shell, maybe there's a mollusc corpse inside ... too bad, you start again, squeeze in beside...' and Bukayr weeps, 'I'm the kind Beelzebub, you see. Throw it all down – better luck next time...'

*

Loulou's a sceptic – but who cares? A job's a job – and Adnan won't come back. There's good slants to everything, but – don't be misled, she doesn't care about the good, no more than Bukayr does. Destruction? However much you'd like to see it, and the new appear – like mandrake flowers – they won't be responsible. Old guys will do it, and they don't need you at all. They're old beasts rutting – they say it's all a trap, they all want peace. It isn't true. There is no trap. They like the sound of falling bricks, is all.

She came from Africa, and when that's gone, there's nothing left she cares for but herself. It's a con, but everyone believes. Loulou – you're wrong: you have to care for nothing, or for everything. 'There is no middle way – if you walk there – you will disappear, down through the crack.'

*

'Loulou,' I say: 'I told you – you're at the centre. You wait, you pour the poison in the sleeping ear...'

'Oh fiddle,' Loulou says, 'it's all humdrum. There's thousands of us, willing a destruction. A message or a massacre – it's all been planned. It's what you are, not what you say you are... You skip fine writing, turn to the end. That's where the colour is: the beast with seven heads, those whores, the burning city, tourists' panorama, the clapping and the clap: the flames, my dear! Our species put it in a book. The species ends. Then comes the interval, a million years, another species wriggles, slithers, to the plate, awaits the skittering pitch – a strike! home run! Another book, or something like, and then the End, the victory. All that, is plotted in our sleep...'

'Oh come!' I say. 'Loulou! That may be wisdom, but it isn't love. Let's stop and have a drink...' And so we do.

'You guys,' the barman says. 'You come in sad. Go out – as someone else. But you forget – there's deathwish, like the Master, Sigmund, said – but there is vanity as well. The will to win, be right, notch up a victory. Be just – just be, as Irma says...'

'Oh,' I say, 'they all troop in here... Bukayr's crew?'

'When they're on mission, yes,' he says. 'Riya needs stiffening. She has the blues, and so she takes the blue.' And he swirls the Bols.

'Babies are wise,' he says. 'They don't communicate – but they know enough to grow – become wise, bigger too. Die in the best way there is. When you're young, you are a fan – state, heads on coins – then you get wiser still, and try to cheat the state, and laugh at heads on coins. You two,' he says, pouring to us, 'could have a baby. Wisdom. You don't need love for that – but love is habit, refuge. Lots of luck and nothing special, no freaking out, no trip. A come-down, rather...'

'We're not here for that,' says Loulou. 'No baby. We want to take out what we brought in, nothing more.'

Loulou's much taken with him: he's stronger on wisdom than on love. Certainly, wisdom trumps love. The smart money goes on wisdom.

'You could work with us – Stéphane?' she says. He has a badge.

She goes on, 'We're planning to eliminate the big powers, making them fight. It's not just, in the first instance; but justice comes after, we believe.'

'You're wrong,' says Stéphane. 'It looks like that will happen, but it never does. Some disappear, then who's left will carve you up.'

Loulou is indiscrete. I tell Stéphane, 'You could work the bar in the *balera*. The thinkers come down for drinks.'

He's not a barman, probably. But – if he's a spy, it's normal. Humans – the basis of all – their brains, relationships, playing exotic instruments – poetry, even the hermetic kind – all rests on spying. Only the autistics – they don't spy. The rest ... that's how they catch you, put you in jail, read your messages. As for the instruments – the *kora, erhu,* you can spy to be authentic, but mostly you use them to put yourself into them, not draw the music out. The best spying – would mean you knew everything – the humans, the dance, God, how the universe is fastened, what works the rollers that it runs on... Stéphane's poetic trinkets – Mallarmé resisted when his wife went visiting, but you need to spy to get it out... All metropolitan, nothing on empire, guys hiding in the trees. It's banal, not even politics, not like the holy wars you undertake when you have spied on God – complacent surely? What's the point of being God if you can't be known, but make it difficult, like poetry, like mastering those gourds with their twelve strings.

Fail – and it's flames. Or jail, or every kind of firing squad.

Everybody wants to reach the end – then, when it's near, they don't. It all links up, so every little thing's about – everything.

It's a throwback – you're culled for what you haven't thought about for years. Too bad. It's life, and when you're out of it, no one calls you to account.

*

'He's not my lover, Irma. He has a poet's name, it's true,' says Loulou, 'Stéphane. But there's no poetry – he's just dumb.'

'Justice is when no one has nationality,' Riya explains to Stéphane, pushing Loulou aside. 'No one is counted, no one's part of an agglomeration, there's no majorities or minorities. You believe in what you want, and don't try to find others who believe the same...'

'Get rid of him, Loulou,' Irma says. 'He has the look of someone who sells secrets and protection. He wears a ginger suit – barmen don't do that.'

'I have an apron,' Stéphane says. 'So I can stay the same when the rest are being someone else. It hides my legs – I'm not going anywhere. I like a drop myself, so long as the rope's round someone else's neck.'

'Yes,' shouts Bukayr, 'he's a barman! Throw him out. Who asked him in?'

'It's Loulou,' Irma says. 'She's enamoured – she told him we want to start a fight between the big guys, start it all again, a new, a winning hand...'

The three women cluster round – someone pinches Loulou; their faces glower, blotched still with dust of butterfly: there's treachery, and trust and justification too...

'You idiots,' Bukayr shouts. 'No violence! The big guys – already they are fighting everywhere, there's spies abound, and reading mail and shootings in the park. It isn't us that starts it off – it's what they are. They could back off. Implode's the word. Dumping the pilot, forget the Gott mit Uns ... Loulou! You're in disgrace!' He weeps – Loulou was to be his star, his moon, that he had hoped would be a refuge. Dear flighty Loulou ... what a fall...

Stéphane resists. He chants, '*Me voici libre et fier parmi mes compagnons*', he hugs all three ... and goes downstairs. No guilt, and no repentance. Sends a report to guys who know it all...

'A spy,' says Bukayr. 'That is what he is. We're what we are – unarmed: for justice... For a return, a better start... No Eden – no divided labour, women spinning, men with the fork: a proper garden this time – flowers and butterflies...'

*

There's a new barman, where I go – morose and solemn, like they ought to be.

How beautiful they are, Riya, Irma, Loulou – clean, powdered, perfumed. And Bukayr too – never had anything, and he's lost that too. He didn't want to work the land he never had.

'If there's the war they say,' the barman starts. 'Where will you go? If you're not exactly gay, my friend, I don't see you in a barracks. What will you do?'

'If you've a cause, there's not much else to do,' I say, 'but follow it.'

'It's work, of course,' the barman says. 'You need religion, the documents – all must be right, or it's the worse for you. In every country, people – lots, sometimes a few, say they are free. For sure – in the army, you are not. But often you are safer at the front than in your room...'

'It's a puzzle, yes,' I say, wanting silence. Poor Loulou – how she flapped her mouth...!

*

'You should visit those big guys,' Irma tells Bukayr. 'Meet, and counsel: – hide your hand. Them, the bandits, every bandit, every chief – talk to them all. That's what they do – they sniff each other out. It's like *suma* – the fattest wins...'

'No, Irma,' Bukayr says. 'For me, it would be pain. I'd sooner take first lessons on the *erhu.*'

'You're wrong,' says Riya. 'The music's not a pain alternative. The *erhu* is an instrument that reaches deep – if it's an electric one, it transforms you, behold! your bones are made of melody, your blood of whispers – deep in your soul it goes, and tells you you will die alone, no one will weep, "a leaf falls off the tree/the tree feels free".'

'Find me a teacher, then,' he says. 'I could play and have the music change Loulou.'

'I'm what I am,' says Loulou, taking Bukayr's hand and weeping in a spate. 'Everyone knows everything – but lots they don't believe, so what's the difference what I say and who I tell?'

'If we're told – we're spies,' says Riya, 'If we make it up – we're what? experts. You must know which is what, and choose your audience, Loulou.'

'She's still a spy,' says Irma, cold. 'A spy on spies. The worst kind.'

'It's a puzzle,' Bukayr says. 'Perhaps you're right, my sweets... The Teacher says – "fiddle on the *erhu* strings – how long will it take to touch a soul?" He says – fifty years. You're my assistants – so, assist! It's your task to venture out, each one alone. The meetings with the powerful – they are up to you.'

'Who will hold your hand?' asks Loulou, trying to ingratiate.

'Oh, Stéphane has two, always beneath the apron I expect,' says Bukayr. He mocks: '"*L'ennui d'aller en visite avec l'ail nous l'éloignons*" – only my excuse will be my violin. We'll bid you farewell, Loulou, Stéphane's favourite: – "*La chevelure vol d'une flamme à l'extrême Occident*"... Off you'll go to the States, hanging, dangling out there, pioneers ever, on to their last resort, their sails full of the wild onion breath of God, blowing hard, hoping they'd not come back, the slaves in turmoil in the hold...'

'Stereotyping, Bukayr,' she says. 'I'll have every kind of adventure – meet every kind of person...'

*

Oh no, Loulou thinks: If I speak my language here, or any other one I know – they'll throw me out. There's liverish guys in suits and monstrous ones in uniform... Bukayr was right... I can't spend time talking about justice here, my world, the *balera*...

I have no home, she thinks, But how I miss it!

'It's exactly like the movies, Bukayr,' she says, when she is back. 'You'd be amazed – the detail! Like the movies! And they speak so well to camera! They're friends with all the wrong sort, though.'

'I know all that,' Bukayr says. 'Everybody is.'

Has she purged her treachery?

He asks, 'What did they tell you? Did they look at the last chapter?'

'It's the one we all know,' says Loulou. 'The one that's in the book. Flames.'

'That's no use,' says Bukayr. 'They gave no confidences?'

'You know how it is,' says Loulou. 'A few drinks, a passage on the *erhu*, a line from something you once heard – and you get intimate.'

'Not everyone is trustworthy, Loulou,' says Bukayr. 'Anyone can use those things to make false entrances.'

'Oh, they soon tell you what they think,' she says. 'They don't care what you think. Remember Bukayr, when you were at home, back there... There's places that are yours, but,' she says, 'you only go once a year, and see if there's a harvest. Over there – you stay all the time, but there is nothing on the trees for you – you might as well go off somewhere else, anywhere, at harvest time.'

'That's all romantic,' Bukayr says. 'What you say, Loulou. Everywhere's pecarious – you'd be an idiot, counting on your trees.'

'I see no trees here either,' says Loulou. 'Nor where Adnan went...'

'What's this rural stuff, Loulou?' Bukayr asks. 'It's not our thing. Try to fit in where you are.'

'I'm not disloyal, Bukayr,' Loulou says. 'Maybe naive – it's said to be attractive.'

'Did you really go there, Loulou?' Bukayr asks. 'America?' – looking far beyond her, the sea, wrinkled and hot, cruel winds skimming over.

'If I hadn't,' Loulou says, 'it would have been the same. Those guys aren't your local councillors – they're appointed, come from where you wouldn't be let in. They're not standing by the door, waiting for your curiosity to knock.'

'I don't know where you're from, Loulou,' Bukayr says. 'I've been here so long, I don't come from anywhere, I don't try to get in to other places.'

'You've found you believe in music, though,' says Loulou.

'Yes,' says Bukayr. 'There's nothing to fall off, no danger, only of not getting it all right.'

'You used to be bad, Bukayr, bad towards everyone,' says Loulou.

'I'm still bad, Loulou: bad towards everyone. I believe what's in myself, all bad,' says Bukayr. 'I'll make bad, don't worry, no compromise. Smash and start again, or smash and have done! I don't care so much. You sentimentalise about the music, Loulou, to cover up what you haven't done. Don't!'

'It's good to have a job, Bukayr,' she says. 'But – you know – you don't make much sense – even if this is what they tell you, what the talk is all about. Be patient: fear the flames: join in. Like on TV.'

'No violence,' Bukayr repeats: 'Have them do that by themselves – my bad part is the bringing on, not stopping anything...'

'What could you stop?' asks Loulou, much upset. 'The violence? Our parties? Good guys, bad guys – they all have awful stuff – setting the sea on fire ... crumbling the hills ... what's your contribution to it all, Bukayr? Next time. let's make the theme – predators.'

*

'You should rise up,' Stéphane says: 'He's gone all spiritual.'

'We love him, naturally,' says Irma. 'But – I'll never go to China. They're so neat and wear white gloves. Let them do just as they please – I'll not wear a hat, not to satisfy someone. I'm me, as I am.'

'Well,' says Riya, 'when I went to Moscow – there was a platoon I saw – they wore white fluffy trousers, white shapkas with a single feather, red: – they're ghosts. And, yes, Irma, they wore white gloves too. They did no harm – they sang. And the rest – they wanted to be ever more beautiful. That's hard. And the grannies did the work... They were big empty cities there, like you'll see in China too – waiting for someone to come – mosques and domes, and cinemas. Apartments – your clothes and photos all hung up, a family bonsai on the sill...'

'Your chief,' Stéphane goes on. 'He's ignorant – he can't produce a proper sound, a ripe sonority – he squeaks and grinds his *erhu...*'

'You're right, Stéphane,' says Irma. 'He is confused. Justice to his land – it would be hard, harder than injustice. What's to do? Not everyone can run away...'

'Settle somewhere else? You're always tied. Adnan tried it, and he finds the land is everywhere polluted, arid, covered over...' Stéphane says. 'He and Bukayr were complementary – and there's nothing left to do that way. Faust and the Devil – a good show. But – there's no surprise. The Devil must bring justice, save the innocent. It's terrible! The wronged redeemed – the rest...? Gallop and gallop – down the horses go, into the cleft. Big powers – they are as they are, and if they start to rock and shimmy – out come the special cops. They billy you, and that's your end! It's like that everywhere. That's how they are. There's no good end.'

*

'If you're as bad as all that, Bukayr,' Stéphane says, 'you must be immortal. So – why bother?'

'Not at all,' says Bukayr. 'You must all try harder. Eternity doesn't come into it.'

'We're trying to be good, Bukayr,' Stéphane says. 'Being right – that's what religion's all about, and now the politics.'

'I might be right, and not be good,' Bukayr says. 'That's what I think. Or – I might be good, and not be right. That's what you think about yourself, perhaps, Stéphane – but that's not all there is, of course. Not right, not good. Get rid of them, the terms!'

'You could try poetry, like I do,' Stéphane says. 'I quote, I don't compose. You, Bukayr, your name! Makes you a poet, certainly!'

'Oh no,' Bukayr says, 'that's an Old Nick name, no more. I've been killed once, for sure: It's enough to think bad thoughts to be not good, not right. It's always so. It makes life hard, you walk crabwise. Things fall down around.'

'It's true,' says Stéphane. 'That's what you are – not even what you were.'

'Come on, Stéphane,' Bukayr says. 'It's clear that you're a spy. Tell me what you have to do, and I shall do the same.'

'It's strategy,' says Stéphane. 'We'd like you on our side.'

'You wanted to be rid of me – now I only play the *erhu*, my lovely assistants do the work,' Bukayr says.

'You're on everybody's side,' says Stéphane. 'We want you exclusively.'

'I'm not the exclusive kind,' says Bukayr. 'I'm not used to being on one side.'

'Well, that's the deal,' says Stéphane, polishing thin glasses. 'And you could try cutting a rug down here too.'

'Spread myself around – that's called dilution, Stéphane,' Bukayr says. 'After the devastation, what shall we both be?'

'After the devastation – nothing grows,' Stéphane says. 'There is no after. Remember where you were, where you and Adnan came from. Play along – or else you're right; there's no one left to share it with.'

'Well, there it is,' Bukayr says. 'You said it. Dirty hands. No hands at all. You choose.'

Nothing happens. It's repetitious. Everything's suspended

'Time for another party,' Loulou says, picking worn shoes from the floor – wood, bast and deerskin, all worn through with rhythm.

They ignore her.

'Look, Stéphane,' says Bukayr, 'you're the most important person in the building, probably the most important I shall ever meet. Whoever you may be. Listen – I don't want cities – flat, grey and brown they are – look at the glass that breaks, the frames of doors and windows – some blasted out, all thrown on the tip in their due time ... the roads pocked and oily... Landscape too – a smear of grass, a slough of watery brown, a corkscrew tree... What matters – all that matters – is what people say. Not how they look – there is no fixed form, the clothes are changed, the bellies boom and bust ... the noses skew, the eyes melt, mouths droop, skin flakes and pouches, orifices drool. No – they are what they say. No humanism, of course, no trust, no parsing... Just the common sense. That's how you know where people stand – there they are, stumps in a field: then flux. They flow, it all flows, lovers hate and haters form a corporation, the president drops his bomb, plays pinochle, or else it's trictrac and a drone... Be modern, Stéphane: listen to me, don't squint at me – I have no tits to watch, no childhood's visible under the skin, just take in what I say. If I give you figs or flippers – they are not grown and killed by me – I buy them in a store. I do not love you, Stéphane, you're not starving, you're not sick – my gift, my gesture is an attempt to ingratiate – eat them, enjoy them, don't think they'll talk to you.'

'Oh, I know all that,' says Stéphane. 'What you look like doesn't matter – not a fig, and not a flipper.'

'We could join the dance,' says Loulou. 'Mostly they're not gendered – there is no stereotyping here – you don't need legs or arms – or even heads. And – what's wrong with Stéphane, Bukayr?'

'He sees things as they are,' says Bukayr. 'He doesn't mind if that's the way they stay.'

MELANIE

'Mister Bukayr!' Stéphane says. 'We don't often see you here. And the news – confirm it, please!'

'All empires die,' Bukayr says, reaching for a bottle in the bar. 'We – and they – know that, but, they don't know which, and which one first. My news – is: "only one of you survives". There's panic. Fight it out – or back off, quick! Usually – most survive: – at least, there's more than one that does, they change the shape but keep the rhetoric. This time – just one. I won't tell which...'

'It doesn't stimulate, nor yet deter,' says Stéphane, writing something down, and posting it upon a screen.

'I know which one,' says Bukayr. 'And for how long.'

Melanie is sitting at the bar: 'Why don't they let us smoke in here?' she asks: 'We're so behind the times. Smoke and drink – they go together. "Bib and brace", "seal and hat".'

'American ciggies are so strong,' Bukayr says. 'And in some acts, seals don't wear a hat.'

'That's not the point,' says Melanie. 'I smoke Macdonalds A – they don't kill everyone. And even if they did, without exception – it still wouldn't be a rule. Mister Bukayr – if you're an Arab, I'd so enjoy a night with you, I love you guys...'

She slides a milky arm around his neck. 'I gave that up,' he says. 'Identity? We Arabs never won a match.'

Stéphane says, 'Melanie's the most lovely person you will ever meet – moreover, entry is by ticket only, you don't need to be introduced, have gone to school with her, or use perfume and shave ... you book, but you don't have to read...'

'I have assistants,' says Bukayr. 'It's they who worked out which empire has the longest life. They're good at wisdom – can you know if they are good at love? What would that mean, I ask myself... Maybe – you and me, Melanie? It's on your mind, I see. I'd not hurt you for the universe – but it's no good, it wouldn't work, none of it. I don't dance, I don't pay for sex. My perspective, Melanie – it's a kind of anarchism... After the fall of empires – they'll want to start it over, build it up again, the same guys, same ruins, stood on end again. Is that the history you want, dear Melanie?'

'You fill my mind, Bukayr,' she says, 'to overflow.'

'No!' Bukayr says, 'you mustn't be another one who follows me! There's a horizon all around, space that will be filled after our deaths, that is what you see beyond the smoke and dust. A line that demarcates a space. 'No God, no chief, no hero!' Start doing something for yourself, Melanie: clear away the smoke, the smokes! See – I started drinking here today – the first time. Now, I give it up. Take control, Melanie, like me. Consider something very primitive, very refined. Organised anarchism – true communism... I shan't be here, of course.'

'The communists,' says Melanie, narrowing her eyes, 'killed the anarchist guys like you, and then they made a state – bigger and stronger than the one before.'

'No one kills me!' Bukayr says. 'The vanguard disappears – the state remains. So – you can try again, to go beyond. Don't think to follow me. I'm not the lead, the bagpiper who goes before, advises chieftains when to fight, and heads the troop, first off to war. I'm the cartographer, sat way back – a tent, a Tabriz carpet on the earth, a jug of schnapps and sharpened pencils in a jar...'

The little band starts up a czardas. Bukayr goes upstairs, Stéphane prepares to tell his boss Bukayr's big idea. How will they react? Will they react?

*

'Of course! Melanie!' says Riya. 'Poor Melanie – down there amid the gigues, the jazz – I long to free her! Down there, it's rules and rhythms all day long, her nature's all squared off and nailed. She could be one of us – I'm timorous, and Irma's wild, and Loulou's a deserter... Melanie – could be our marketable side – our face turned to the sun ... while we are round the back, like rats beneath the barrel.'

'You're wearying,' says Bukayr. 'Do what you must do, be what you are – I can do no more, my plan is circulating... It must be conceptual – Adnan says all contested land's polluted, waterless – to the victors only what is spoiled...'

*

Melanie's a fascination. Her, and all her crew. They never dance, come in when trade is down.

'The fire-eater, and the mask. The lady with the little dog,' I say. 'How far they seem from commerce, and the calculation, Melanie. They don't dance in here, but outside, in the market – it's splendour among the stalls. They are quite other, all day long. And then they come and talk to us, and tell me how Palmyra was, and Bangalore...'

'Yes,' she says. 'You're not serious about anything. You'll never be. It's a great protection, a great gift. If you lived for ever, you would never change. How irritating! We tumble with the acrobats,we inhale the flames, the dog runs off – the man with locusts in his cap sees them fly off and multiply... You don't! You stay while the tragedies revolve...'

'You're one with them, Melanie,' I say, entranced.

'They're flowers,' says Melanie. 'They have a pepper smell. At night – they sleep bad, flop like wet silk sheets. Not where you'd want. Night crawlers, you might say,' and she laughs. 'I'm alive, though: mothy, deep.'

'Yes,' I say, 'you're too delicate to dance, of course.'

'I dance to the *kobiz* – that's my instrument. I come from Tartary, you see,' and she laughs.

Well, why not? You wouldn't do the cha-cha, if that were the case.

'The world's a sprcad of storics, Mclanic,' I say. 'Evcry ruin – bursts to tell its tale, be inhabited; deserted villages – can't contain themselves.'

'It's as I say,' she says. 'You'll peer through every holey stone, and every keyhole – butterflies. That's what you'll see. Your lashes – and a flitter. You'll never put together anything – it's all a patchwork.'

'Maybe Loulou could come down here, Melanie,' I say. 'Permanently.'

'Does she have an act?' asks Melanie. 'White doves or suchlike? There's some people stay here all the time, and others show up once a year, say, when they dance Hutzulski, or there's a special day. Loulou'd need be here all the time. She'd do better in the market, with a show. Cards or shells.'

'It sounds quite dull in here,' I say. I hadn't thought.

'It's not one thing, nor yet the next,' says Melanie. 'It's like the seventh century, our era: it was quite obscure all over – big, big armies, no trade, no shoes ... gritty bread.'

'There's always trade,' I say. 'If you can't sell some info, you can sell other people anyway.'

*

'I think you should go downstairs,' says Bukayr. 'It's fluid. You'd feel happy there.'

'It's not at all what I would want,' says Loulou, starting to cry.

'We don't trust you, Loulou,' says Bukayr. 'Besides, things get worse – you know how it might be: balls juggled by a clown. The ones that's dropped – they raise a laugh, or you pretend it's all contrived. If you've rank, some service, Loulou, a uniform, major or colonel? – you'll feel more at home with Melanie.'

'Oh absolutely,' says Loulou, crying more. 'Bukayr, you're off your head!' She says sarcastically, 'Oh, of course, I'm some foreign spy! Fantasy! Can't you see that I'm a thinker? What d'you imagine – that I'm a squaddie? A codifier?'

'I wanted you just to be a foreign spy, Loulou,' says Bukayr, apparently unmoved. 'You seemed to be on too many sides, is all.'

'Just think, Loulou,' Irma joins in, 'if you were in a tall cement block, in China – now, that's frightening – the way the wind blows through the grey, how the ground can disappear ... all those chairs, no one to sit on them. But downstairs here – there's a whirl. It's like Berlin. Always new people passing through, off to more exciting places.'

'I can pay you in a while, Loulou,' Bukayr says. 'You don't need to sell tickets for a dance with guys – not now. If there's someone else who pays you, take it.'

'Going this way, Bukayr,' says Loulou, 'you diminish your own significance. Ours too.'

'It's true,' says Irma. 'Maybe we should poison you, Loulou? Renting her room is nothing.'

'You're still with us, Loulou,' Bukayr says. 'With us, but detached. We can't explain to Melanie, of course.'

'You've made a story of me,' Loulou sobs. 'You gave me pips – or crowns, maybe ... and now you're stuck. You all are spies – so, what's the new. Suppose I get a salary from somewhere else – you're envious, perhaps...'

And down she goes, and so it stands: she doesn't dance, or sell herself, she's down with Stéphane, but she cries all day.

'I'd planned,' she wails, 'a whole career – deceit, treachery, knowing the undersides. Now – everyone's clued up, takes snapshots of the everything – and all I have is Stéphane, with his sorry tags. It's all gone binary – rich and poor, hungry and thirsty, barman and drunk. Wisdom – oh! it doesn't lead to love...'

*

'I'm innocent,' I tell Bukayr. 'I didn't plant her there with you. She looked so cute – I picked her up, she dropped me – there you are! From not quite love to not quite wisdom – there, the whole journey is revealed.'

'You're still my heroine,' I tell Loulou. I don't know what that means – she does.

'I'm down here, in the whirligig,' she says. 'I'm made for intelligence – instead there's this...'

There's couples, then there's rings, go whirling round – some stick, like oiled-up cogs, in corners – 'Move on, move on!' shouts Melanie, forcing the pairs apart, finding new partners from thc losers sat along the walls... There's dancers in their faun suits, Isidoras in loose wraps, girls in plantains, girls in their skin, men farded, men from Grosz, dances from the Atlas and the steppes, stomping from true north and from the sand – 'No animals in here,' shouts Melanie, 'alive or dead or in between...' and yet each pair, each band, hears just their music through the rest, and does their sacrifice 'as if' the creature was to hand – and people of all parts and every gendershade, they join the dance, indifferent to its geography and faith, still less to family and friends – they follow rhythm and excitement, patterns in the sand – sand for sprung floors and sand of desert land...

'It makes my eyes spin round,' says Loulou, clinging to me. 'Save me! – my sailor on dry seas!'

I free myself: 'If Adnan returns,' I say, 'he will be with you.'

I've no idea.

'He's a lost cause,' Loulou says. 'His plan? People settling in sterile lands? They'll live in houses not their own – they're ghosts of who was there. Ghosts who prowl and seek who they had known – and other ghosts take over wherever they had lived. What will Adnan be? Ghostmaster, shepherd of the shades. Seeking the living and the dead indifferently? Why should he return? Why, if he does, should he find satisfaction here? This mechanism,' and she points over to the sufi group, churning like crown wheels on the floor, 'is motion perpetual and constant. It only tells one time, but that's a strip, a belt of infinite extent, never repeating, never doubling back, reflecting... Adnan needs a sundial, every dawn it cancels out the day before, and sets the day back to the first – what you always see's the primal landscape, the colours just invented: the people spilling out the house – are always prototypes, the moulds endure for ever. They are their own history. And so it goes, on and on, the memory cancelled every day, but in the dawn – there! It returns, not in their mind, but to be relived afresh... Each time – the first time. But the arm, the hand, is sculpted so although you don't remember how – it's perfect. Picking the fruit, harvesting – there can be no other way. But this here,' and she sweeps her white-gloved hand over the ticking sufis – 'This always changes, and it always modifies the day before, a deeper gouge upon the steel, a wearing out, recording, lengthening a nose, thinning hair and closing orifices... Adnan knows all that. He won't come here... This fleets… There is no setting back...' and she weeps for someone she has never seen, will never see: just like us all.

'It's true,' I say. 'Take someone's house – and you're at once its ghost. Some have no houses, but all the same they're ghosts. Those sufis – persecuted, rotating for the tourists, bobbins ... fibres destined for no cloth...'

'And when you die,' she says, 'you go back, you start again, from where and when you had to flee, that very day: you're always dropping on your cord of life, a spider in freefall – waving all those arms and legs... Who'll come? Who'd help? There's no one, ever, ever...'

*

Upstairs and down – my! they're suspicious, and they're glum.

'Of course there is no atonement,' I say to Loulou. 'All of us, we die in that wood outside Athens. Motherfuckers, parricides, unclean, unloved. What can you expect? That striding all alike, on to the same fate, should it gives us comradeship? Look at the couples dancing here – they don't mix, they don't talk. They join each others' rounds, that's all.'

She puts her arm round me: 'Don't mistake,' she says. 'This is a gesture, nothing more. It's what they say you ought to do, to show you're *sympa*, just like Stéphane says. He can make poetry from a pair of gloves; dropped beneath a chair.'

'I know, Loulou,' I say. 'You're far outside my range – so what would be the point? This is the most we'll be together.'

Melanie leans over, says, 'Some people go for mismatches – because they will not last, because they are a wrassling on the mat. But you—' and she punches my arm '—you don't have the muscle for it, nor the charm. You're a Pandarus, that's all. You, you do the introductions. Then you leave.'

'We leave, always,' Loulou says, 'because time forces us – there's no alternative. And it's true – we all lie dying in that wood outside Athens, men and women, dressed this way and that. All mainly innocent. The dying's real, but it's in a legend, which is not. That's why there's no way out.'

'Enough, Loulou!' I say. 'What I understand of what I've said – I'd sooner not believe.'

'It isn't fatalism,' Loulou assures me. 'You must fight, for the right, the right side. Even if you lose.'

'You must be on the right side,' Melanie agrees, 'but you often aren't.'

*

I could help Loulou, and Bukayr. A little treachery. Expose the plan, denounce Loulou. Make news, accuse. Friends as before ... Make up with everyone, make up – everything...

I inform. I tell the cops. There's no violence, there is a plot. Better – a *Weltanschauung*. Lots of them. Nothing has happened, nothing will happen. They flee from an impossible situation –

land, justice, peace, bread – it's all there, everyone's involved. Nothing happens, everyone is innocent, the Devil alone brings justice – but no one believes in the Devil, so justice is not done, everyone's relieved, there's no way out, you can't live alongside the evil ones, but there's nowhere else to go.

The cops take it all in. Of course, they'll resolve it all.

They're taken off, Bukayr, Loulou – and then – they're back!

'They were futurologists,' Loulou tells me, 'not cops. You bastard, though! "Everything has its argument," Bukayr said. Of course, that is their job: guessing what comes next. Bukayr didn't spill his magic bean... He didn't say who would survive, and for how long... Probably they didn't want to know. As for me – I tell the tales. Who's interested in my stuff? But you – you turned us in, to places where we might not return with our skins whole...'

'Raising your profile, Loulou,' I tell her. 'Getting you known. Even to a small authority – must be worth the bother.'

*

'Only the devil knows the future,' Riya says. 'Me and Irma – we each only know the half. That lets us out. It's up to Bukayr, putting halves together ... but it spoils things, if he tells.'

'Loulou?' I ask. 'She knows everything – she's paid...'

'Oh, Loulou's cute,' says Irma, coy.

'In the *balera* I'm a Ganymede, it seems,' I say. 'I've been everywhere, done it all – useless! I know nothing. Melanie's in charge downstairs. Am I her sidekick?'

'Oh no,' Irma says, 'Stéphane pours. He has the class. The aim. That's what true poets have.'

'Then I...' I begin.

'You are a Pandarus,' says Riya, laughing, 'If anybody wanted sex. But – we can manage for ourselves.'

*

'Loulou stays here,' says Melanie. 'She betrays. Riya is delicate. You'll have to take Irma. We'll tell you if there's another party. Tell us what you find, if you come back...'

'I hadn't spent time,' I say, 'thinking what I am. I'm the empty jar waiting to be occupied. Some thief...'

'This is a bad idea,' says Irma, holding my arm and striding out... 'All the people, all the difficulties – we're not the ones who'd set them straight.'

'It's a novelty, Irma,' I tell her. 'After the butterflies – it could be predators. Or simians. There's loreleis, mermaids too – and going on that way, all kinds of chimera, wills of the wisp, gorgons, medusas of all kinds...'

'No, no,' she says. 'There's a big change – Bukayr is closing down. Everyone goes downstairs now. Bukayr dropped his findings, dropped them on the powers... Who will remain after the conflict, and for how long...

'It's made no difference, had no effect. The information is quite accurate – it's not an inference: it's sure. and all the allies, occupations, irredentisms, racist boasts – all those too – are attested, notarised, absolutely concrete: who will last, who crumbles into archive... No one cared. They all have charms – some magic or religion – they think will twist them out of certainty...'

'So,' I say, 'Melanie will boss the lot downstairs?'

'There's a roster,' Irma says. 'She just turns the wheel.'

'A Wurlitzer?' I ask. 'Whirling everything there is!'

'I see that makes you sparkle,' Irma says. 'The point is – Bukayr's idea rests on what we three, me, Riya, Loulou – had worked right through. It works. They laugh at Old Karl, Sigmund, their Revelations – the telling what has been, what is, and certainly will be. The bricks, my dear – of what we are and what we'll be and what we thought we were... Then, there's the new guys, labrats – saying how the whole shoot will fall into the sun... The food runs out, the water too, the animals die, there's wars all round, and millions spilling up and down – all that is credible, and believed. It's true. Expect no messiah: no hero – no refuge. Admit no gloss, no "maybe they'll find another way, maybe the others..." And yet – Bukayr is not believed.'

'It seems,' I say. 'He is believed, but all the truth's discounted. Everyone proceeds "as if". As if it wasn't so.'

'That's right,' says Irma. 'Riya's in crisis on account... but, there it is. They'll find a haven down below, in the *balera*. Cut their rug...'

I shout up at the window of the *balera*, '*Proshchai*, Riya, my summer! Goodbye "Walls, mothers, womankind..." She leans out: she knows, of course, what happens to Russia, the bottled gherkins, the bothies, the hooch and the laughter... It was not to last, it had its special time, its knowing. Everybody knew – that was it, till the finish: no forward and no back, but good enough for what it was.

'I can stay here,' Riya calls down. 'In the *balera*, with all the rest who've left themselves behind.'

'We'll be back,' I shout. 'Irma too. It's not a relationship. I've been all over on my own, and now...'

'Now,' Irma says, 'you've made another awful choice. Off we go!' And, arm in arm, we do!

*

'Just we two?' I ask Irma. 'Then it's to say goodbye. It didn't work, the human project. You had it calculated. You were paid to find it so, but you still researched it all. Nothing was invented. The information was the best. No imagination was involved, and no emotion... It's right that we should make the trek, and then *proshchai*, farewell to everything. But all the other people? The *balera's* full. Always.'

'Oh,' she says, 'I expect the dancers already left their place, their origin, and said goodbye. That's it. It wasn't safe, back where they were. No one tells you you should stay. There's buses out – planes, if you've the cash.'

'I don't believe,' I say. 'We wander. Humans have no home, they've nothing *ur*, no habitat. They're smooth and unpredictable,' and I think of Marina's machete – out of the divan, out of the blue.

'It's evolution, spooling back,' she says. 'Back to the start. They looked beyond the ridge, saw the void, and so ... back to Africa! Somewhere like that, invented. The *balera*: that can be the Africa. You and I – we wander. There's every kind of old and unknown we must say farewell to... It takes a lifetime. We don't dance, we two ... that's not for us.'

'I might do the figures, Irma,' I say. 'But it's the case – neither of us wants to live out life on the floor, waiting for our tune to play. The natural life attracts – who'd want to spend existence in the circus ring?'

'Don't exaggerate,' Irma says. 'The dance is good. The music's opium. Sometimes the others bear you up, there's food, applause...'

*

'Don't misunderstand,' Irma says. 'We're not here because we're brighter than the rest. We're here because they don't like us. And I told you – Riya and I – we don't get on.'

'Well,' I say, 'I always did what they wanted. I can't imagine they take exception to me...'

'No, that's it,' Irma says. 'They didn't ask much of you. You're limited. In some areas, you could be a bigot, but probably – you just haven't thought, imagined. Or just not been, not heard, not even wondered. Being self-sufficient – it doesn't make you *sympa*, and no one thinks you're courageous or sensitive. They didn't want to spend the rest of themselves with us.'

It's a blow, of course – but you get over it.

'Then there was Senegal,' says Irma. 'Was that what you are, or what you think you are? What you'd like to forget, and no one else can.'

'Adnan,' I say. 'He wants to start off something new – not through charity... It's a labour. Dirty too.'

'It's that Dostoevsky thing – if things go wrong, up rise morals like a picket fence,' says Irma. 'You have to get away from that. Start again – the same thing. No introspections.'

She's an anarchist – out of place in any city, especially the one we're in – big modern tenements, higher than the sun, magnolias not quite making it at corners...

'If you follow someone else,' she says, 'you must go right to the end. Life, or mostly death.'

'You get set up for flags and presidents that way,' I say.

'It's up to anyone to follow – but not me. You don't see me, nodding in fours, fronting some band,' she says.

'Adnan failed from the top,' I say. 'Founding villages, harvesting, addresses, asphalt streets. He might have won people to follow him – maybe unhappy, certainly poor: perhaps driven out and injured, worse...'

'It's best to start failing from the bottom,' Irma says, 'and keep on failing, because you – you at the bottom, you can't win. It's a truth, a certainty. It's not so bad.'

'I'm somewhere in the middle...' I begin.

'That's nowhere,' Irma says, 'a middle's geography, or maths, somewhere two real places need to have, to separate them.'

I can't answer. Irma says, 'Everything I've said is true. But – it isn't me. I want something else, that isn't part of someone else's scheme. Bukayr's idea of the collapse – all true, but a manipulation. A programme, a moralism... It will take centuries – the last Adams, on the last island in the universal sea, the last bullies, the last pistols, Le Grand Macabre on tape ... all hocked to some bank. That's how it will end – the last coconut, last cute bug – fought over... No one we would recognise around. The last people marooned from everywhere, thinking the same and all in different languages. Salty and hot.'

'If it's true, Irma,' I say.

'You haven't understood,' she says. 'They all must climb that ridge – it takes them many many years.'

She pushes me, off the track, down the crevasse, a deep *burrone*. 'And do I want you with me, tagging along, a walking foil, an unreliable patsy? Quite unnecessary,' Irma says.

That's what you are

Good, thinks Irma, I've got rid of him. Now I can take the next steps on my own.

First – seek immortality. Of course, you never know if it's been properly installed. But you need time, to watch things all come down, or have your stay in jail and not be bored...

Then – you're no hero, heroine, and you've no land. So – no romantic turn. Resentment, jealousy – in an immortal, that's beneath you. Human rights – immortals are already halfway out of that. Poets make the humanistic speech as mortals – but, on the notepad, the birchbark walled up in the cave, there is immortality nudging, indifferent to content, sentiment, and so... What's written down perhaps survives. The writer won't, Irma knows. What lives? A celebration of this, of that, of walking in the rain, a bottled message 'all will be better, just you wait and see.' Of course, it's immortality you need for waiting, though – see how the land mass shrinks, the islets sag under their human flesh like rusty cargoboats, sailing from Durazzo or from Tripoli...

*

If you're immortal, you don't need a banquet – some asparagus, a marigold, will do – but it's no fun. You have no option – you survive. Then, with no struggle – on you live, alone. It's good – but there's no project. Hope's not abandoned: it has never been. I – you – are a museum piece, examplar of a species now extinct. There's perfect peace, no one to visit you, bolted upright in your perspex case. You're the history encapsulated of everyone there's ever been – the unique survival, no heroics, and no epic. A reverse messiah, come to close the shop, the last, the only, miraculated survivor. No one is left to look you up or worship you – sure, you could really be immortal, but who'd know? You're the last, after all, the story's yours. No one can sneak on you, even if your eternal realm, empire of self-love, lasts just five minutes...

On the bonfire goes the everlasting flower, lasts on as dust and ash...

*

'This looks like my street,' thinks Irma. 'Though with the buildings knocked away, it's now a road.'

There's youths, revving up their bikes. 'What's the game?' she asks. 'Where does the road end?'

'Not anywhere we want to go,' they say. 'We race, up and down. To see who's fastest. What did you think?'

'What if you've no fuel?' she asks.

'There's donkeys, and there's skates,' they say.

Irma is light, she's slight: she has the worst bike lent her, and the worst opponent, though he's sure he'll win.

She lies along the machine, a salamander. It's easy to go fast if you don't care... Or don't want to lose.

'Don't give me a helmet, I can't see with one...' she says. She wins. She's so low, it's as if she isn't clinging there, just factory paint. She wins and wins, and they get bored. She's a circus rider, that's for sure.

'I've done it,' Irma thinks. 'Immortal!' You just have to concentrate, and choose the line.

She asks, 'All this stuff, the bikes, the clothes, the flags, the gold and silver cups...?'

'It's all been left,' they say.

'You could plant trees, and have the dates,' she says.

'It's dirty here,' they say. 'We shan't be round in any case, to pick the fruit.'

She's no idea how long it takes to grow a tree.

*

Winners ought to get a prize, champions should leave something of themselves. Take a gold cup – and that might draw unwelcome eyes. What could she leave? Strip off, flash herself, a moonbeam. So quick, it's an imaginary. That wouldn't cost. Frivolous and vapid, though, a throwback: and free – she's free! Otherwise, here, do they expect theology – you take a serpent that becomes a stick, and strike a rock and make a stream?

*

'You herd the pigeons,' says the guy. 'The room – if you do well, it costs you almost nothing.'

'I'm not sure it's even yours,' says Irma. 'But it's high up, hot, so small it is unnoticed. Good.'

The pigeons spiral – every tenement sends up a thermal – the pigeons would sooner wheel than climb – they could see everything, but it's no use to them, and it's them returning Irma needs.

On the next roof, there's a guy with a net – he catches anything that's flying low. If they go too high – there's hawks. Also when they perch.

'Patience, that's required,' says the guy, Adnan. 'You can know your destiny, dear Irma, but it's the timing that's essential...'

'That's what Bukayr says,' Irma says. 'Now, he's a wallflower. They say devils have the best tunes – but some don't want the tunes at all. Devils are in fashion now – back to claim their place. Anyway, Bukayr played the *erhu*, though it doesn't fit in the *balera* repertoire. Persistence, sounds at the limit of humanity. He must have a golden heart – that's the hardest kind... The beat goes on, but you can't sing to it.'

'An everlasting wallflower,' Adnan says. 'Riya beside to prop him up – she'll be an old dry stick. Beast and beauty – waiting out their time.'

'They're both immortals,' Irma says. 'Bukayr writes fragments, Riya does the puff... The scent, the pollen – she's responsible. It'll all end – I don't remember when.'

'That's it, then,' Adnan says. 'Immortals, when time ends, they don't exist! My time is not yet come. I don't have what I wanted – but none of us, my friends, is jailed, or tortured, nor a torturer. It's a success. The people here – they cling. They don't feel up to starting other countries yet...'

'One forward, two or more – back they go, but they're not steps to what they say was, or will be, wonderful,' Irma says. 'Drill for the infantry. I'll move on. The pigeons will go round and round, wider and wider, until they find the grain the people left. I've had my adventure – I know what I am. I'm a racer!'

She has a gold cup, but she doesn't show it.

'I'm like I was at the beginning,' says Adnan. 'In a dead land. Ready to start again, with what I think I am.'

'Take all the pigeons, Adnan,' Irma says. 'Start from there. Fly them round and round – they'll attract others, till you can have all the pigeons in the world. It's not stealing. No one will try to take them off you. They don't belong to anyone.'

2

MY COUNTRY

AIR, walking, smiling – there's many schizophrenics here. They stroll up and down – they used to be shut in. It didn't work. Even earlier – they were chained: that was no cure either. What cure do they expect? They're not war casualties: no one need feel bad about religion, massacres, or uncertain about Americans, or any foreigners. The schizoids – they can't hold the line, that's all. These illnesses – they're just a pain, for everyone, worse if you haven't got it but someone else has.

Cheating and disloyalty: that's bad, not in itself because it's normal here as well, but because it leads to settling the score, for good. Not everybody goes to jail for that, of course.

Being angry – it's stupid, unavailing, let's you down – you have to keep some cool.

The teacher – supposed to teach the kids. 'Open the lid, switch on,' he says. 'It's a forest. Deep and black: who wants to see the satyrs, down inside, out of sight, pleasuring the nymphs? Smell the tulips – moist and woody...'

It's not tulips, naturally.

Maybe a fungus.

'Belinda,' the teacher, Egeo, says. 'Remember those foxes, living on the island. Evolution hadn't taught them to look up – so when the eagles landed and took root, they were all snatched, eaten like candy. Well – everything you've learned, everything you've tied your strings to – it's all melting, disappearing. Everything familiar – the people, the buildings – all evaporating.

Soon, the people you love, they'll all go in the wood. You open it – down, down inside – your life is there. Dark, deep in the roots and where the light creeps up from below – you'll look at them – disporting, spreading their arms, rubbing against the bark. All the rest – your hut, the fire, the woodpile, the animals ... not needed any more...'

He's not a real teacher – he's a technician, teachers don't talk like that. He wants to see if Belinda cries. She doesn't. Maybe she's relieved, attracted even.

'Then we won't die,' she says. 'No cemetery, no stones.'

'Oh,' says the teacher. 'Of course you won't. There's nothing there. What would be left, to hide away; who'd dig those holes?'

'That's good, very good,' Belinda says. 'I like clean endings.'

'If you ever get a dog,' Egeo goes on, 'remember, you have two souls there. There's the abject – who pees and craps while you walk it out, look at the panorama, see to Greece, to Libya, Amazons and Phoenicians in their boats. Then, there's the hidden one, the wolf, *in pectore*. Clean as a stone. Friendless. That's the one you value, closed safe inside. You see its shadow, naturally – usually it's hidden in the dog – but in the sunlight, there you glimpse it, against a wall, flitting past a tree, grey watercolour.'

'The forest's good as well,' she says, switching on, and going deep inside.

'You gotta believe, Belinda,' Egeo says, earnestly, 'even if it's all quotes. Planted in your head, for ever, till you die, and then what's in there – that won't be dead. You do understand, Belinda?'

'Of course,' she says, 'but you'll get into trouble, Egeo. We're only nine. Though our heads are bigger in proportion than they'll ever be. We're at the top.'

'The truth's the truth, Belinda,' says Egeo, 'even if you're nine. Besides, you've been right down there in the forest, seen it all.'

'Yes,' she says, 'but maybe I didn't understand.'

'That's why people get into trouble,' Egeo the teacher says. 'They don't understand. Probably no one does, ever, and most people have been nine, passed through. If you understand, of course, you still get into trouble.'

'You're trying to corrupt me,' says Belinda. 'I am fascinated. Naturally. You'll come to a bad end, Egeo.'

'That's for sure,' the teacher says. 'But I – perhaps alone – I'm innocent! Think, Belinda! If you were a monkey, at your age, you'd be grown up, part of the family – not learning what's the longest river, what's Titan made of, and all that. Reflect! There's two kinds of monkey countries: the warriors – ever upward, struggling towards a goal, because they are too rich and have no other thought: or else too poor: your prospect is eternal war. Then there's the other sort – the suffering and contemplative. Subsistence, reproduction, poetry and whittled sticks – that is your lot. The groups exist apart, but they aren't alien – they all climb down, from that same monkey tree. And on they go, like that; they don't collect the broken stuff like us and put it on display, don't bother writing down what's evident and learned when you are hiding in your mother's fur... Those are the heroes; the monkey types wise people worship. Belinda – our species,' and the teacher wipes his eyes, 'Thinks we're an advance: – the best of predators, the smartest warriors, the most sensitive; pacific too... It's a fantasy! We took the wrong turn, Belinda dear. Evolution – gave us swivel necks, like owls. There's nothing more than that. That's the whole truth. We've swarmed. We're eating everything, our massacres don't make a dent, the populations move around without a grip – we pullulate, Belinda, bindweed. We're parasites, cochineals, tall rats...'

'I know,' Belinda says: 'That's what they teach us now.'

'I thought I'd seen what others wouldn't tell,' Egeo says, much disappointed. 'You've fallen in, Belinda, dropped down, into the forest. There is no way out.'

*

In a small time, Belinda's grown, is something else. 'Egeo,' she tells friend Mirko, 'shopped me. He window shopped me, told me everything you need to know, so whatever I do now – he can betray. He knew it first. My secrets are his, for ever. Who knows where he has gone?'

'Things you don't tell aren't secrets,' Mirko says. 'A secret is valuable, and that's why there are none.'

'If you were smarter, Mirko,' Belinda says, 'you'd run from me, me and what I know. The more intelligent – they keep away. But I can't run from you, you all, from everyone who sees the cover and can't read the book. So – I'm your torment, I'll give you what I can. I can't, though, give you understanding.'

And he doesn't understand.

Things really aren't so complicated, and besides – the strong guys cut the knots with laws and bombs and threats. If you're just weak and normal, someone who pulls in fish and serves the bread – yes, it's incomprehensible.

'All our exercises, the machines, the drugs, our lurching towards immortality – we're shamans, Mirko. And we're quacks,' she says. 'It's good. Best be that way, not too serious. Everybody here invents their own universe. It's intimate, one you can travel round. Start believing you can make trips up to the stars – all you create is tanks and rockets. You know, Mirko – the poor people, they get killed in ones and twos, they say the rich guys aim at them specifically, or else it's neighbours settling scores. But us, here in rich country – we won't die like that, won't need to run, or battle for a drink of mud – no, the rich ones have the answer. They'll take everybody with them – they've explosives that can end it all, better than injections, better than a plastic bag tied on your head... You can watch it on your screen, every second – then it's upon you. The wrath...'

What I'll be, Belinda thinks, is what they call a grand reporter, one of the *grands*. But I shan't write things down, like you're supposed, and walk away. I'll give cash to those who need it, give counsel to the guys in power. I'll make and shape the stories, have a following. I'll colour everything I see with crayons, like when we were all innocent, small, and knew the happiness...

'Leave me, Belinda,' Mirko says, 'and I'll harass you. Disfigure you, all your life.'

'That's good, Mirko,' Belinda says. 'That way I've no more fear, and I'll know too what the figure was, the original, that's blotted out, disfigured. It's good to have you stalk me with your bow. You are my enemy, you don't have the nerve to shoot...'

*

Downstairs, it's a fine hotel. There's real storks in the palms. The rooms are crap, but if you sleep, you don't see what creeps out by night. Belinda is a journalist, a storyteller, shaman, explorer, knows what's underground and lives on. You can bring up a soul, stoppered in a terra cotta bottle like a moneybox, you talk to it through a slit, 'How's death? What are your plans?'

Then, suddenly, there's battle on them, the four sat round, Belinda's minders, guardian angels – some guys with clubs – as handles, set on them. Belinda runs out to the motor – 'maxillary' runs in her head, it brings relief, remembering the word for where they've hit her, a remedy, a cure, maybe. She's in the back – don't go there in a two-door car, that is the end, this one has four, it's good. The rest jump in, all dented and alarmed – 'Shoot, shoot' – she shouts, as the clubbers run towards the car. 'Fan it,' she remembers. 'Fan the hammer back, you idiot,' a phrase recalled, fits the kind of gun, you need do that before it fires.

'Is this what I want?' she thinks: the brain articulates so well, indifferent to a broken jaw that transposes tongues and teeth, limes off the words that now for ever drop and blur. 'The famine, axes with heads, cutting heads off – someone wants revenge, catastrophe, that is for sure. Those rabid guys, they had the rage ... far greater anger than I have. Truth – it must lie all around – can you feel passion for it? Writing it down – what does it add? Then, you see the thugs that's paid to beat up on us innocents ... my brothers, all of us, God's Slaves. Everything and everyone – has its reason, except for time and wear.'

Off they drive – shooting at the clouds, the press is free again, the ambush thwarted, hope regained...

It's more Mirko's country, throwing acid in your face, than it was Egeo's, peeking at the patinated nudes.

*

'I will go on,' Belinda thinks, 'even if, like Egeo said, it is all quotes. But, the brain articulates, it's perfect. The way they set my jaw, though, it's kiltered off; it's not a lisp, I have the enchanter's voice: behold the sphinx! the oracle – unique. I understand it all; no one can make out what I say. Is my incomprehensible a secret then? Or the banal future everybody must endure? I'm an Ophelia, letting go, a wanderer between the thought, and speech.'

*

Besides, you can't go on camera with a facc all skewed. Journalism, the prince's counsellor – that's done. Finished. Something else...

'I'm not a *grand reporteur*,' Belinda tells the doctor, 'but I want my straight face back.'

'Well,' says the doctor, 'you must still see the funny side. If we can't laugh about it all, what's the point of all us being here?'

'I can snigger,' says Belinda. 'A guffaw's far out, way beyond my throw.'

'I'll try,' the doctor says, taking a hammer from a drawer: 'A smile, at least: your sneer is irritating.'

'My brain can see the joke,' Belinda says. 'It's the way I just can't tell them.'

'Think of what you most believe in,' says the doctor, smashing at her face.

'Oh no,' snarls Belinda. 'Now the other side has gone.'

'Oops! My swing! I took my eye off your mouth. You clearly don't believe in anything that's strong enough to guide my hand,' the doctor says, replacing the hammer. 'Things were bad before – now they're no worse – it's just the therapy to put things right, is doubled. But the price agreed, that doesn't change.'

'Oh, wire me up and switch me on,' Belinda says: 'It's destiny. I've no "good side". No one will profile me now, good doctor.'

'I feel,' the doctor says, 'a bit responsible. You are the beast I made. Belinda, you are my monster now. I drew you as you were, should be – perfection, desirable, electable – a power for every land. Now, somewhere we must fit you in. Everybody has an act, a scene – what will yours be?'

'Yes,' Belinda says, 'I had high hopes. Truth and power. Now what?'

'Well,' the doctor says, putting his arm round her, pressing her to him, which she doesn't want. 'Now, you look funny. But we mustn't laugh. So – you're invisible. You are not what you are – you're a mistake – the mistake that comes out of my mistake.'

'That's what my teacher said,' Belinda says. 'About creation. A mistake you mustn't laugh about.'

'I'll have to take you round and show you off,' the doctor says. 'Not my responsibility, of course, though I feel bad, so bad. You are my thing, my *Ding*. The good news and the bad news is – you don't look as you do from history; no self-deprecation, no jester turning aside the blade, no stand-up clown for fear of falling down: no, Belinda, you're unique. You're what we all would want to be – true individual, in and for yourself. No freakery, not a lady, not bearded, and not fat – original, unique, invisible. Incoherent too.'

'I chew as if I am a sheep,' Belinda says, 'but nothing tastes of grass.'

'Everything connects,' the doctor says. 'Now you are mine, a part of me. The tongue links to the taste, the taste – to what? To reason or utility? Fashion? Happy end? Tales of people who can make the best, or somebody's grand friends they write about?'

'Everything is flexible, good Doctor Alban,' Belinda says. 'Sheep eat the grass, their flesh – it tastes of meat. When you were small, you longed to be a smith, and shoe the horses – wield the tongs, the file, the hammer, see white iron turn to red, red into orange, smell the smoke of burning hoof – then all the horses went, the smithies closed... So – it was doctoring: the tongs, the hammer and the phial, the white flesh runs with blood, we all are steel, we burn with purpose, clean, no smoking, and good tempered ... and off we go, we gallop off: the road! The road! That is my destiny!'

'I can't feel responsible for ever,' Alban says. 'Enough! An accident – you must forget. I can start to see your deeper flaws, Belinda. Take Mali, now: you should know all about that – look at the fractures! The north and south – and see – the crucial lines – Niger and Chad, you ought to know about all that, French Africa – you, Belinda, *grand reporteur*, say something, profound, important. Those aren't accidents, my dear, not like your face, your trauma – speak!'

'Oh,' Belinda says, 'of course, I am half-educated. I know about the music – the politics I can't do anything about...'

'You see?' says Doctor Alban. 'None of that's my fault. You're not half-educated. If you know nothing, you're not educated in the slightest... Knowing half the alphabet, half a diploma, half the one-times table... You can't go on the road like that! A quarter horse, maybe – but half a horse! That's pantomime, and not well paid at that.'

'You're wrong, good doctor,' shouts Belinda. 'A half-horse – is a mule. That's me! There's a sadness I can understand. There's my road, there's the dead end...'

'It's never so,' the Doctor says, whispering confidentially. 'And I know exactly how roads end – at a sea, a swamp, a mountain top – it's true, how they all end, they seem to end ... or else, if you're the perverse kind, roads have only starts, beginnings – in the end, the origin. When we're extinct, Belinda dear, whether from being rash, or catching something – maybe a rash –' and he curls with laughter, 'or hunger, thirst or massacre, discovery of something you smarm on – you're happy, but you croak... I, Belinda, I, my genes, are in a box. I can be recreated, I'm the young Adam, the ur-man, the Mister Lucy. If they should decide to start it off again, our species – the best, first specimen – is me! But – the expense... And will those creatures lurching after me – conserve? You, Belinda, you could be my Eve. It would be you, but with your accident effaced, your face restored and flawless once again.'

'Forget it, Alban, lose the crap idea,' he thinks he hears Belinda say. 'Maybe that's history, circling round, a pair original starting it all off, a thousand circuits, from Eden to the flames, the judgment. Not for me! A mule I'll live as, as a mule I'll die.'

'I thought to offer,' Alban says. 'If you wanted, you could die and live again – infinity, the brain wiped clean each time the roundabout swings round...'

*

'It's all their sense of guilt,' Belinda tells her friend. 'They fuck you up, and tell you they've an invention to transform the world. And all it is – a telephone, a space-ship – something to impoverish, for sure.'

'That doctor Alban, dear, is quite the best,' her friend, Alicia, says. 'He trims your aspect to your destiny, they say. He forms your outside to the inner shape... The future of the species – that is in his grasp...'

'That may be so,' Belinda says. 'I found him trivial. And his aims are hit and miss.'

'We must forgive their errors,' Alicia says, severe. 'And hope – expect – they'll find out things that bring us happiness and fuller lives.'

'I don't see that,' Belinda says.

'Look at all the top class men you have,' says Alicia. 'Mirko, Doctor Alban – you, with your horse face... There's others who would swap with you... I'm only joking, dear,' she adds.

Belinda says, 'I laugh at lies and laugh at truths – they say all animals like some fun, but it's the laugh special to us, a kind of whinny, you would say. I wonder why...'

'Belinda, you're a pedant,' Alicia says. 'It's so annoying. Truth and lies – we get enraged by both, it's true...'

'Symmetry attracts,' Belinda says, 'and so does difference – what interests me is why the laugh evolved – and not just one, but every kind, fitted for all occasions. Like words. Or metaphors.'

'You've become one of those who can't be understood, Belinda,' says Alicia, irritated. 'Maybe it's your accidents.'

'Go away, Alicia,' shouts Belinda. 'Learn to accept!'

'I should be quartz,' Belinda says, as Alicia leaves her – 'Quartz would resist, and all the rest – we could be printed out as books, if there were someone who would read us – small books, and everyone alive would fit into tiny pamphlets made of our genetic spirals, fit into the trunk of a big car... So what? – whatever's inside the leaflets printed out and stored unread, at least by humans, and whatever eyeless, earless sneaks a peek into the messages that make us up belongs to the alarming universe of properties and whizzing things, invisible and hatched a depth of years ago, tiny to non-existence, eaters of matter, with no guts; hunters of air and colours without arrows, without mouths... Science-fact, they say. I stand between the world down there, of crap precarious work that when I die I shall not leave a stain, not figure on a plaque to millions of my similars, my brothers, sisters, eliminated, remembered digits inside chains of zeroes... and the world up there, of rich invention, of speculation on nutrinos, holidays spent stealing amber in Ukraine, sailing with lookalikes on soupy seas... between a mass that has no class and hates its boss, its capital, indifferent to its mates – and richland, riding on that bisque, the Biscayne Bays, couscous and beys – perched on a nautilus, pulled by a quadrille of lobsters till they tire, and down you go, a last thrash, out of yourself, a letting go, not a bubble left, gristle dissolved, your soul free of all ligaments, ascending in a blooming of medusas, undistinguished, undistinguishable...

'And so, I read your thought, your mumble-tumble?' asks the man across the aisle: 'You're wrong. This isn't richland, and you don't exist, my dear. You underestimate the huge machine that's everywhere – the troops of trojan horses, molochs that turn you into shit, the tides and droughts of wealth, the sun approaching and the universal cancer undiagnosed and flowering in the dark where no one sees, my girl, my girl ... in the dark, in the dark ... the sickness unimaginable...'

'Yes,' says Belinda, 'I like ideas like that – we strain to push it round, that machine is made of boilerplate, so tall the armaments hide up in the clouds: it turns out chocobars and aztec seeds...'

'What you don't see, Belinda,' says the guy, sitting beside her, lifting the veil that covers up her martyred face, 'is, though you push – that juggernaut, it has no wheels. Vanity, sheer vanity: it's a machine that's built so huge its obsolescence means – the end of everything ... the flowery bridges, oratorios, the spray above the falls, the maple and the chestnut, old jokes and sugar squirrels... So, Belinda, have no fear – wherever struggle leaves you – gravity will have you in the end. The pit, my dear, that's falling into other pits, until they reach the buzz where nothing's visible and all recedes as dizzily as if the universe has drunk a bucketful of schnapps...'

'Yes,' says Belinda, 'I started off so well. And now I know. I am a mule. That's it.'

'Come with me, Belinda,' says the guy, Jean-Luc. 'I give counsel – and it pays. You'd think they knew it for themselves. But it's like you, Belinda: I understand you perfectly, every word that you think's blundered, but instead – it rings upon the counter when you rap it!'

'No,' Belinda says, 'I'm not interested. Those counsels turn out wrong.'

'I see you're not a gambling mule,' Jean-Luc says. 'We give alternatives – the opposite may occur, and often does. You need to hedge your bet, Belinda.'

'Go away,' Belinda says. 'You crook.'

'Don't worry,' says Jean-Luc. 'There's no crime any more. There's no property worth having, it's all made to depreciate. Money? You do it in a flash – two fingers and a nudge. The other crimes? It's all politics. There's millions involved, with families and cash: no one is ever guilty, and besides, you don't remember. Everybody dies.'

'Go away!' Belinda shouts.

'That's right!' Jean-Luc says. 'I knew you would accept. No more Doctor Alban; your stalker sniped and snipped, off with him too!'

'I'm a witness of great crimes,' Belinda says, 'performed on me, quite personally. It's quite too bad – although there's nothing I can do. I'm nearly dumb, but not a prisoner of family; I'm no princess, Ophelia jumping in the pond. I need to find the ear, the right one, that hears what I've to say. I'm sure you hear me well enough, Jean-Luc! You're my last choice, but time! Oh History! Oh taste and fashions – just let me make my speech! Remember – I am the last one of my kind!'

'We all are that, Belinda,' Jean-Luc says.

'I shall not go to waste,' Belinda says, but – that's the end: the hole, the urn, the river or the pyre. Nature – out you came of nothing, into nature now you go, to make the sunsets and the maples, the syrup and the capsicum, the sweet and sour, the jolly steamboat and the skewer.'

*

'Here's where you work,' Jean-Luc says.

'Why, it's a paradise,' Belinda says in wonder: there's an alp, with Heidi flowers and cactuses, depending on the genre, and blobs of sheep or tumbleweed, and on the ranch-style house – it could be by le Corbusier, or Mies too, of course – there's flags, of every nation, some just rags on poles, and some all holes...

'How come you found this?' Belinda asks.

'Oh, everybody knows a paradise,' says Jean-Luc, cool and masterly. 'The problem is, nothing dies here, but nothing grows. There are no eats.'

'These insects, though,' Belinda says, 'they sting!'

'It's their paradise too, of course,' Jean-Luc says. 'Now, here's the office. If you stamp your feet, the roaches go off back to bed. See – all this paper and more precious stuff – it's riches unimaginable. There's railroads never built and prototypes of planes that crashed – they're worth a fortune now, just takes some geek to tweak the plan – some of this goes back centuries. Whole calves went into some of them, the parchments: edicts, certificates and bonds, patents, permissions – imagine! Birchbark too – with the inflation of a thousand years...! The records – as big as zeppelins – you just need blow them up...'

'What exactly is my work?' Belinda asks, reluctant still.

'Oh, soothe the worthies, unworthies too. Dignitaries, indignitaries. Find what they want, make them sign a trust, a deed. Promise the return – then in the file it goes.'

'Is there no more?' she asks.

'There's the advice, of course,' says Jean-Luc. 'And the caution. Lots complain. Tell them to pray, obey, and go away. If they are comely – they can love me. It all, of course, everything they try to take away – it comes to naught. It's what I store up here that counts. You see, it all amounts to fortunes – held in trust, of course – for heirs and corporations, if they ever come... It's not an easy ramble, this! Remember our trip, Belinda – over the fever swamp and up the glacier, over the scree and down the sheer. The few who get here – you need to be in form, in shape: no corporate body's lithe enough to scale and bounce and do the butterfly among the lily pads...'

'And you're alone here, Jean-Luc?' asks Belinda.

'Oh, the women, they come and go...' he gestures: 'Corseted, veiled, the lot. Here's not to everybody's taste. Ascetic and devotional, no chatter over cups of tea. The men – it saddens me to need to stereotype – but, the men hate solitude, they want their toys spilled on the rug and biscuits with their milk...'

And indeed, the huge windows show a cerulean sky, with puffs of cloud too ephemeral to presage lightning, thunderbolts...

Unless you have a faith – there's nothing up there except wasted space.

'And, Belinda,' Jean-Luc says, taking her arm, 'it's true – here's populated, but it's also sparse. You could say,' and he whispers, 'I'm Mister Lonely too.'

'And, might I ask,' Belind asks, coy. 'Where d'you stash the cash?'

'You haven't understood at all,' says Jean-Luc, angrily. 'The cash goes obsolete. Why – I dump the copper cash down in the well, the gold I melt to hold the patio stones in place. Capital, my dear! We hold a slice here, what you might call a golden share. It's history, and future too: the poetry, the science, oil and water, fresco too... Worlds of imagination, imaginary worlds – that is our capital, on paper, canvas, marble... Surely you were taken off from elementary school to see the banks of statues, deposit boxes filled with gewgaws... That's our capital in concrete form. The originals are here...' Jean-Luc waves around – from the parchments faintly comes a bleat, a moo...

'If I work here,' Belinda says. 'I'd be amidst just everything. Public investment promoting private gain: shifting capital from here to there, creating the satisfied, and then the rich, or twisting votes the ways I want... Making space and stoppering holes... And, Jean-Luc, all compensating for the crimes I wear... my face…'

'Oh no, Belinda,' says Jean-Luc. 'The scheme's immense and contradictory, of course – but it transforms the world. Continuity and constant change – long white beards, wrinkles – interest is paid, and wanes. The crimes? – no, I don't think there's a relief – not forgetfulness, nor punishment, not pardon, nor remorse. You're fortunate – the crimes are on your face and in your words. You won't forget. But – maybe there was no guilt, and no intent. What then?'

'Then – I'll get tired of paradise,' she says.

*

Belinda starts to heal. It must be the spell in paradise.

She keeps her twisted poker-face. People everywhere: – she meets – discards. No full house without its warmth's in sight.

What do all these people mean? Is that a question than can hold an answer? Paradise. That's the furthest you can get. But Jean-Luc – he talks funny, but he's just a station on the route. Nobody is angels.

If you should see a person beautiful, with an accent – maybe it's class, or from a place. There's the sounds gyring up: round a twist in the œsophagus... Or, it might reflect money, or a servant, a tutor: – being abandoned in an orphanage or in the desert; walking with your tribe in Ethiopia... It could be too, that person, bored with the scene, had fled, intent to spread around the world mundane, profane, their fragrance and their vowels, their elevated characters. If in paradise, the rewards are not enough – that is Belinda's fear – you'd likely root out the cause. It must be Jean-Luc! He seems quite without a personality, pays lip service to loving and tolerating ... but he's on his own. Maybe he feels lonely, though it's not important – he'll always be a loner, he holds Belinda, squeezes her arm, maybe they make some love – just for a month or so – it's paradise, after all ... and then there is indifference. He could be a caring angel or a devil, rather bored without his togs and tongs, the fork, the talk... He and Belinda – they could both be Mister Lonely... They're people it's unlikely you will ever meet, and probably you feel they're so atypical there is no message they could carry, or worth reading if they did.

You would be wrong.

'Belinda,' says Jean-Luc. 'I've long thought the model of revolution that convinced me once – was maybe not so right. There's a dynamic lacking. Too much state. It clogs. The vanguard, and its party – where does it end up? Of course, paradise is one place you won't find a revolution. So many start with cutting off a head – no use doing that, or even cutting off some thousands more. I need a change of air, Belinda, new ideas...'

'It's so,' she says. 'Even the simplest things have grown more complicated – the military finishes its works, no one else seems able. But – revolution, whatever it might mean to you – perhaps you have a plan? A provocation?'

'Oh – it's something cultivated folk must have opinions on,' says Jean-Luc. 'Part of their baggage.'

Belinda packs some papers – certificates and contracts, some are centuries old – into a bag.

'It's time to go,' she says. 'I'm sure I've done all I should do here.'

'Before you sneak away, Belinda,' says Jean-Luc. 'Please help me dig the pit.'

'It sounds as if there should be one of those already, older than paradise,' Belinda says, anxious to be off.

'I have to make a hole and put the documents away,' says Jean-Luc, 'before the owners come to use the place themselves.'

'I thought...' Belinda says.

'I was the owner? What a thought!' he says. 'I squat here. That's a thing that paradise allows you to. Then the proprietors come back, and you'll have gone, you never see them, who they are, how many, or what they'd think of signs of occupation. My guess is – they're too big to care. Or else – they're always on their honeymoon. It's always been a mystery to me, and now it's one for you.'

'How I shall miss this,' she says. 'This paradise. It's civilisation – without this, there is none – and you, Jean-Luc, without you, not even the belief persists that we could sit here, do the business looking at the sky, those immense high windows, the puffs of cloud, like cannon-smoke above contested fields.'

'We'll miss each other,' Jean-Luc says, sliding his long fingers, twiggy as Voltaire's, a last time inside her dress... 'Civilisation has left, it's true. Without a paradise – there's none. There's just a ranch without its cattle and its steaks... Oh well, like revolution, paradise has passed on to the books, been accounted for ... the awful double entry, that made us rich and sceptical. Scribble scribble – all is written down and nothing understood.

'But now, Belinda, you are cured, you speak without your veil, your curtain, it's all clear, and often, dear, it's quite banal. Alas! You're not a genius. True, any idiot can speak in puzzles but, Belinda, don't forget the depth, the smoke, the curtain, the tarry gob that stopped your throat and made you whistle, roar – the dragon's song. People would come to listen to your taradiddles, not your commonplaces. Farewell, Belinda, down from the sky, toting your gladstone full of dry and dusty leaves – where will you wander next?'

*

'I can start again,' Belinda thinks. 'Back in the village – the ugliness that no one sees, the ugliness you love. The young ones – they will give you hell – it is their gift, so no one thinks they have enchanted life, but sad sad like the one that everybody has.'

'"Looking for the golden mean..."' she sings. 'Alicia! Why are you here?'

'Oh, I love frontiers,' Alicia says. 'Here, you age so slowly. There used to be animals on those hills, and gangs of people picking cabbages down here. There used to be...'

'There was fascism, now there's something else,' Belinda says. 'You can be the same as everyone, and no one cares.'

'Different countries,' says Alicia. 'Different clothes and different gods: off they go to fight on different sides in different wars.'

'The children,' says Belinda. 'If I had some, I'd want them to look like me, be the same size, for starts. Here, they all seem cuckoos, rude ones at that...'

'Oh, you're such a stick!' Alicia says. 'What fun – to have a baby, a surprise pack... Besides, children here – they often don't belong. There are some swaps, and many lies. It's like no one dies what gets called a natural death – the suicides are classed as accidents, the murders too.'

'Yes,' says Belinda, 'it's all true – but there's no further meaning to it. It's all a story, just what happens to be fitted to the characters, the plot. It doesn't signify. Just random lives, adjusted to the winds.'

'You could be happy here,' Alicia says. 'Like I am. Or be critical and move.'

'Go away, Alicia,' Belinda says. 'Paradise – was the worst experience of my life. It makes the rest seem mediocre. Truth and power – can these, my country, give to me?'

'Every place set on the world,' Alicia says, 'is made at the same time. You think you come back here, to your country, so that it drives you off to somewhere else. But everywhere, it has the same, the simultaneous, origin. The morning that the planet formed, everywhere is one: there is no brother and no twin, no place autonomous. Flight, Belinda, is unavailing. Whether this was underwater at the start, or in a flaming hole – it's all the same.'

'Is that profound, Alicia?' Belinda asks. 'Or just wrong?'

'You'll be here when there's the festival,' Alicia says. '"Birth of the World". You can join the dance.'

So long as Mirko, the stalker's, not around...

*

The organisers of the birth – they don't bother with the empty years of cooling down. The era of amoeba, then big lizards on the hop ... the ash, the monkeys teetering, on the upright to get near the fruit. Then, the hominids with pointed sticks, pics in the cave. All that – a dumb show, and passed over in a blink.

'No, no,' Alicia says, 'that's all for kids. It's when the show begins! Us, Belinda! Dancing before the ark – maybe with animals inside, like there was conservation then, not only ones to ride and eat...'

'All I'd take from the dance,' Belinda says, 'is the round, the circle. I want the time when we're no longer man and woman. Having to press skins in and on, the contact so close you can't see anything. I don't seek some phantom body that's a lost myself. Forget all that: – and if you want a laugh – there's books of cuts and thrusts upon the stalls. The circle – rolling back on us, a hoop, when we shall be one of two troops again: the warring ones. And – the suffering. The warriors – they're not Slaves, they know their knowledge won't resurrect them on the battlefield or in the pit, and have them steal another march on some poor sap. The suffering ones – they're stupid, slack... They tease an image from the skies and from the pods and teasels, the sheep's eye, the gasping cod... But – it's just echo. It's only words and stuff you could invent, floating in bed, without the pain, without pretence there is some tie between your tongue and all that goes on, underfoot and overhead. There is no listener, Alicia: no idle buyer who pays to spy your sensibility. No, my friend, there's no one there but who you see that walks away, bored, abstracted...'

'I'm not stupid, Belinda,' says Alicia. 'I'm quite objective – and I've hope. We do the scenes – a stockade for the Pilgrims, and then there's the big shows they do, the Bowl games, and the athletes in their armour ... going at it, head to head, like rams or stags. Then there's the beauty of the scene – the liberation of Omarska – people don't remember what that was – but the silver balloons, the souls – they rise up, wriggling, like spermatozoa, looking for a mate up there. If you're not optimistic, Belinda, you're dull, or else you're halfway dead. Then – there's the music and the dance.'

'Yes,' says Belinda, 'that's what I love. You have to be a communist, living in America, during their wars – it's nothing, but it is the least... Just a symbol? But we must have those – and then you see what's wrong with what you've done, and look at what your exes do... You know what comes, Alicia, after a day? Another day.'

'Maybe, Belinda – but you can't live like this,' Alicia says. 'Always turning them, your dry and dusty leaves – nothing would be harvested, nothing slaughtered, nothing planted. See – over there, the necropolis. Here, the lake, the prirogue. Us, the aunts and uncles, celebrating the birth, the baby, the what we were, the what we have survived...'

'It's not enough, Alicia,' says Belinda. 'I don't rejoice.'

The loud music starts.

'Kronstadt, Alicia,' Belinda says. 'I'm a sailor, but I don't have a ship.'

'I expect it sank,' says Alicia, 'but you can still be a sailor.'

The loud music – it's so loud, it rocks the ground!

'Dance with me, Belinda,' says Alicia.

Why not?

'I love you, Belinda,' says Alicia.

'It's starting again,' says the presenter. 'We celebrate the birth, birth of our world!'

*

That was just cosmology. Nothing special.

Belinda's a reporter now – one of a special kind.

The track is mostly grass, and up they go.

She's an investor too, looking out for ways. And an explorer: the guardians with her in the car – they'll make the films, the stills – and when the news is done, they'll have a doc to sell, supposing they've not all run away if things get bad.

'What's in that bag?' asks Claude, trying to open it.

'Oh, secret orders, stuff like that,' Belinda says, fending off. Never abandon a document, she thinks.

There's no one to be seen: 'There's lots of internationals around,' says Claude. 'But these indigenous guys have to do it all themselves. The more they'll resist, the worse it is for them.'

'We'll be witnesses,' Belinda says. 'Or if not – martyrs for the cause.'

They have to stop often, getting out to pee.

'Like all the other heroes,' says Claude. 'It's not about us. We're the gods – it's other people ending down on the sand. We have longer stories.'

'Let's not go up to the ridge,' Belinda says. 'Let's stop here, where the rise begins.'

'No, we must go up, look down the other side,' says Claude. 'Huts smouldering, perhaps, the scurrying, or no one. It's our duty. It's our job. Our reason; our reason for being here.'

'We know what there'll be,' Belinda says. 'Now or later. Now or never. Look – there's a shepherd. Let's speak to him.'

'Oh, shepherds,' Claude says. 'Here they still sleep in the fields, beside the sheep. They're marginals, they don't talk to anyone. You have to watch their dogs. And there's no religion there, the work, the killing wolves – it's on the side of people; but the people – they don't want to know.'

'All right,' Belinda says. 'You're right. Everything is as you say. Let's just go back.'

*

'I expect you've dirty business in your minds,' the shepherd says. 'As well as truth, of course. Maybe you have a handle on some power. Profit, at least. Your contacts ... paths to your ambitions. The wealth you see around you...'

'It's not my field,' Belinda says. 'I don't see any wealth. Of course, sheep fetch a price...'

The shepherd pulls her in a cave. 'See,' he says. 'My collections. My fine arts.'

'It looks like broken stuff,' Belinda says, trying to read the dark.

'They dig it up, the animals,' the shepherd says. 'Rabbits and such. They burrow in the sand – and here it is – horse clothes. Parts of cataphract. Look – this is bronze stuff: bits. Bridles, and that could be a caparison – I thought the armour was of bone, but no – it's metal strips on leather: no use against a point, but good against a slash. And here – there's ivory. They put plaques on their furniture ... *yakshis* – see, that could be a leg, an arm, a nipple... Fine work, but of course the wood has gone...'

'It's wonderful,' Belinda says. 'You just pick it up? No need to dig – the rabbits do it all...I could manage that.'

'Nothing is whole, of course,' the shepherd says. 'But yes, collecting is a human thing. There's just some birds that do it too – they've more gifts than us. They fly, and while they fly, they sing. That's how we know there's angels everywhere.'

'It seems quite random,' says Belinda. 'Like writing history, or doing science.'

'You could pass your time well, cataloguing here. After all, we each have an idea of what truth is,' the shepherd says. 'And bossing people – not everyone's attracted. You'd stride beyond your truth and power...'

'Oh, I must seem such a butterfly,' Belinda says. 'It's fun, the flittering, that's true: but people expect you to steer so straight a course, even if they're on a waver by themselves. Collecting – yes, that I could do. But – I'd choose a spot far far from you.'

'You'll be giving up the best,' the shepherd says. 'You might remember – there's a discussion about stirrups. I'm quite an authority on those. I've never ridden, but I know there's things you can't do without those on your feet.'

'That's what the Cavalry believed,' Belinda says. 'Those Plains Indians – they should have watched their adversaries more close. That's how you learn survival...'

'Rabbits and foxes, don't forget,' the shepherd interrupts. 'Watch them! The rabbits build more extensively, but the law says the foxes eat them all the same.'

'What interests me, shepherd,' says Belinda, 'is why they made you watch the sheep, and threw you out the village.'

*

He doesn't answer. Maybe he's a bit crazy. Shepherds are, quite often. 'Stay with me here, in the cave,' he says. 'I'll teach you about collecting. You will be the first. The first exhibit.'

'Shepherds can't be trusted,' says Belinda. 'Too many silences. The animals... Those eyes, those tongues: so eloquent, so mute. Then, there's the secret of your expulsion... They follow you – tens, thousands – all sheep, all alert. It's like tribes, settlers – all followers – but much much older, down through the ages. The Bible's full of you fuckers. The Qur'an too. You don't do any harm, it seems, you're the magician, the piper. You have the love of all those eyes. And you deliver them, every last one, their kids, their warmth – the knife, good shepherd! That's what awaits them, that's why the villagers throw you out – those sheep are spellbound, and to the butcher you deliver them – no wonder the people don't trust you, and give you their treasures to protect... Perversity, necessity. Their wealth, their guilt, hung up on hooks.'

'You talk like someone exalted, Belinda,' says the shepherd. 'But – I've never heard a thing more obvious, more worn and trite. There's troops of wolves around, you can't imagine ... thousands! I keep the sheep safe. I can tame the beasts, put collars on...'

'Oh fiddle!' says Belinda. 'Pipe your pipe – I'm not your violin. The sound comes out from me – nothing goes in. Women love me, shepherd, not the men. To make a sound come out of me, you need a bow, and strings – a body and an arm. You need an Amazon to draw that bow.'

'I still don't see...' the shepherd says. 'My cave has room...'

'No!' says Belinda. 'It isn't what I want at all. The end is clear – the knife...!'

*

'Oh no!' says Claude. 'Belinda! Not cataphracts. What will they do, our eyes and ears, Blaise and Tamara? What movie? Rabbits?

Foxes? Nature docs? We should have viewed the massacre, therein lies our truth and power.'

'If it comes to that,' Belinda says. 'Here was a massacre: the innocent, the sheep.'

'You're so predictable, so trite,' says Claude. 'Human nature, human accidents? Your take's predictable. They say – "you've nothing – you're a victim, easy". That's the tale. "You have lots – we'll come and take it off you." No, Belinda – there is more than that. There's philosophy. There are turnings in the road.'

'I'm sure there was a city here,' Belinda says. 'That's why there's all these burnt accoutrements. We'll make a documentary.'

'Nonsense,' says Claude. 'There's been no city here, it's just a slope, with grass and sand now where once were trees.'

'Well,' says Belinda, 'we've the camera, and sound. We'll make a city with our film. I'll write the story. Then we'll sell it.'

'A story about the Hyksos,' says Claude. 'That's what we need.'

'I must get away,' Belinda says. 'Forget stories, forget you, Claude. Where can I go? This is always where I came from, always my country, my village, copied...'

Making a movie's more complex than it looks. Belinda's no idea. Claude's her guardian angel, the fixer – that's all that he can do. Are those her people, relatives, under the hill? Bigots? Scared? Just resources? – away with them, and quick.

What's to report?

'I know!' says Belinda. 'Paradise is useless – it's the place you never get to so they can throw you out. The secret, Claude – it's herding. Most ancestors: they did it, mine for certain. Down the chain, done to animals; and up the pyramid, they themselves got herded. Milked and skinned. That too – is something I could do. The truth is knowing how to be the good, and then, when the time comes, the kindly executioner – hanging on the legs of suffocating men to give them dignity; what the rope can't. Sheep and goats, Claude – you need to tell which is which; the character, the characteristics. And yes, you need to tell when it's the time.'

'You're wrong, Belinda. I know the good life. You need be surrounded by people just like you, not isolated in a field,' says Claude.

'Yes,' Belinda says. 'That means herding, that's for sure. That's your take. But collecting's not just about consuming. It's about the spirit too. The shepherd spoke about the winged bodies – the feathered angels. The holy fowls, baked in a pie. Maybe he didn't think of Aztecs when he thought of cannibalism, bodies in feathered cloaks... How we eat most creatures! Gods, angels – my! we're gourmets! How beauty shines through sight, "since we came to earth": how beautiful the thought! ... Yet we don't see wisdom through our sight, for wisdom would arouse a "terrible love" if we could see it. I've never known a terrible love, Claude,' she says, suddenly terrified – 'Have you? I guess not... I wonder if I've seen anything at all, collecting junk and thinking it was beautiful. I haven't started off anything at all...'

There's no use saying this to Claude – Claude's quite limited. Beauty and wisdom are quite incidental to the good life, if they figure in it at all...

'You should be thinking about sex, Belinda,' Claude says, 'before you decide it's too much bother. And reporting on those poor people killed, out of sight beyond the crest.'

'And will it do good?' Belinda asks, now quite confused.

'Don't be misled, Belinda,' Claude says, and tweaks one of her breasts through her fatigues. 'Those feathered things – they're not from up high – they're lizards in disguise. Beauty – it's not a thing you'd buy at auction – no, it's the way they sneak in law and order. Try not for beauty, dear Belinda, but for ugliness – the pitchfork and the tail, the flame that leaps, divides, and warms. Those shepherds – they're the ones who nurture you, then take you, every one, over to the slaughterhouse; then go, collect some more, your brothers and your sisters, quite indifferently.'

*

'Is it nature, then?' Tamara asks. 'That's what Belinda wants?'

'It's the second choice,' says Blaise. 'You are the eyes, Tamara. In theory – they're the prime, the primal, instrument. They see the beauty, so they say. But – there's a trick. Who gives us eyes? And why are ears, my instrument, a gift, but not so great? What do they grasp? I'd say "the real", in all its limitations. Eyes, Tamara. Are they so innocent? Mirror of nature – or do you make the contexts? Filters and distances – quite arbitrary – and you spoof with time, see in the dark, blown up, blowing like the wind on maps – you impose, superimpose, and then you make it move, dissolve and fade...'

'Yes, Blaise,' says Tamara...

They could be the greatest lovers in the local literature; a place for ever – neither wants it, each would rather be with someone other, or just quiet, in dark rooms or booths as tight as tight. 'Sounds we don't make ourselves – they are suggestive, but they don't cohere...' she says. 'Are there languages around us we don't understand? Musics that shift from tree to tree – you graft a backing on another thing, words and music by... What a mystery, poor Blaise – you don't see what you tack together...'

'Foxes and rabbits, that's the deal, Tamara. The snap of bones...' says Blaise.

'Here, Blaise,' says Tamara, holding out a pill. 'Here's consolation. This will knock your fences down – swallow this! It's written on. All becomes a movie, melodrama – think up lies, spit in your lover's face – it's all your chemistry come undone, unravelling. That is the mystery, my dear, the sphinx, the cave, the oracle – my eyes, your ears, the brain obedient, colluding – wisdom and beauty, that's what it makes up. Hallucinogens, my love: that's what we live by, otherwise life's a dull picnic on the grass. Our brains need tickling up, my dear. Plato didn't even know he had a brain – he thought his gut would do the thinking. Years spent round the dining table ... making smarty talk. We're just the mechanicals, so, Blaise, we're here to make them laugh at our naivety and silly lies, our tender copulations... Remember, Blaise, don't be cast down: the humans, our directors and producers – they are neither wise nor beautiful.

'We're in luck, my dear – those dead babies over there, beyond the ridge – we don't need go and lay our film on them. This time, we get to shoot the animals! There they run, they hop! – they're architects, they're lovable – how they love parenting, and stand against the sunset, quivering and combed. Then – comes the fear, the predators that sneak or dive, and so, they're eaten up, but that is life, and on and on it goes, and we are wise, and they are beautiful and eaten up...'

'Oh quiet, Tamara,' Blaise is laughing, his life is easy now, the sounds can all be added later on, there's no interviews to do and no complaints. 'Yes! You're right: our principals – they're helpless, they screw, sit dopey in the sun, then there's the fear, and they are bombed or snatched – there is some creature wiser and more beautiful than them, skills more refined, black belts as predators: off go the silly ones, the bunnies; nursery tales aren't all of life, Tamara dear: maybe it's parable, maybe it's all lies... And in the end, there is the end. How fortunate we're good at moulding tales – we do it or we don't, it's all the same, but if we don't it's something we shall lack, something we shall not have done. Our legacy, Tamara – it is our document, our documentary. That is our banquet, where we sit, and we don't eat – there is no menu; we discuss, our host must win the arguments, the slaves – they cook and stand behind our chair, the stuff goes cold but still we listen and record – and that is it, Tamara! We have done our job. The rabbits? Here they come again, another bunch, they're on a cycle, on a line, off with the grannies, on the baby ones, ditto the foxes, best be on their side or neutral, trusting in diplomacy... It's life, Tamara, on both sides of this hill, but here at least we're safe, there is no friendly fire to dodge, no heart to harden, and no brain to count the costs...'

'Can we bring it off again, dear Blaise?' Tamara asks.

'High fives!' shouts Blaise. 'Eyes on stalks, Tamara! Down – into the burrows, into the underworld. They're all ghosts down there, you'll light them up, make them glow green by night...'

'Oh Blaise!' Tamara laughs. 'Those ghosts don't come out in the dark – we have to fake it! Ears pricked, dear Blaise!'

*

'Get started,' Belinda says. 'You two, Blaise, Tamara. What you don't see and hear does not exist, it lacks good reason. In this case, beyond the ridge, there's nothing happening. Nothing to see, nothing to tell. If there was something – it's happened, all over. Get on with it now, Blaise! Hold Tamara's feet while she goes down the hole. Those pills – you let them speak for you – their story never ends. You're in freewheel, melodrama, you make up endless tales, go before the judge, and swear and swear, bankrupt your gran, beggar your pa... You druggies – spread it around, invention's never-ending. Consolation, dears? – it's always necessary...'

'What do you want it to mean, what does it all mean, Belinda?' asks Tamara. 'Our film?'

'This. This is what it means,' Belinda says, stamping on the ground.

'No,' says Blaise. 'She doesn't mean the big "it". She means the foxes. Are we for them? Do some rabbits escape? That would be literature. Or do they train and fight? Maybe we step in, with a hospital, an orphanage...'

'Do the hard thing, Blaise,' Belinda says. 'You are best at that. Leave things as they are, leave it all as you have found it. Don't pick up a gun, don't even anything out, don't give a chance, don't improvise. See how it all works – you only do that if you don't take part. Efface yourself. Caring? – if you do or don't, it's all the same.'

'Blaise!' Tamara shouts. 'Let go my feet! I must go down, be free. Why, it's so vast down here, there's even room to dance!'

'Let her drop, Blaise,' Belinda says. 'For certain she'll be up again.' Then she thinks, 'That should be me, down there! It's a story, that's my job, my destiny must be to fall, go down into the burrow.'

But it's too late. Tamara's disappeared, the camera too.

'I don't hear anything,' says Blaise, letting down an ear on wire.'Maybe it's a hole that doesn't end...'

He starts to cry.

'It's her adventure,' says Belinda. 'What she wants. She must take from it the good or bad. That's what you must try to do, and if there is no bottom to your hole – you fall eternally...'

The holy books don't mention that,' says Blaise. 'At worst, there's noisome creatures waiting, hungry *buongustai* who suck you out but leave the shell to be refilled and sucked for evermore...'

Tamara – she's not seen or heard again.

They even wait for her. Make a report.

It's true, that journalism is a craft where mystery abounds: dangers and fantasticals, you never know where searching for the truth can lead. Especially if you don't want, don't have, a power...

'This is another movie,' says Belinda, 'quite different from the one we thought we'd make. Tamara's found her habitat.'

There's more room in the jeep for three, as they head back.

Belinda writes her piece about some sects and tribes.

Tamara's Adventures Among the Rabbits

'She's a true Columbus,' Claude says. 'We'll let you know how it turns out. A new world's been discovered. New people, far beyond our good and evil, primal innocents...'

'Now it's my turn, Claude,' Belinda says. 'I'm the lead. Those new worlds get filled up with all the old. Back to my country: that's my starting point.'

Tamara falls and falls – soon she gets used to it, she's packed some food, there's television and a chair, she plugs in and it's home, there's all the planet in her lap, some children too...

Columbus comes back, pretends he's found new stuff. Really, there is a void. You fill it with the history you know, or bits and deals you have remembered.

Belinda's forgotten many of the friends who're not around. Her stalker; Jean-Luc, and Lenin; Alicia the satisfied... Her country? Most people talk like middling poor. It's wrong – the real poor are more eloquent, they've enemies and loss, songs that go on and on. Here, there's enough – it's the aimlessness that seems a poverty. She doesn't know the details, what golden cloak's above them, suffocating; who has sex and who has debts. Some want socialism – but if it's not there, it's not a thing you miss, not like a lost dog, or respect.

All those planes up high – are they flying off on holidays...? It's not a subject you bring into your chat...

Tamara: forget the rabbits – she's among the bigger stuff. The hunter, the giraffe: the morning star, the pole, the cross... When you have done your fall, you are yourself, and only that, sliding through dry nothing, arms, legs swimming, a water-fly – a star not yet conceived, a blob on an astronomer's magnifying glasses... You needn't breathe: rest those folded batwing lungs.

Will gravity provide?

Something big, she thinks. Throw Claude out the door. When you are young, it's all molestation – things you don't want, don't want to hear, things useless and things upsetting. Everybody takes a hand, paws at the front, the back – in through your ears it comes – the woman rising from the waves, the lady into fox or into tree... What you might want to be. Leopards and measles, every kind of pox.

*

There's room for a goddess. Forget Babylon, no more; and whores. Scarlet – is Belinda's shade. Maybe not divinity at first – a mediator, a message: keeping the people fired until the last. Not love, not war. Something to dance to.

It was a mistake, she thinks – the movie, the ears and eyes, assembled from a kit, music to come, and me that writes the script, some other guy to cut it up and have it make some sense. Instead, it should all be made by me: divinity. The spirit. A script that is my life, my statements that come biffing in your teeth – a language fully formed, incontestable, that's what I said and that is what you hear. A language you all, out there, repeat. Repeat so I can hear – not word for word, but library by library.

Of course, it's solipsistic; I need an ego big as the world. Modestly, big as the species; less modestly – big as the universe. The thing is – when yours is the grand voice, you don't listen, not to anyone at all. It is all you. Chinggis knew it. So did guys better and worse. Am I, she wonders one of the better ones? Or the worse?

'Get out, Claude,' she shouts. 'Out of my house!'

He's dressed for bed: that's where he is – but it's a casual walking suit as well, one you might wear to go and watch the swans, run from the cops or practise on the *kora*. And out he goes.

'Vanity!' shouts Claude. 'Belinda – everything is sewn up, it's a shroud. The wars you won – are always on your back. Better to lose, accept someone's new history. All that you do, or want – it's life! It comes, bidden or not, helter-skelter, hugger-mugger. Senility, Belinda... That's your sentence – at your birth, and it's for ever, stronger and indelible...'

It's his curse, Belinda thinks, his insult. 'It wasn't us who fought,' she shouts. 'We were the soldiers, that is true, but we were ghosts, centuries before our deaths... Maybe it's true, all that you say. We're in the web: what I want and what I'll get, it's all banal...'

*

'Not love,' Belinda says. 'That has been tried. Maybe free trade? For sure, I'll not be what's expected of me – my voice, it is the oracle's: basso profondo, from the smoke.'

'We have bombed everyone,' the guy, the salesman, says. 'Nazis, communists, dictators, democrats, nationalists, secessionists – Christians, Muslims; probably some atheists are in there too. For much, I'm in agreement. Others – I'm sure I made a protest. What you need, Belinda, if it isn't love – promiscuous and opportunist, interclassist, cosmopolitan...is what I have here on the lot...'

'Yes,' says Belinda. 'To discriminate – have influence, that's what I need. A bombing plane.'

'Of course,' the salesman says. 'They're all uncomfortable. Vibration, noise. They didn't think you'd need to make trips back. This Lancaster – the worst!'

'I don't care,' Belinda says. 'I don't talk *sympa*; don't expect it, I don't do what you would want. The takeoff – will it do it from my street?'

'I've seen it in the movies,' says the guy: 'Of course, you'll need a crew, else you won't see where you are.'

'I sacked my crew,' Belinda says. 'His habits! Body, mouth – and thoughts! How can people tolerate each other...'

'Oh, you will always find a crew,' the salesman says. 'And as for airfield – this is capitalism, dear, exaggeration is allowed. So, I can swear you will not need one, that's for sure – this beauty flies from anywhere... Like a butterfly, off your hand...'

'It's old and worn-out,' says Belinda. 'Are you serious? About the price?'

'Assert yourself,' the salesman says. 'Greater your will to power, greater the debt you'll bear. Don't be a cheapskate. We're all going to lose everything. Soon. You could become fictional, but it costs, isn't secure, and no one looks you up.'

'Oh, I'm real,' Belinda says, 'You can find me with a nudge. I'm in lists too: – black boxers, the guilty freed, the innocent imprisoned... Trust me! I'd take the aeroplane except one's not enough: you need a gross.'

'That's something might interest the mafia,' the salesman says. 'A fleet of them. Except it's noisy, and more than a little crass.'

'Oh,' Belinda laughs and says, 'This place is much too poor to have the mafia.'

'Well,' says the salesman, Dave, 'there's an opening for you! Bring the money in. Then, you can skim off – and help your neighbours too.'

'You're caring, honest,' Belinda says – she doesn't know, of course, nor care. Those are the things you say when you're about to dump someone – it means they won't turn and bite the foot that urges them away, away...

There is a pause: then Belinda says, 'Look, Dave. To be honest with you – I deal in metaphor. I don't have cash. I'd no idea you could buy the stuff and make yourself a power.'

'Oh,' Dave the salesman laughs, 'I'm just the entry level. You must have a mound of cash, an idea to match. Ambitions, and a will: do you have that, Belinda? It doesn't seem... There's competition too...'

'My life,' Belinda says, 'supposes a cosmology...'

'You're wrong,' says Dave. 'You're merely planetary. The universe, Belinda – that is not your oyster either – its future is unsure. Better – it's certain. It won't last. What's not clear – is when it ends. Go back a reasonable distance: to monkeys. They're thoughtful, complex – familial, Belinda. They set great score by copulation and by lineage. They talk about it, move accordingly – in and out the group. They are the opposite of you, Belinda. It's true, they're bushmeat now. But we're their sons and daughters.'

'It may be so,' Belinda says, quite shaken, 'but they're threatened. They are shuffling off the stage...'

'Ah yes, that's so too,' says Dave. 'It is inevitable, alas. There is no cure, no happy end to work towards. But it's the truth, it's what you're given.'

*

'If you want help with your mafia, Belinda,' says Dave, stretching out on her chesterfield. 'I'm your man. I know you think they're thugs and stupids...'

'No, it's worse. They're all related,' Belinda says. 'And can't spend the cash – or only on flash stuff, or tatty houses underground. Not my taste.'

'Relatives?' Dave asks, drinking her tequila. 'I have lots. All in Siberian towns. They have them sewn up like shrouds,' and he laughs – it's a phrase he'd like to make his own, exclusive.

'No, Dave,' Belinda says, 'I stand with Lenin. That arm that points – it shows me the direction.'

'You're wrong, Belinda,' Dave says, taking off the other boot. 'Lenin pointed straight to me. He was a rightist – if that has a sense. Continuity, my dear: authority is of the right; collectivism, the root's the same: "collect".'

'Fiddle-faddle blah blah blah,' Belinda shouts, to drown him out. 'I've heard that facile stuff before.'

'It doesn't matter what you think,' says Dave, trying to keep awake. 'Mafia beneath, bankers and commissars above... All twins, Belinda, have something of the Siamese. The rest, the opposition – is only bureaucrats and anarchists, who'll never make a decent pact. The left? It's Judy to a Mister Punch. That is the truth, Belinda: there lies the power. Get wise!'

'Fuck off, Dave,' Belinda says, tipping the divan, so he rolls off on the floor. 'Army surplus – that's your stock, your trade.'

'Don't mock,' says Dave. 'Trade – is circular – round and round stuff goes, annealed and burnished, fitted out with knobs, the fuel, the batteries, the stencils painted on or sanded off, the motor boosted... The chain is long, Belinda, long as writing or as speech; and I'm a link that's always there...'

'Off my couch!' says Belinda, 'and now – my floor!'

'You must accept, Belinda,' Dave says, seeking another perch. 'You're *facho*: if you don't feel so, it is still your destiny, your crutch, your stilt. The *Neinsagers* won't get you anywhere, and anyway, you're not one of them. And – beauty, truth, wisdom, justice – those are horses, Belinda – perhaps they drag a wagon, "power": they're harnessed, but atop the diligence is coachmen, there can be outriders too...'

'No, Dave,' says Belinda, 'you're from another scene, another genre,' but she is shaken, certainly. 'Of course – it isn't what we think that counts: the thought we think is ours, our marker – that's all been around its ancestors, and handed down. The thought could stick some place, and after years you'll find someone who's tried it out. They won't have understood. And it won't work. Besides, it isn't what we think – it's what we are.'

'Oh yes!' says Dave. 'You're getting there, Belinda. It's what we are. What we do. I even see you, yes – in a Sukhoi. The first! Very rare! And slow. But I won't try to sell you one. We're partners, if you want.'

'Too slow!' says Belinda. 'And, though I've no tribe, I see myself, swinging along, singing side by side with allsorts on the march – they are nothing special, but they plod, they fight, they win. What luck – they are not family! I remember how my mother said to father, "*vous me dégoûtez*". That's the spirit! Truth and contempt – the seeds of freedom! That has set my life, its compass. But, Dave, you too must have mates...'

'That's right!' says Dave, stretched out again: 'But – you want to be a yagbo, a leader of a tribe. No! There is no vacancy for bosses – I and my comrades, we don't trust the chiefs.'

'You're workers, then?' Beldinda asks. 'If not the wretched, then at least prepared: the decisive struggle?'

'That's about it,' says Dave. 'We're scrap men. Scrappers. People – they mistake their gold for brass, Sheffield for solid stuff... But we assay, we accumulate a stash...'

'And yet, those old aeroplanes, of wood and skin...' Belinda says.

'They're for collectors,' Dave admits. 'The modern stuff – we strip it down, and on the heap it goes ... we junk the robots, otherwise they'd see us as a pile of junk, and throw us on the heap!'

'How refreshing,' Belinda says. 'Analysis!'

'As little as I can,' says Dave, changing to grappa. 'There's lands where it's all tight and uniformed. You might climb up a ladder getting guys to vote for you – but what a bore! Then, there's the cloudy places – dust and handshakes, your sisters in silk baggy pants – and you could be a yagbo, leading your tribe down the Elysian field, a copy naturally, where the statues are of solid gold, the doorkeys are of platinum... Perilous, Belinda, but more fun, and more extent ... the pottery windtowers twisting unexpected, up out the stinging sand... If you want enough, you can get in anywhere – ballot, bullet, it all depends on accent, on your dialect. And in the end, my dear – nothing but vanity. Or – just nothing.'

'I don't know where you're leading me,' Belinda says. 'I want to be where I can live by principles, my principles ... nothing more.'

'You're speaking like a yagbo,' Dave says, and laughs. 'A chief. But – best be warned. Don't take insurgency as the lightest choice. If you want to get along, to maybe change some things – you need accept the rules, laws of the state. The state, as is and as will always be. If not – there is no space for you. You'd have to carve one out, a gummy space – you'll be provoked and you'll do things that's terrible, that aren't your principles at all...'

'I'm not into that, Dave,' Belinda says. 'If not the state, then anarchy: everyone in charge. Easy! I don't know where you're taking me, what you propose...'

'Well,' says Dave, 'I'm just setting out the scene.'

'Is this how you started?' asks Belinda, 'with this band, this gang?'

There's totters, with a horse, one each: then, there's what you call scrap merchants, with a yard.

'Those are flash cars,' Belinda says, 'I guess that's what you call them...'

Then there's guys who're rich – maybe they deal in metals, maybe they steal them, or smelt the bits, maybe they dip the chrome, or have green boys that do it: maybe they have foundries now, some disused, where they rent rooms for guys that's fleeing, or wandering, with families, or hiding, on the lam, or just with nothing better.

'There's the Sukhoi,' says Dave, patting it. 'If ever you should want – I'll take you up, we'd go and see the snow, and then the river spread out on its stones, and swoop, so the cattle beasts run off like crazy fools...'

'You start like this,' Belinda says. 'Where does it end?'

'Oh,' Dave says, 'it doesn't end, it never ends. It goes as long as ever you would want.'

*

A classy guy gives her a card: it's titanium, it seems; no name – just SCRAP: FERRAILLE: SCHROTT. 'All you could want,' he says. 'We collect and we distribute. The whole cycle, past and future. Plastic strangles, ether annihilates. The worst in metal is the rust: fatigue. Surely you can take the risk, Belinda, live with that?'

'Old iron?' says Belinda, laughing. 'I can do better than that.'

'Oh,' says the guy, 'we're always there. The Great War. Mussolini and the farm machinery, the Americans now – going to produce more and more – on the battlefield: the houses bombed – beams, steel, always more... In the crucible, in the muzzle – bang! Off again. The cycle is complete...'

'Dave loves the Sukhoi, it's mostly wood,' Belinda says.

'Yes,' says the guy, 'wood survives, sometimes. '37 it was made – it didn't go into the furnace. It's Dave's lesson. Wood isn't scrap. It doesn't make good bombs.'

'So, you chum up with presidents?' Belinda asks. 'You're in the cycle.'

'Heavy stuff. You need the weight, if you're to drop it on your mates,' says the guy, turning away.

'He thinks you're a featherweight, Belinda,' Dave says: he doesn't laugh. He looks disappointed. 'You don't seem to understand – the bomb, the bullet … power, Belinda, comes from the barrel of a gun. It's what you asked about. If it hits you – that's the truth. Beauty – if it misses. Think of that gun, Belinda – the metals singing – if you record the detonation, then stretch it out, slow it down – it becomes an oratorio. A bang – and then it's scrap. The *ferrailleurs* – they know it all, Belinda. Schrott. That's the cycle – and we ride it: from shiny magnum to a lump, and back again.'

'It sounds like you're a fine battalion, Dave,' Belinda says. 'I guess those medals too...'

'They're made from casings. Iron rusts,' says Dave. 'You need the bronze – with iron, you have to keep renewing...'

'I liked the one about the wagon best,' Belinda says. 'A totter can't start the round without the horse. You're rather taken with speed, bullets – as if you can't wait to get it over. You miss the meaning, Dave.'

'Oh,' says Dave, 'cart, carriage, bolt and pin – it's very much the same. I just don't see the meaning people want to take away... It's all like a piece of music, or a picture – safe in itself. What more does it have to mean?'

'Dave, you're crazy,' laughs Belinda. 'Of course, every picture tells a story! Hadn't you been told? It all has meaning – you look and look, then comes the dawn.'

'To me,' says Dave, 'it lifts and flies, or – it does not. That's all – it's how you know if something works. The things that don't – they get collected. It's true of all living things, Belinda: whatever they mean, or do – when they're dead, all you can do with them's collect. That's the meaning, that is everything.'

'Is that a religious sort of view?' Belinda asks.

'You collect those too:' says Dave. 'Of course, there's some are dull, and some are crude – that's the trouble with collecting: dross. But – in any case, I am a *ferrailleur*. Once you are, you're up there, up with the big guys: comrades.'

What is there for me? Belinda thinks – driving a truck, or in the back office filing stuff...?

*

'Your friend,' Aubin, the smelter, says to Dave. 'She doesn't seem so smart. The fire – that starts it all – it can't provide her purpose, it's ineffable. The fire consumes, the fire creates. It's everything, it's life. That is the motor, Dave, dig down, and there's the heart. Surely she sees – we miners, gatherers and smiths – we are the alpha. The cold, the snow, the white, that's death. Let's not speak the word, that means the cycle's broken, at an end. We make the forges and the furnaces, dear Dave, the iron wheel, those are our creations, and we're bound to them...'

'Yes, yes,' says Dave, 'I know all that.'

Belinda pours him drinks. 'Dave,' she says, as he goes down, 'you can't believe all that about the fire. You're an air man. It holds you up – by themselves, those stubby wings would take you into earth – then, there's your lungs. Dragons breathe in the air, and so their blood heats it all up, and out it comes ... smoke...'

'I know,' says Dave, 'all that. The great fear is – the earth. When we – the *ferrailleurs* – when we die, we go into the volcano – those burial pits, they may keep off the frost, but they're not warm, not a little bit. As for the air – you guys keep coming up with that. It isn't so, it's no alternative. It has its use. It feeds the fire. It's food, Belinda, nothing more. Free too, like grass or water. You add nothing to it, you don't change its application.'

'Take me away, Dave,' Belinda says. 'Not in that plane. You're too pissed to fly, though maybe then's the best time...'

'I know,' says Dave. 'You'd feel safe with me. You think I am a renegade – "air man" you say. It isn't so, Belinda. Nothing can save you from the shrapnel. The air – it comes to you as blast, it knocks the cities down. I could fly above it all... Maybe you could too, with what you call "a religious sort of view".'

'What's coming, Dave?' Belinda asks, a little desperate.

'What's coming, Belinda,' Dave answers back. 'What's there to fear? There's nothing but the words.'

'When they're anywhere, they're here,' Belinda says. 'Answers are given. Fears confirmed. They're not coming up the street – they're here already, next door, every corner with its television...'

'You're safe, Belinda,' Dave says, poking through a closet to find a coat, it's raining in the street. 'You can't mean those guys with beards from centuries ago, other cultures, other friends?'

'Hypocrites,' Belinda says. 'All of them. That's what's special in our brains – say a thing, plan another thing. Only with language, Dave, do you get the chance to simulate, to lie.'

'Of course,' says Dave, 'but we – the *ferrailleurs* – we have the bigger stocks, the most variety of metals, the casings that you need – those are essential; even if you put your fire inside a car – it's still the metal round the fire that makes effect...'

'It seems,' Belinda says, 'that evolution doesn't count in this. Egeo, my teacher, saw it as a boundary. Ever before you, you must cross it, then there's something more, better perhaps; but with the metal cycling round – it's an iron ring ... here and back again... The river and the dwarves – except there is no halflight, it's forever dark...'

'Yes, evolution,' Dave says, peering down her dress. 'Don't bet on that. It's not improvement, just adjustment. But – in the stream – there's sparks. There's light – comes from the fire, the forge. There's a beginning, when the earth is born aflame, but then...'

'Then – you and all your mates arrive,' Belinda presses on. 'You are a secret society that everybody knows about?'

'That's it,' says Dave.

'Well,' says Belinda, 'where would you think of taking me? How valuable am I to you...? It's not that you would pass me on, recommend me to some friends...?'

'Be wise,' says Dave, 'recognise your limits. And – the world is one. It only comes in discreet parts if you fly around, and study some bit, some bog where you might come down – hugged in a plane, that's slow and not too stable. That's excitement – not knowing where you will come down, hit the earth – and then the flames: they put in a bigger motor, so powerful the wings come off at speed; it burns, becomes a clinker...

'See, Belinda – you have quality, you're unique. But – being unique means you're not reusable. You're a prototype, like everyone; you don't fit, don't work. Your country sentences you to life – and nothing more. You have no second chance – you put up a statue of yourself: remember Jean-Luc, all that Lenin bronze... Off to the heap! A battleship? It's even worse. You rust, you lose your plates. A book? Hmmm, yes. But the book itself informs you how it's rust, or moths: corruption. You rot. You're eaten.'

'Why fuss with that crap plane, Dave?' Belinda asks.

'1937 – rising from despond: the skirmish with the Japanese; then the Nazis. If it flies, Belinda,' Dave says, 'we beat the fascists!'

'I didn't think you'd care – you and the big boss, Aubin,' says Belinda.

'Oh, it doesn't enter into trade,' says Dave. 'The dwarves go on hammering the same, and whether you say your name or not – who cares? The dragon doesn't puff? – tomorrow perhaps she will – flames from every seam, blue and green... It is my hobby, flight. Something that might interest – only if it flies and lifts, of course. If the plane goes down – our bones are good for flutes. Our heads for Halloween. You take your chance, Belinda – something your teacher didn't teach.'

'All my struggles, my experience,' Belinda says, 'should make me much more human. But instead – I just grow old and flat.'

'I could have told you so. The devils like them young and full of gravy – that's why your nickname comes in infancy,' says Dave. 'And so you jump, you crawl, you swim, you twist and fry, a salamander, when you are in the womb: earth, water, air and fire. To make a metal, you must be all of these. Mostly, you've only one element that's your home. You, Belinda, maybe you have none. It's all a quota, nothing is chance, all is dug up and every spadeful counts.'

'Except for the flight,' Belinda says. 'That's chance. It seems a risk too big to take.'

'A risk's what you take. Accidents fall on you,' says Dave. 'It's an easy choice.'

'You're very plausible, Dave,' Belinda says. 'But in my country – we accommodate. We don't recognise a principle. Nor a recurrence. You're all principles, Dave.'

*

True love is not the truth. A flight for love – you do that on the ground, in the maquis, not in a plane. Belinda – goes nowhere with Dave – both are rather glad.

It's inconclusive, the relationship.

*

'Ticktock,' Aubin says. 'Belinda – we'll go to see the President. You'll be my watch – I can't imagine why there's all the fuss about expensive ones – me, I wear the sun. When there's clouds, I stay in bed. It's all the same.'

'We're talking about dull things,' says the President to Belinda. 'Aubin and me. Go and see my presents, dear Belinda...'

'Oh,' says Belinda. 'I didn't think to bring you one.'

'You'll find you did,' says the President, and laughs. Aubin laughs too, pushes her forward.

It's dull, being so close to power, and that's the truth. You don't get justice in this country, maybe not any place. Beauty? When you're stretched out on the couch, you're looking good, but no one can believe that for long, when what comes next. The President is overweight: the big ones win the vote, like walruses.

'You could be my lady,' says the President, holding Belinda down, 'or concubine, which would be best.'

'No, no,' Belinda says, 'you're making a mistake. I'm not nature. I think, not nurture either...'

It's no use. His member – she'll remember, as she wishes it could be dismembered – is green with verdigris, like a brass projectile left in the field too long. 'I can't, I can't,' she whispers, 'I am not a culverin.'

The word – for the President, it's new. Now this novelty! – after Aubin's chat on tungsten, on what will bind with what, on silver solder, alloys and alliances, soldiers with their mortars, stoned or drunk, pissing through the barrels, burnishing the sabres, brandishing the tulwars. 'You've no idea,' Belinda says. 'After those old aeroplanes, balloons, the rockets and their many sockets...! And now you stumble on a word that everybody knows... What do you propose, President? More countries, places to conquer, then you can't go there without an escort: it's scary – suppose the limousine takes the wrong turn, and there's some paid guy, woman exalted, waiting... And you can't duck! Can't look afraid, or even prudent...'

The other qualities are shot – justice, beauty: only truth remains, supposedly the best. Belinda sees that everything around is true. There is no consolation: 'Tell me,' she says, 'that I shan't be a present for another, just like you, maybe with hornsilver on his prick – internalised, his treasury of copper wire, zinc brackets he can boast about...'

There's no good answer to all that.

'You have many of those bombs – filled with air?' Belinda asks. 'The End?'

'Yes,' says the President. 'Air and fire – like dragons. You have to use those carefully. Imagine you're in the theatre, or on a set... All fall down – and all stand up again, you hope...'

*

War games are off! Don't fool around. There's no case against first use: why wait? – it's bombs away, when threats or daring allies call the shots – deterrence has failed, you dump out all you've got and maybe hope you won't be there to see the end. The end in any case will come...

*

And there's the President, postcoital, pumped out, jaw a hogmouth like the Duce's...

'My country!' Belinda shouts. 'Traduced. Now me: bad sex! My village – where all was worked out once, the inconvenient expelled, the feisty ones ignored, the grey exalted; peace...! What concerns you, President – is despotism. *Schrott*! Ordnance; melting the railings, smelting the wedding rings, the harrows, digging up dirt, making it glister so that when it's dropped – it flares like phosophorus, like Greek fire, Bengal lancers, Roman candles, Vesuvian *cipolle* ... getting up your nerve to loose the big one; after that – no return, no criticism, the bad guys and the good all griddled, flat as drop scones, everybody ladled in the crucible, and you – the last one, a look around: the desert, pleasure: no one to boss you, no one to criticise...'

She shouts on, the President laughs and says, 'Aha! A humanist! You walk that springy bridge, belief in men and women – the suspension: it tosses you so high! – and there's the waves that beckon you like Loreleis... Here's the knack, Belinda: if you want to reach some other shore – you shuffle, waddle, over the bridge, senile in your socks...'

'Let me go,' says Belinda: 'We've been through our time together – hard, difficult... Now's the end.'

'"Great moments", Belinda,' says the President, holding down her arms, '"in history". Write speeches for me: what to say. Long, sonorous sentences, no quotes, all quotable. How many? I could live another forty years: how many will I need? One? The big one – and a voice alone, giving solace in the wilderness? No one is left, no one will come! Or will there be many, tuning in? A multitude, crying for parasols – the heat, the thirst? The occupation? Soldiers around so long they don't seem foreign – and you pay their wage. Slave mercenaries: they've always kicked and whipped you guys. Write, Belinda – something I'll remember.'

*

'All his ladies are invited,' Aubin says. 'They must speechify. It's his collection. Great inspiring words. The memorable speeches... Then, he has the best set up and framed. It's an honour. It may not seem so, you might even blame me for the unwanted favour I have done you – my sweet Belinda, my sweetener, my selfless gift…'

'No,' Belinda says, 'as if you care! It's unforgivable. If it matters – it's unpardonable. Reactionaries like you are, Aubin, your thoughts leave a scum, and you are never clean, and what you spread – it's oil, Aubin: crankcase! The enlightened – even if they urge me further than I can ever leap – they're clean, and they leave me so...'

'Think, Belinda, of the very bad things that never happened to you,' Aubin says. 'There'll be a lesson there, a consolation. Am I reactionary? Are you? Don't take it all to heart, my dear. People who don't reflect continually – they're the ones who grow, psychologically. They're the attractive ones. You aren't one of them. you're with the other kind: – they ponder. Change their minds. Your brain gyres with the world, and you – you don't make roots or flowers. No scent. You're always fresh with new confusing stuff.'

'I know,' she says. 'Beneath the surface, there's more surface, under that wagon stuck in its pond – there is a storm, and billows, doodlings and triangles, slabs of red and black.'

'No,' Aubin says. 'Not surface under surface: it's door and room, room and door, a long procession, galleries, the same people in each box – sometimes eating porridge together, exploring their bodies, praying, balancing on the sill ... just sitting. Combing the cat.'

'Oh, I died weeks ago,' Belinda says. 'I'm just a bad smell now.'

'Don't despair,' says Aubin. 'I'm not good for you, that's all.'

'Is that it, then?' Belinda asks. 'What have we reached? The end? How awful that would be! Always finishing on the wrong side and being patronised. Winning would be worse, and – anyway, what is the game?'

Aubin laughs. 'You villagers! I love you, love you all. Your funny customs, fresh eyes on the values. I believe in you. Of course – there's some as may be traumatised: those events you all went through, awful, just terrible.'

'Oh,' says Belinda. 'We know how to settle in. And give a good account, if someone crosses us.'

'I can't doubt that's true,' says Aubin, not impressed.

'None of these children is mine,' Belinda says, as they pass by. 'And I'm glad. I'm too old now: besides – no *da capo*. They're no good, the kids: rude and frightened. What is mine? Where is my country?'

*

'I've missed so much,' Belinda says.

Here's someone you can talk to – a teacher, not at all like Egeo, but someone trained and emptied out. Is he from heaven? Or from hell, like Springheel Jack, omnipresent, all-knowing: warning, canoodling, tufts of poetry growing on his palms, algorithms tattooed, sucking the marrow of ignorance from the innocent bones...

The longest river in the world – that, you must know, even if it's dry. Pink dolphins dried on racks.

'I never had a band,' Belinda sobs. 'I can't even sing. The ashram on the hill was closed. When they dug the pits – I wasn't there. I didn't know who was missing when that day was done. Now, it's too late.'

'I had all those things,' the guy says. 'A group, tattoos – tattoos you can take off; the band falls naturally into forgetfulness. They're ordinary things, you don't regret, unless you expect them to be revelations.'

He's called Ariston. 'People have fridges called after you,' Belinda says. 'How will you face the things, quite terrible, that'll happen to you?'

'Things?' asks Ariston.

'Your death,' Belinda says, enjoying it a little, 'when you're very young, it seems like singular – when you're mature, it's complicated.'

'Metaphor.' says Ariston. 'Winged things.'

'My bad thoughts,' Belinda says, 'when I believed, I wished for terrible things. When I disbelieved – terrible things were what I wished.'

'Nothing,' says Aritoston. 'Everybody to and fro's with that.' He jumps up and down – circulation. 'And what did you believe in most,' he asks. 'What you believed in or what you didn't?'

'Oh, what an old folks' question,' laughs Belinda.

'And did you kill more people for what they believed, or what they didn't?' asks Ariston. 'And was it for what you did believe, or didn't? And in what, exactly?'

'Oh faddle, Ariston,' says Belinda, cross. 'You don't have the choice of that. The most you do is patch guys up, send them back in.'

'I've no doubt,' says Ariston, 'your villagers had a happy time – probably before time had been invented and all laid out. Not exactly *your* villagers, of course, not their kind of happiness. I mean – generically: and not a time they weren't around in but they say they were told about, so they remember it, sort of. Sort of not. All they can remember truly – wasn't happy. Now, we can reinvent it all: time, and happiness. It's history – especially time; and happiness is something you record and pass around ... poetry pasted up...'

'Oh Ariston,' Belinda says, 'my teacher said all that, when I was small: but in a realistic way. I knew then – I'm an actress, that's the real me. That is – for me – the top: but for the species – it's not good. It's even cheating, being doped, a dope. A species, when it's at the top – it counts no time. Dinosaurs, Noah, Methusaleh – time misremembered. Each champion awaits the next – and when the limit's reached, there's no new champions – that's it. The countdown's started long before: but when there comes indifference, or killing of one's own – that is the end. We – our species – lost. Then, we must sit, relax and take our pills or smokes, and wait for some new wise amphibian to slither out, neither *frère* nor *semblable*, and eat our melons; figs and apples snagging its feet and tickling its crown... And you, Ariston – you're an accomplice, not a critic. You see it winding down, the system full of lies and bosses ignorant and crass ... children devoured; the dead lie unburied underneath the bed...'

'Belinda!' shouts Ariston. 'This is fable! Good times? Once had – they don't exist, they don't live on...'

'Power to my imagination, then,' Belinda says. 'I'll show you how it works, Ariston!'

'The big bad men, Belinda,' Ariston says, not wanting to listen. 'It's true – they're big. But they only did little bad things to you. I know, it all adds up, makes a sum. Some – the bland ones – haven't started yet... There's their fuse, unlit,' and he pushes himself forward, strutting old-time sex, perhaps... 'In time...'

You'll find love, Belinda, even though it's not a thing you're looking for...

'You want to reach the bottom,' says Ariston. 'That's supposed to be wisdom – but it's the bad of bad as well. When you reach the bottom, you've arrived – even if it's so deep there, that you've drowned.'

'No psychology, Ariston,' says Belinda. 'Trying to be clever – instead, I wear you like a cowl of sadness.'

'Ah yes,' says Ariston. 'Your teacher. The first. Pouff went your innocence – virginity's a metaphor, but innocence comes in barrels, ready to be ladled out.'

She hasn't forgotten the schizoids. There's nothing to forget. The old doctor used to say – you must coax out that second voluble person chattering within, the unreal voice that answers yours, tempt the doppelgänger from your body where it's lodged ... kill it, pin it on the barn door. Then, there's nothing left to understand. Life's as it ought to be – a monologue. Most everyone subdues the other voice – it's better so, already there is violence all around, you shouldn't need to kill your invisible, your unrelated, twin ... those suggestions, stories, cock-and-bull...

*

'*In carrozza,* Madame,' Ariston clowns, 'there's only us two in the world.'

'Where to, Ariston?' asks Belinda, clinging to Ariston on his Yamaha.

'You've no country now, Belinda – you have been agglomerated. It's good,' Ariston says: 'All you have left is funny costumes, customs invented, memories have slid beneath a sheet of glass...'

'Oh, how banal,' Belinda shouts, against the wind. 'The past! It's grit beneath our tires. On, on we go. The more unfamiliar it is – the better so!'

'Faster, Ariston,' Belinda shouts. 'Faster!'

'Too fast, Belinda,' Ariston shouts back, 'and you won't see. They'll take it from you, and you won't see what it was, can't read the lips, the labels, the crawl's all blurred...'

It's like they found that bomb – the one that leaves the people, kills the trees and birds, destroys the building, the pylons and the launching ramps, the corrugated iron, the razor wire, the simply barbed...

The people here are black – that must be good? They stand and stare – intrepid Belinda, clinging on, and Ariston shows off. 'Are they waiting for some work?' Belinda gasps.

'No,' says Ariston, 'waiting for something – maybe rain, an official, or a bus. You risk all sorts of stuff, standing around all hugger-mugger, catching something probably un-named, and the kids – you can't cuff them, reprove them; let alone expect an alphabet – maybe their language doesn't have one, besides, they're rude and frightened, those little urchins. Belinda – I could show you things that move you, desolation – you would cry, but then – you know it all. What you've not seen you've heard or read...'

'Banal, banal,' Belinda screams. 'Show me what I haven't known, and do it fast. Or do it slow...'

The track is grass now, and they bounce, higher and higher on their seats of pleasure, quite rhythmic, love just around your corner – it's better than springing on a bed, a desk, a carpet – if there is one; and the floor if not...

'Yes,' says Belinda, 'this is travel. This is how it's done, the best... Such an excitement. But – the black guys – taking me that route – it's crass...'

'Not crass,' shouts Ariston. 'It's trite.'

*

It's true: this is not at all a moving tale, no drama, no emotion.

They're going fast: if it was slow, everything would be the same. Some awful things – they last for minutes – even for an hour: or longer still, if there's diplomacy, or if you live it through and never feel a pain first time, and back it comes quite unexpected... It isn't, naturally, the same, whether it's fast or slow, or up or down: that's *qualunquismo*, fatalism, mini-facho – even worse. Looking for some guy, some rule, that makes it all endure... But on a trail bike – you're never all that sure that you'll cling on until the scheduled end...

'Faster, Ariston,' Belinda shouts. 'This landscape – grey and brown, and beets of red and white in line; and ah – the purple; not murex – aubergines! Make it a song, Ariston, make it all blend like in a mixer – I can't do it for myself, I can't write the music, do the rhythm, can't speed it up. But, after all, I am a happy sort, and I resist.'

'Faster, Ariston,' Belinda shouts again, and hugs him – her tongue won't reach to his ear, but thinking it – is worth a giggle, and he feels her pressing on his back, and eager, so he doesn't see the bump, that maybe isn't there, just too much speed, an excellent machine –

'I'm flying, flying now!' Belinda shouts.

3

MORE PEOPLE YOU WILL NEVER MEET, BUT WHO KNOW EVERYTHING

ROXANNE AND FLAVIO

NO ONE has heard of these people...

Flavio talks to Roxanne, who seems not to be listening.

'"A *passeur*: when caught, is buried alive." That's a media source. Nothing else is closer to the truth.

'A pain artist – cut out the running and jumping, the straining and the arnica and the dope – just show us how it hurts and how you suffer, more and more – skewers through your cheeks and up your prick.

'"They're famous names – Holly Barn, Octave LeNain, Benito Robinson: aesthetes and *coprophages*. Dung beetles." All media sources. Praise for the runners and life-sculptors.

'"I had become the old odds-and-ends man... And on my chest I felt the weight of a woman's dead body." From the book under review.

'Can't end like that.

'"Be a critic – make big bucks."'

Roxanne says: 'Not the end. Read on. It's the sea, without end. Read! You've been taught how.'

*

'Too flavoury – pink satin humbug dress, makes you salivate. As seen on TV. Now being worn.'

'It all sounds plausible.' Flavio says.

'They won't pay you for saying that,' Roxanne says.

'You tell me I'm bourgeois – there should be solidarity. I don't want a job – I want the money: the jobs I might get – they're terrible.'

'You'd need to be a boss. Then people would spit on you. You might get to enjoy it.' Roxanne says.

Even the bottom wolf gets to eat the leftovers.

'No! None of these species diatribes. Enough!' Roxanne says.

Is this the only book we have?

'It's written simple – say you discover it. Write some lines...' Roxanne says.

I'd sooner go there, sit in the gardens. No flies and no cadavers.

'The cat stays here. No "travels with a cat" for you,' Roxanne says.

She'd walk better if she was more outside. Her limp would improve. The cat, that is.

'No one need walk today,' she says.

'Which ground for discrimination should I blame? My setbacks... Sex, colour, class – or attitude?' asks Flavio.

'You think you're as good as all the rest...' Roxanne says.

If I drink this – I disappear, like in the book, leaving you to be the baby and the mother. Or – the baby and its coming child.

My life starts where yours comes to an end.

Go away. It's nearly over anyway. I shan't lay heavy on you, not at all.

There is no cat. It has no limp. Everything is as it is, no utopia, no dystopia. That's maybe bad and good. There is no parting – there's always parting, and there's no new world to step into, there's the old people in fresh clothes. Some in rags.

*

'There's ways to help those *ivoiriens*,' says Flavio's friend. 'The addicts, the *microbes*. They're dependent on those machetes – take your arm off at the shoulder, even if you're wearing canvas. They make a living, and so don't have to face the Libyan police.'

'I'm not with Roxanne any more,' says Flavio. 'She laid heavy on me. But these guys – of course, I've a soft stop for a hard place... Côte d'Ivoire! All those elephants...'

'Smithing,' says Flavio's friend, Auguste. 'A demanding substance, sucks you down, sucks you in. You don't ever want extra, no sleep, no peace. It's you and the metal. It cured you. Turn them around. You're always doing it. Cure them.'

'Maybe it's not me,' says Flavio. 'Steering – it's not easy. You end up following other guys. Not me!'

'No biopolitics,' Auguste says. 'No diatribes. Start it off again. Heat. Hammer. Think Thor, think Wotan – chase the dragon, forge the sword. Skill, not symbol, Flavio. That's where you tumble – in discriminating. You fear doubling back – there's only forward!'

'We clean the *microbes* – the heat makes buboes grow upon my groin...' says Flavio.

'We send them out,' Auguste says, 'to work for smiths and be exploited – then they can choose between the anger and servility. Maybe you can have them both, and live to be a smith yourself – start a new clan of them...'

'It's odds-and-ends,' says Flavio. 'All curlicues and nails and hinges – all we make is crosses and those heavy tiny boats ... symbols to toss back in the oddments box...'

'That's good,' says Auguste. 'You don't see it, but you make a chain. We're all in it, each twisted round the next, a viperous knot, the stingers and the crawlers, the creepers, they eat, we eat them and we're eaten... You, Flavio – you make the good, the beautiful: all is invention, fusing a discarded piece, it turns out art, religion, some technology ephemeral ... that is your task, you're in the flow, this is humanity, on and on, keep your eyes well down: water, earth, fire – that's it, dear Flavio... Don't scratch your groin – that's what the monkeys do... Round and round the people go, with this clangour, there's not much to say that you can hear...'

'Peace, Auguste,' says Flavio. 'Rest, space, distance. The people. Set me free! I'm in a lump with everyone, let me float loose, let me be molten and then separate...'

'Yes,' Auguste says. 'You want to be a *microbe.* That's good, that's very good. It shows humanity is one – a common substance, taken rootlike from the earth, then heated hot as hell and beaten flat – in any shape, the more you beat, the stronger and the brighter...'

'My afflictions,' Flavio says. 'They make me howl. And – I'm a volunteer – you ought to pay me, dear Auguste.'

'Ah,' says Auguste, 'the universe is full of "is", but I can't see an "ought". Those scholars – they'll soon know everything about the "is" – deeper and deeper, further – off they go, the star-hoppers in asbestos shoes, on hikes that last millennia, they too want space and distance, a new home, maybe with pineapples, no reptiles – those dinosaurs, d'you think they asked, dear Flavio – "What's it all for? Why are we here? What is our destiny?" No, the "ought"'s a good invention, like the poppy and the leaf, it opens up an inner void, maybe a cellar, dim racks and presses, wine and oil... If you're a *microbe* – down the steps you go, into the cool, alone: forget the wine, the oil, you're down there with yourself, with all the ought you need to soothe your groin... Some smiths, Flavio, forge a sword – you – a needle. Sell, dear friend, don't use!'

'I can't sleep, Auguste,' Flavio says. 'Stretched out by the forge... You must have friends, a cot, a mattress...'

'Don't whine!' says Auguste. 'I have friends – they have a daughter who's locked in: Célestine. The French disease. She's self-referential – can you unlock her? They'd find a floor for you...'

'Of course,' says Flavio. 'Keys, tumblers – that's my stuff ... the oilèd wards. How apt.'

She's better. Flavio bends and moulds her. She lives like a cat – the parents like the change, she eats her food instead of throwing it, she smiles – 'But don't insist,' says Flavio. 'Don't have her married.'

The parents – love her so much – she's unlocked, she doesn't scream, doesn't trash the room – but she's empty. Full. Full of mystic knots, you see them if you live here. Now – that's beauty; they say it is a tragedy – how do people get to see like that?

Bad luck – that's the great force, the discovery. Célestine is five – she always will be, that's good luck, and bad luck too.

Flavio gets taken by the narco-army – really it's more a sect, whether you use or sell; a militia. It's all gangs, in the dust, waiting for capital, your office and the cool air blowing the paper on your desk.

Dear, lucky Célestine: she doesn't understand, she's all alone, she does what she tells herself to do – but she knows to smile at Flavio, and not be married off.

'Auguste,' says Flavio. 'Look at me. I'm finished. What more is left for me?'

Auguste – is quite black, no wings – face like a plum trodden and spurted in the grass, not radiant – but an angel nonetheless. Some come with wings, though there's much cheaper flights on hand, less stress: some bearing a sword, some a needle and a spoon.

'Well done, dear Flavio,' Auguste says. 'You have done good. Worked for the others, suffered, been taken down to where good people stay away or walk around you where you sprawl, or lurk in wait... Yes, you have done enough for several lives. What they call your journey   you could call it done. They'll look you up, the angels. All in a book. Côte d'Ivoire ... hmm, not an easy place. If they find your name – and record-keeping is not great – they'd say you'd paid the trip. Your trips.'

'Yes, Auguste,' Flavio says. 'I've lived two lives or more. But – death...! It seems a drastic end. I seem to miss the fun, the spectacle.'

'There's always funerals,' says Auguste. 'You're loved by smiths. You could be buried in a replica – white-metal Rolls. A Daimler even: the springs are so much kinder.'

'It's not at all...' Flavio says, and starts to cry.

*

Dear Célestine. So young, so mute – for ever. How she loves Flavio. How he loves her – in silence, both. Nothing to be said. Love: and love.

So what.

'It's not like you, Flavio,' Auguste says. 'Eternal sentiment. You're iron, not sugar-coated.'

'Yes,' Flavio says. 'Iron rusts. These tears – there's salt. That's what corrupts.'

'Rubbish!' says Auguste.

Célestine – she loves Flavio, like a cat does, absolutely. You don't expect a dialogue – maybe you will waft a speech, an aria – embarrassing; a soliloquy that no one hears, not Célestine, no audience. Air into air, that's all. Some cats, the loving ones, go on loving you, even when you're doing something else. Some cats are buddies, some are lodgers. The cat that loves you – it could be your angel, hurt, but not offended if you push it off. Love without arguments, without betrayal, without a cooling off. If you're not around – of course, they forget, cats.

*

'She'll always be here, Flavio,' says Auguste, hurrying him along. 'Until she's not. That's your big experience: Célestine. Now – on to something else.'

'I can stop, whenever I want,' says Flavio.

'The machete,' Auguste says, 'is not your thing. When you're in Algiers,' he says, 'ask for the ride onward, say 'Marsiglia'. That's the word, the key: so, if you're stopped, they'll know you're from elsewhere. The place, your destination, is your kind of place exactly. You're a psychologist, your papers say. All officials have concerns about their mental health – give a prognosis, and they'll bless you, let you go.'

'It's a sticky journey,' Flavio says.

'You've half a talent, Flavio,' Auguste says. 'That's the most anyone can get. Half unlocking Célestine... Genius! So long as she stays exactly where she is – too small to rape, too happy for her suicide.'

‘It’s the sand,’ says Flavio. ‘It’s time. If you fall off the truck, they won’t stop for you – they’d bog down when they stop. The same over the desert if you’re in the air – it’s glass. It holds you.’

‘Ah yes,’ Auguste says. ‘Your friends, the Touaregs – down there, in their tents or in their technicals.’

‘They are what we are,’ says Flavio. ‘The desert’s like the Amazon – all the first peoples. We can’t escape them, what they do, we do, we are. We’re a bit different, we write down about ourselves, we settle and we think the chairs, the sex, will be secure, that it will all go on...’

‘There’s no analogy...’ Auguste begins.

‘Don’t argue,’ Flavio says. ‘I’m with them all, especially the Touaregs. Algiers – those immense concrete buildings, rearing up like in the movie. How you long for space! But – no one trusts people who move around.’

‘It’s the epidemic,’ Auguste says. ‘People don’t mention it. You’ve read about it – and there’s several now. Spreading all over, never eliminated wholly, not in one place. Keep your mouth well covered up.’ He swathes Flavio, his eyes, his face. ‘Remember,’ he says, ‘don’t say you are a smith – they’ll beat you and expel you.’

Célestine! She saves me – her brain, mine – in love!

*

‘Périco!’ says Flavio on the plane. ‘My friend! We held each other on the truck!’

Périco pretends it wasn’t him.

There’s a movie showing: animals, pretending to be actors – there’s a mottled snake, eating, oh so slowly – a fine green specimen, a lizard with green arms and legs... Oh no! The snake has engulfed the head, the arms – and paused. The hairless head, the knobby eyes – that’s easy – but the arms! Were they folded? Flailing, or in prayer? The lizard’s going, going, gone inside the cave – but digestion falters... He’s the banquet, in the cave, there’s shadows, but he’s the honored guest – what’s the subject? Justice, Phèdre, the République? And – oh dear – that infinity of tail, can’t leave a yard outside, and yet it doesn’t slither down...

Flavio thinks, 'It's quite embarrassing – I'd hate to be the lizard, half in, half splayed and motionless, but still outside, recognisable as one of us.'

'Being eaten, says Périco, 'is humiliating. We think quite readily of ending on the pyre, or in the loam – but not the belly of the snake. And yet – consider, Flavio: the snake brought us sinful in the world and it is right that he should take us back. Cycles, Flavio.'

'I remember, Périco,' says Flavio, 'it was you, on the truck, you clung to me. I thought it was for sex, or brotherhood, or maybe so's to steal the cash sewn in my pants ... so close, so tight... Really, it wasn't you...?'

Périco admits nothing. 'I am your *flic*,' he says. 'See that as you will – protector, provoker, accuser, fixer, framer. No one believes your tale, dear Flavio. No one believes your journey's innocent ... you could be anything – against any regime or none, a critical critic, a bigot or a warrior. All of this – like all of us. Maybe if you had more brain, you'd be my *flic*. No, Flavio, politically you're a straight. Perhaps you want salons and aristos, or just to play with scaffolds, dress up your lovers in those loose black clothes – just see the eyes, all the rest's adventure... Or brawling, playground tumbling – in your head or on the dust... My eye, dear Flavio – is on you, as you come the perverse way, from south to north...'

'I'm the green lizard,' Flavio thinks. 'My long thin waist, mucus-oiled... I'm half in, half out...'

At last the plane ... except Marsiglia isn't North, nor South... As Auguste said, it's in-between, both and neither. Nothing's decided, nothing is resolved.

*

'He's with me,' says Périco.

'This looks like a cell,' says Flavio. 'That guy Auguste – he told me, "Either live according to the rules, or by what is right. Otherwise, you'll split in two."'

'This makes it difficult,' says Périco. 'What you say – and the photo of Célestine ... to show the cops.'

'I haven't one,' says Flavio.

'Exactly so,' says Périco. 'And – you're white as tripe and come from Abidjan.'

'Algiers,' says Flavio. 'Unless you told them otherwise.'

'Oh, fiddle your harmonics, Flavio,' says Périco. 'Details on details. You're just a spy, like everyone... And then the sword of justice – you'll find it one morning in your hand and run amok with it – those elephants in Côte d'Ivoire, alas, they're only dreams of tusks, and all there's left is must of pachiderms, the instinct – water! – back to Africa and make our home...'

'If only...' Flavio says.

'Now,' says Périco, 'don't be paranoid, or we'll be here for ever. Yes, this is a cell, for our own good. Fulvio! Have you never thought, or planned, something that some regime might have objected to? Omission, commission – fantasised? – or hidden someone who has done or thought an awful thing? – have you invented some scenario of cataclysm, long before it had occurred to someone else...? Or thought of how suspicious something innocent that you had done might seem? Assume your culpability, dear Flavio, and so you'll understand the fears and the precautions of my colleagues here... But – don't let on. Keep quiet about subversive thoughts. Don't confess to what you've thought and haven't done, or we shall not get out...'

'But, Périco,' says Flavio, 'you want that I should spy, and that's a necessary but a putrid thing, for which I shall be paid and praised. But – the deceit ... it undermines the basis of a polity, the trust, equality, the brotherhood, the personal autonomy, that all in theory should desire. You want that my spying should be my alibi, although – it's vile. Betrayal of the whole. But – that will make me free! And what I haven't done must be concealed, to guarantee I seem a guilty innocent like all the rest...'

'Yes, Flavio,' says Périco, tugging at the window bars. 'That's it, that's what we read at school. Do the bad so's to avoid the worse. Let them rough you up, it gives authenticity to what you say.'

'I work metal,' Flavio says, 'not the bendy stuff.'

MARSEILLE

'Here we are, here we are...' sings Périco, stamping some mattresses flat. 'Freed! Remember Hugo, "*Les adieux de l'hotesse arabe...*" We pay rent to her, and we pay it also – more Hugo – to the "*fiancée du timbalier*". Hear those bongos? That'll remind you. They collect for the "*charmant gazon*", the lad on the motorbike down there. How the French value their culture! Victor Hugo was the richest man in Europe, but he never forgot the poor. They made him richer still. Remember that, Flavio.'

'For sure, I shall remember, Périco,' says Flavio. 'I'm tough. The people here – they're tough as well, with more experience of being here. I ask myself – will all this experience do me good? Is it the best thing, diving right in? Experience is diesel – you need it but it doesn't change a thing, except it brings more black. And in the end...'

'Oh come, Flavio,' says Périco, 'would a dinosaur ask that? End? "*On s'engage...*" I've heard you say it... Aren't you excited? What will happen next? What's the mystery, how will it be worked out, will you resist, transform?'

'You're right, Périco,' says Flavio. 'A dino wouldn't ask. But maybe that smart green lizard in the movie on the plane – oh, how could it be so stupid, the lovely all-over suit, and head first into gastric juice ... maybe the brain dissolved by now...'

'Vainglory, Flavio,' says Périco. 'There must be rules: it didn't look, it walked right in...'

*

'We are all orphans here,' the Arab hostess says, making her farewells. 'Don't talk about where you're from. You'll feel at home.'

The snake is outside, you can't miss it, as you walk out the door. You have to leave your room, or else you'd starve; you couldn't pay the rent.

Life is slow – 'Wait, wait,' says Périco. 'Establish yourself, you're a poor sap. It takes time. The street will suss you out. Register your moral flab.'

The guys outside – don't look as if they care: they'll find a place for you, or maybe not.

No chance. Nothing, nothing at all. No work in crime, experience required: informing – all full up.

'Those Parsee funerals over our heads,' says Flavio. 'And then the wings...'

'That's an augury,' Périco says. 'A mariner! That's you – think albatross.'

'I don't think that's what they are...' says Flavio.

'Be a sailor, Flavio. Just for a night – transferring urgent medical supplies, from some big boat, into a little one,' says Périco.

'I'd be on track for goodness,' Flavio says. 'Except ... the sea. It swallows you. Every piece of crap – it ends up there. Those whales – they glide about like turds. They squeak and mew – everything is there, it's true, but like in a mirror bent from side to side and top to ... a hand is not a fin, but – there it is ... those eyes don't see, that nose, it doesn't smell, and then there's all those yellow viral things, like in your brain and in your gut – except, that in the sea they're out, and swimming round and having kids and playing ducks and drakes with gender, things that live in other things...'

'No, Flavio,' says Périco. 'Just do this job. The only time that you must be precise and care who's standing close, is when you're doing crime. Then, you must be careful. Don't drop things, don't ask for credit, remember vendetta's real and imminent, you must respect the boss and follow his instructions, not grope his women, but do walk his dog, and if it bites you – don't complain. Life in the other world – where people say there's honesty and doing right – it's *farabutti*, Flavio. Liars and deceivers, wastrels, puff-fish galore, gurus on the take, and speechifiers, idlers and incompetents... A Crime, Flavio, is where there's nothing wasted, everything is counted right, omission and commission counts, is punished. Get it straight. Which world you live in – that is up to you. But trust me, Flavio: those goods are needed, they will have a sale, and if they kill your customer, well, they'll have been warned...'

'That's theft and property resolved,' says Flavio. 'And all the rest? – the guttings and the mutilations, all that's done under licence, or as concessions, by kings and queens and presidents, all for good causes, or at least for historic or for pressing reasons, pretexts, all that tale – and...' Périco puts his hand over Flavio's declaiming mouth and says,

'I know, you're going to say "The Barbagia"! The *codice barbaracino* – the sheep-stealers' code, the lex talionis in accountants' terms, shepherds' honour... Hegel said, I think, everything is honourable, or else – it's a mistake. You can't punish a mistake, and honour is repaid with honour... Something like that...'

'I know,' says Flavio. 'I've just been waiting for the chance, an offer from some guys to make my living where there's life and feisty guys who hold the world at bay! The other world, the world of patient idlers – that has jammed. There's no work there, and everywhere that guys still hoe and hammer – that is coming to an end. I'll take to sea...'

'You need to hold your breath,' says Périco. 'You have to dive and search and swim and float, you need to dodge and go quite dark, turn off your phosphorescence, your poet's lighthouse, that critic's nose all luminous...'

'I know,' says Flavio. 'There's stealing by intent. That's what we two aspire to. But also there is stealing by being slack and greedy, ordering stuff that no one needs, building a bridge that takes ten years, pretend humanity...'

'Exactly,' says Périco. 'It's all to make a buck. Intent or inattention, the bandit captain or the clerk: is one so good, the other bad? This is our humanity, our activity, dear Flavio – everyone here's at it – the predation. And then there is another sphere, where there's no theft, no massacre. So lofty it is usually invisible. Getting the high notes in that Zelenka piece... Nothing there to steal, nothing to denounce. Heard or unheard, it isn't stolen, it's not for profit: – or, if sometimes there's cash, it doesn't go to you, you, standing fooling there, your hunting horn primed, stuffed full of nerves and clams... You see, there's a whole universe, extending far beyond the stars – where making livings doesn't mean so much, and criminal's a hollow word: – the category is non-existent: – there's no work, no effort from some guy – it's forces, bits of string. All there's ironed out, and yet it's travelling fast. It's all not bad, not good – and not political...'

*

The sea is all around. Tales of the sea are all around. Tales of the Côte d'Ivoire are everywhere, in the Côte d'Ivoire, and all around. Flavio turns off his light, dives down in the dark dark sea.

Down among the slaves, fish weave in and out and through them all.

*

'I'm a subtle person,' says Périco, 'I understand: but – you'd find it hard to tell all that to someone else. In time, the thefts, the slaving – that's all just a tale, not good or bad, but something to be told.'

'For me, it's the diving that is difficult,' says Flavio. 'The sea is full of everything you can imagine, and stuff that's been thrown in and roams around. It's like the desert where you follow those invisible roads, except the sea is filth.'

'You found the cargo, clever boy,' says Périco. 'And everyone is pleased.'

*

... an old workers' quarter here once, it fell down and disappeared – these kids can't even write, brought up to murder and suicide ... brought up to obedience and a contract to play football for a week...

*

'You're too old to be interesting, Flavio,' says Périco. 'Guys here think they're making new states far off, somewhere else, at least. That sounds big; it would be big if it wasn't all so intricate... More delusion and more myth. No one takes you seriously, Flavio, or anyone at all, except yourself.'

Real estate – that's what fascinates Périco. Acquiring the top floors, and charging rent.

In Flavio's line, people get hurt, lose everything – 'I'm not weak,' says Flavio. 'But I'm scared.'

Fear's hard to price – the cops are frightened too, like soldiers always are. Many are in love as well – so what? Flavio thinks: 'It's trade and cash. If that's crime, it's too dull for me, too boring for a life.'

'Oh,' says Périco. 'It's kids and soldiers too.'

'Maybe,' says Flavio. 'But it's just like life up in the other sphere, the futile one. All I get's enough to pay the rent.'

'No, Flavio,' says Périco: 'I won't expose you to yourself. We're all slaves; after all, some boss instructs us – invisible or often not... But – there's the law, and there's the crime. When you're in crime, you'll have done everything, or been prepared to do it. Just like the perfect cop is ready to face all sorts of naughtiness ... so too the diver, the wide boy, with his cosh, his cash, his shiv, his dose, his dart – he's all a-quiver, his every arrow tipped, the tipsters at his elbow, odds quoted, backed, he's done it all, the good, the bad ... ready always for another shot, another venture...'

'Enough!' says Flavio. 'I live in nature. In a pack, drawing my territory, ganging up to eat... It isn't me, but it is us: the natural life that everybody talks about. The leisure parts are quite desirable – the preening and the bowers, the dance, the rut. The prancing naked in your fur. It's not like that at all, that part's the ad. Everyone hunts everybody, all the time. There's never mediation. You can hire a cop – but nature: it's there beside you in your lair.'

'Well,' says Périco. 'Your burrow's yours to be kept clean, dug deep. It's the other guys – the exalted ones, who wave the guns around, and have a plan ... they're dangerous. I'm innocent, dear Flavio, I don't believe in much, but I don't want to change the scraps I do, still less get in the way of someone's scattershot...'

'Of course, dear Périco,' says Flavio, 'everyone's an innocent, if it's not their show, their heist.'

'You're right,' says Périco, 'they're all too young now. It's not like when Alain Delon ran the city – how they sang the song, "To arms, citizens", and they set it up, republic, empire, now all that's left is Côte d'Ivoire. And Mali. And their long war against the Touaregs... You're not part of that, Flavio, you're ignorant. I feel these things – I'm ignorant as well, but I have premonitions. I feel the history coming, sharp against my skin and rough in my throat. This place – it isn't you, today's already too much for you. Anyway, I have a solution, bought for you with cash hard earned.'

'A boat?' says Flavio fearfully.

'Like that, but better – no water,' says Pèrico. 'A mobile bar. Go where you want – *birra* and *pannini, pressions* and *baguettes*. Sleep on the floor, travel... If it isn't you – hire hands to do it all. Go, Flavio, go with the wind.'

'My time is up, Périco?' asks Flavio.

'It's orders, dearest Flavio,' says Périco, starting to cry.

LUDIVINE

'This is the worst part,' says Ludivine, heaving her hindquarters as she scoops fake ham from a can. 'Those unfortunate pigs. It's hard to speak of fortune when there's none, none at all for them. Oh, how I feel for pigs – my father was a pig...'

The customers admire her for the flow of smooth and runny talk. She says, 'Your friend, Périco – he's a big name in real estate.'

'They make a banner for you – any size,' says Flavio, lifting up from his nest woven from army blankets on the mobile floor: 'Agents. Everyone needs them. I'm yours, Ludivine.'

Pigs out of luck... Ludivine's vision has freed her completely – you'd not think of asking her to lie down with you on the caravan's floor, though of course she might – she's thrown off her personality and all its pettiness – while you're still in your niche, your box, your tunnel. Ludivine, though – she's free; the everyday, the moral, are around her like a garden she need never leave because it grows as she advances – new, newer fruits maturing, buds revealing flowers not seen before, not ever. Tucked into those baguettes.

Ludivine is in the world – it's not hers, though, doesn't belong to her, so she can't say there's rules for everyone and everything, there's good and bad because we're in the same boat, on the same sea... Not being number one doesn't mean you're number everything, and Ludivine's not in a boat. Sometimes she is, of course, rowing or stretching out, sometimes she wants one to save her from the waves, sometimes she's eating ice-cream on the shore, and there are ships and sailors far far off.

'The clearest vision,' Flavio says, 'is sheer transparency; is nullity. Everything is clear, revealed, but it can't be paradise, because for that there's judgement, and after that, you and your friends are separated – alas, you don't go there, not into paradise. Too bad, you were not told, or you had not believed it. Everything is clear as glass, but nothing's labelled good or bad. Heaven and hell, they look the same – but they can't be... And yet – the clarity! It must be all around, your eyes are made to see it just like that, exactly as it is... Nothing depends on you, even your eyes are not your self ... and yet...'

'"The contemplative life",' Ludivine sings, laughing. 'Lying down there so's I do all the work, Flavio...'

'More cash, Ludivine?' asks Flavio. 'What difference would it make?'

'None,' says Ludivine, laughing more. 'We'd buy more gas and have it take us further on.'

'You'd meet more people,' Flavio says. 'You must have met most everyone – every point of view, that is.'

'Yes,' says Ludivine, 'I listen. You argue. Some of the people where we were – they saw streets full of bodies, just lying there. It's like you don't believe those scenes, just boggle – maybe in old prints, the Commune, maybe, there's the same thing, folklore. Some of them responsible, your friends, your chums. People you talk to. What'd you make of that, Flavio? I'm not there, of course, and not responsible – that's what it means, "no self" – it's good, it gives you judgement, you don't have to wait for it,' and Ludivine laughs and laughs.

'No one waits now, Ludivine,' says Flavio. 'Certainly not for judgment. Bringing religion in – it's an excuse. The metaphysics too – forget it, Ludivine.'

'You did bad things, Flavio: then, you excused yourself,' says Ludivine.

'Well, I see you hang around me still,' says Flavio. 'You don't seem so turned off...'

'Oh, I get to see the world, Flavio,' she says, 'and I'd leave you in a flash – except this is not you. It's just a job.'

'Yes,' says Flavio, displeased. 'Hold your nose when you're round me. Once, these sandwich bars, the mobile ones, were all the rage. Music, moulded glass, oysters – the *Place de l'Opèra*, the *Plaça,* Frith Street; they were everywhere. Now, we're a rarity, possibly unique, like the *Orgue de Barbarie*.'

'We could put chairs outside,' says Ludivine. 'A table.'

'No,' says Flavio. 'It would be illegal. People hate nomads, especially when they start to settle down.'

'People are the same everywhere,' says Ludivine. 'We could change the fillings.'

'It would be wrong,' says Flavio, 'indecorous. Against nature.' He's quite frustrated. 'It's trivial, Ludivine. People don't expect much choice from us – the least there is, the happier they are.'

'No, Flavio,' she says. 'Happiness and everything else, emotional stuff, comes from your habitus. History and neighbours. There is no universal rule – I mean, *that's* the universal rule, there isn't one.'

'You just add copouts as you come to them,' says Flavio. 'You ducked around responsibility, and how the collective's not a person, not a human. What is it, then? It makes no sense, Ludivine. You can't abolish self and then make guidance for all selves.'

'Oh,' she says, twisting open industrial cans of grease. 'I could untie it all if I had more education. Hone myself into a point.'

'Money wasted,' Flavio says. 'Your work is modest, but it's danger-free. They say the *passeurs* get entombed alive – not that it worries me... Keeping humanity on the move... We keep our heads down here...'

*

And so they must – there's crossfire, birdshot perhaps, that chips the stemmas on the van. They're at the furthest point of Europe here – there's rivalry, those orchards – citrus of all kinds, and the elusive bergamot. Flavio and Ludivine lie on the floor, embraced – 'Invidia, Ludivine,' he says. 'Envy is the root of all the other sins – it makes our grandeur and our baseness ... it's the motor that can generate the other peccadilloes, the stealing and the sex and murder, discovering more powerful gods, wanting to be good and then the best; the schema is dynamic, Ludivine. It's easier to recognise one big sin than lots of happenstance, fortuitous temptations...'

'But, Flavio,' says Ludivine, cowering as the guns, intimidating, crack away. 'It's all a paradox. If sin is bad, and envy is the mainspring – it's also what drives us to be good and better than the next guy, it's disease and its own cure...'

'Don't go outside,' says Flavio. 'I'll creep up in the driver's seat, and we'll head on out...'

They leave behind a crepitation – gunshots. 'Over this piece of sea,' says Flavio. 'You can see the start of Sicily – a paradise. Paradise spoilt – by envy, naturally. Nothing special – there's always been some bandits here. No point in going further, further south – there's Sicily, and then there's Africa, for thousands of kilometres. Rather too large for paradise – or is it Eden? Maybe I confuse the beginning and the end? the curious fruits?' And Flavio laughs. 'It brings to mind Roxanne, start, finish, all in one: Ludivine, you'll never meet her, she and I had years together. I couldn't bring my ideas together, not to fruition – it must have been a bore for her. But then I travelled – and everything became revealed – a cunning artifice, like those old Krazy Kat cartoons... Once you know you'll go on and on, dodging the endings, the pitfalls and the pratfalls – you see it's all a set-up, actors, cities carpentered and lit, those lamps, white light – I forget the name... White phosphorus? Of course, there is an end – to everything: always the same one...'

'Yes,' says Ludivine. 'The same old corny end.'

'If you doubt that it's an artifice,' says Flavio. 'Remember, what you're after, Ludivine: moral philosophy's the most evidently an artifice of them all.'

'Nothing wrong with that,' she says. 'If it's like the rest, like everything – that's rather good.'

'No, I think it's trivial,' says Flavio, accelerating up a crumbling motorway. 'Anyway, those bandits, they weren't after us. It was just the bergamots.'

'I'm glad you talked to me about Roxanne,' says Ludivine. 'I thought you might have forgotten her.'

'The mafia,' says Fulvio. 'Sells this cement – made with sea water – the salt eats it, its strength. I told you – from the sea comes nothing good.'

'I know,' says Ludivine. 'That's how it used to be. Bandits, though, should be shooting from behind a rock, not selling builders' wares.'

'I like talking to you, Ludivine,' says Fulvio. 'After all, there's nothing else... Of course, there's beer and sandwiches.'

'I'm leaving, Fulvio,' she says. 'Though you can go on talking, as if I was still here.'

In the fields now there's fat blocks of bricks and concrete, quite purposeless – 'Those old Romans,' Fulvio says, 'knew about conquest. They put themselves in their cement.'

*

'You'll make the big time, Flavio,' says Ludivine. 'But I got there first. I do international cuisine – and here – up here in Bologna, I do the history too. Legions from here – they crossed the Rubicon and conquered England ... just taste my larks' tongues ... that fishy paste that burns your mouth with salt. The sucking pigs...'

'It should be "suckling", Ludivine – but you know pigs...' says Flavio.

'The bar, dear Flavio?' asks Ludivine. 'You'll hire another crew. And don't be snide – it isn't you.'

'Oh Ludivine,' says Flavio, his tearful eyes – what a sight! 'The sadness! Our philosophy! Where will that go, what conclusions can I draw? And you – lost in the fluty chatter of larks' tongues. It isn't you! Off you go, my rock, flying through everyone else's space. Alas! it seems our journey's always interrupted, fidgety – the book you take to brighten up your trip, always too short, too long – on and on you go, each strand of time unravels as you try to knit it up...'

*

'The bar,' says Valentino, 'is our heritage. The civilisation peaks there: the apex: handicraft joined to factory: the marriage of the artisan, his sword and musket by his side – with industry: the furnace, trip-hammers, moulds... Put it on show, dear Flavio: those baguettes, they're history too. Stretch the body, re-paint, mount a Dodge power-plant...'

'Yes, Valentino,' Flavio says, 'it's quite a metaphor. It's irreproachable. Ease and simplicity. It chimes with us – we're good. We don't know what happens out of sight. Better ignorance than complicity, my friend... And anything at all – it may, it will, be done. The past's an empty tomb. The present – maybe a radiant stranger with a tale alights... The future – a mystery that keeps us mesmerised ... what's there, just out of vision? A ball of fire? Star colonies? No self? Ludivine will tell you: the world is made of oysters on a silver plate – you choose and swallow, hope it's not the one that sends you early griping to your grave... The staff has checked them out for pearls – no hope you'll crack a tooth on one...'

'I always ask myself,' says Valentino, hugging Flavio's arm in his – they're partners and curators now, guardians, defenders of the hope, 'so we're good – why not? Our bosses too – responsible: but – how far would they go? How far, to preserve the heritage, and all our quests and questions, freely, independently pursued? Civilisation ending on a pyre, pure as the phoenix...'

'You're wrong, Valentino,' says Flavio. 'Civilisation's about lasting and being original, not being civil, still less being kind.'

'I must agree,' says Valentino. 'It's consolation. Inspiration. It's the drum that thrums us into battle: up the temple steps we go – there's the priest, and you're the sacrifice.'

'How much for the bar?' Flavio asks, losing patience.

'Oh, it's unique,' says Valentino. 'It's worth all and naught. Come, Flavio – this talk of civilisation, how banal! The inside serenades the inside; the lover hymns her love, it serenades itself! Look! I've made my own, its quite original –' and he raises up an old zinc door, pulls Flavio with him, into a dark and peopled hall: 'My habitus.'

*

'See, Flavio,' says Valentino, the dealer in old and costly curios, 'I wanted to be good. Our civilisation says goodness lies in helping out the poor that civilisation has produced. But – some say the answer lies in tents, and some in jobs, and some in keeping people where they are and festering, or teaching God or patience, taking arms or using votes... Or all of these... And so I thought – "I'll make my civilisation here." This, Flavio, is the biggest trailer in the world. Your little bar, all glass and splendour, will fit in here, almost invisible. All the guys here – if I didn't feed them, they'd be hungry and be poor. That's how perilous it is, Flavio: life! See, here there's chance, or, to dignify the term, it's destiny.'

'They're slot machines,' says Flavio: there's rows and rows, all blinking, offering some tempting fruits, proffering stiff arms...

'Yes,' says Valentino. 'Got it in one! Then there are other zones – mats you pray on, walls you whisper to... Peep shows. Woods to whittle. Martial arts and physios.'

'I'd try the bandits,' Flavio says, ladling coins into a machine. 'Take the cash, and off I'd go...'

'Remember, Flavio,' says Valentino, 'the theme's precariousness. Your winnings work quite well inside. Outside, they're washers. Some with a haiku, but not currency at all. They're for collectors. What is here, is ours, and stays with us. So – no one here is poor. Everyone has some activity – see, over there the screens where you can find the dead – they call it genealogy, but sometimes up there pops a live one – an Auntie in the States, a cousin on death row...' He laughs. Flavio's quite lost.

'A joke, Flavio,' Valentino says. 'Every culture needs its joke. For Frenchmen – it's the Belgians. For me – my culture's joke is me!'

'I don't understand,' says Flavio. 'You've laid it out, a sward, a trailer parked, a few guys fool around, and while they're here, they're occupied... It's fun, maybe, not funny. You're the philanthropist – a patsy, probably, and spoiled – envied, but not ridiculed.'

'It's trivial, what I've made,' says Valentino, 'and I'm pretentious. So, master of the paradox.'

'You must make stuff for the outside...' says Flavio. 'Export. Useful's as easy to produce as useless.'

'Ephemera!' says Valentino. 'Nothing endures. Except the scuffed and broken stuff, vainglories, junk – what people call a civilisation when it's gone, and stack it on the heap of similars.'

'It doesn't seem a funny joke,' says Flavio, insisting. 'What you're all about.'

'No,' says Valentino: 'You are right. It's not. Now, your kitsch greasy spoon on wheels – how much do you want for it?'

'Enough,' says Flavio, 'for over the hills, and through the border posts.'

'Well,' says Valentino, 'suppose instead I have you drive the rig the whole world over. No question – I can pay. And we can pick up staff all round: everywhere, there's poor. Until we find it. The best place.'

'How'll we know?' asks Flavio, though he knows this isn't him, not at all his thing, what he's been driving to encounter here...

'I'll tell you,' Valentino says, 'when we arrive.'

'Ludivine,' says Flavio, 'she should come to run the bar.'

'Too late!' says Valentino. 'She's with the butter-eaters now. You should have thought.'

'I feel I'm losing on this deal,' says Flavio. 'How's that?'

'You have the licence, Flavio, that lets you drive. I've the charisma,' Valentino says.

*

First, Timisoara, then the pelicans by the sea.

'Wait!' thinks Flavio. 'This is not the way! I've been tricked into driving many times before. It's just continuity. It shows how the same people got to different destinations, and how reality seems to change, though you do not. Périco gave me what he said was better than a boat – a boat's no good without a flood – the water's scarce. The bar – an ark! Although – the animals are all in zoos, or camps. Just me, and Ludivine. Our food and drink, abundantly...'

It doesn't mean so much – on these roads, there's tractor-trailers just as large, full of boxes not for you or anyone you know, some with clandestines within, or runaways... Few, it is true, are feverish, contorted, not like Valentino's rig.

'Suppose we go South, Valentino,' Flavio says. 'See Uruk...'

'Uruk is no more,' says Valentino. 'That was when the gods took part. There was abundance, some malignity. Then they were all rolled up into one, after, booted up into the sky, or in a book! Now, see what a mess, and how we hate each other. Fortunately – there are big minds left, deep pockets too...'

'There's you,' says Flavio, flattering. 'Valentino. And lots of us.'

'Little guys,' says Valentino, 'needing a help.'

'I didn't think of that,' says Flavio. 'Remember the song, "no gods, no tsars, and no heroes"...'

'Your tone,' says Valentino huffily, 'I'm not sure it chimes with me. Besides, you're foolish, Flavio. Don't think of going back, not a step. You know those old far-off places don't exist – and if they did, you know how it all turns out, just a re-run, everything unravelling just the same until you end up here – a maze, dear Flavio: start at the centre – and you come out here, where you went in. Try to reach the centre – and you come out here, where you went in.'

'I know all that, Valentino,' Flavio says. 'Where you are – it's nowhere in particular – Moscow Tennessee, Varna Ontario – an empty city, somewhere in Guizhou, on the road to Moldova: the future's mist ... and so you look back along the track, the heaps of bones and skulls, and you're the only one alive ... you make the traveller's tale, the road song ... and on you go.'

'Exactly so,' says Valentino. 'On you go, Flavio. Drive on!'

'The load keeps shifting, Valentino...' Fulvio says.

'Nonsense!' says Valentino. 'It's people move around. You must get used to that. And, Fulvio – your cosmology, the poetry, the lilt, the chant – you've no idea how many of you drivers over time have sung the same, the very same, refrain. "I want to leave!" they say. "And – ah! how they carved netsuke yesterday: and oh and ugh! how terrible, what went on then and now, maybe we'll go, or maybe stay..." Adventure! Fulvio. *Raus, raus. Davai!*'

Flavio doesn't move – sitting in the cab, he's much much taller than Valentino, who's trying to shut the driver's door: 'Flavio – drive on. Would you join the opposition? To arms? Fight the desert, that stinging atomic sand? Those childish flags? The street? Guns against bombs...'

'Wait!' says Flavio. 'What exactly is it all the drivers say?'

'Always the same,' says Valentino.

'Invidia? Eternal return? The past, the future, civilisation?' asks Flavio.

'Yes, always the same, exactly,' Valentino says. 'It's their litany. Learnt off by heart and then forgotten, out it comes again as if it is original. What I'm taking round the world is something different. You, of course, don't recognise a novelty...'

*

Here's Suceava. Flavio climbs down. It's over. Valentino's mobile world, the sideshow that has no poor freaks. It's impossible.

Suceava. All round, those little forts, chapels, flooded, then repainted. A march, an in-between: or a limit, end – but no! Off it goes again, your trek. Distances immense, beyond belief, into another distance: – aha! the camels, yaks, then cycling into Lianshan. Suceava – a place that seems strategic, people ready to leave whenever there's a call, a push... A place it's hard to walk from, getting to somewhere else quite different.

BEATA

'Come away. No one's interested, everywhere is central.' She tugs at him: she wears a name – Beata – like a dog its collar, somewhere to take her back, always, even when passed out in stupors, lost running wild and free with other dogs.

'I'm thinking of where it is I have to go,' says Flavio. 'I'm like a genre painting – or a piece of music – everything's inside, and no way to get it out. Those walled Dutch courtyards, Spanish kids in flounces.'

'Nonsense,' Beat says. 'You step outside your room, and everything is there, all life. People who look like fish – all sorts, but *every* sort. Even if you drown, it goes on and on. What does it mean – everything you could imagine, a touch away in any street – war, peace, the comedy divine, profane? You ask – everybody does – do you wait for an answer? Your answer?'

'Leave me be,' says Flavio, wondering where...

'You see!?' she says. 'You're lucky – there's a step in front – and to the side: it doesn't matter. A direction's always available, just empower one leg, you're there! Off and away! If in doubt – the luck is yours, the next card's platinum...'

'That's what the dealers say,' says Flavio.

'Your trouble is,' says Beata, looking deep into him, 'you're eocene. Cycladic. People are identical to you, your cult. Some look pregnant, but their noses are the same. A triangle on a flat face. Think Proust: instead, Flavio, you think Plato. Value your gay friends, esteem cross-dressers. But no. It's all pingponging with you: arid chat. We're shadows in the cave to you. You think Homer – they're all clones – some have oily fingers, some are wily, but everyone's an archer or a knitter. You should think Dickens. Now! Each has a quiddity, cute or brute, a jolly ancient or a snippy brat – that way you don't see how the story's always identical, the music goes round and round, but no one gets to kick higher than their height, and if you don't hold on the girl next door, the line, the whole line, just falls down.'

'Well, Beata,' Flavio says. 'What's your quiddity? What do you want? You're too tall to be a waif, and you're not rubicond... You're in variety, but it always sounds the same...'

'Exactly,' says Beata: 'You've seen the trick. Of course, I am a stray! What do I want? A ticket to somewhere plush, a job. Scruffy food to share along the way.'

'I left the rig on a principle,' says Flavio. 'I don't want to pick up crawlies.'

'The principle?' Beata asks. 'That it wouldn't work? A déjà vu? That's the best principle to make you quit, of course, and usually right. Anyway, I've a boyfriend, George the Greek – you'll need to court me, wean me off him.'

'I've no cash for that,' says Flavio, quite tempted and dismayed.

'Oh, George is poor – he doesn't show it though, not like you do,' Beata says.

'Everybody shows it,' Flavio says. 'Even if it's all they show.'

'I'll help you start with nothing,' says Beata. 'If you've something, you're already going somewhere that you don't know where it is, but you have hopes, high hopes. Spend what you have on me, my dear – and off you go!'

Everything's so cheap here, thinks Flavio: and no one has any money. That must be why. But...

The bus is nearly free: but beside Beata there's a youth in white and sandals – 'Who's that in my place?' Flavio asks, knowing it is George the Greek, who doesn't speak, besides, knows no language but his own.

'I told you,' says Beata. 'Don't be a stone. Court me, win me, let adventure flow...'

'I could unlock George,' thinks Flavio. 'But maybe I won't.'

He asks, 'This George – if he wants, he talks? It's not just being Greek and having to look back, over a shapely shoulder? You're right, Beata, having nothing is the best.'

When the coach stops for eats – George says, 'Chicken tikka.'

Beata laughs: 'Budgies that pull cards, horses that give the numbers. Hens that lay to Haydn – he can watch the hands go round, the clessidra empty and refill – mechanisms obsess him – he sees them everywhere... Mechanical birds and monkeys, robots – "Down with school!" he says. "It's over, didn't work. Forward, machines – do the grunt work – let us humans be our natural selves, creatures of passion and vendetta. Down with intelligence, the intelligentsia. Long live life! So, we can rejoin our comrades, the animals, our brothers: instinct, routine, procreation – resignation, speak, don't speak: it is our logic, our true selves. As for ratiocination – our machines will do that for us!"'

'He says all that?' asks Flavio. 'It's like "potatoes" – for Japanese, that's an enormous joke, a wonder of the language.'

'Oh yes?' says Beata, unconvinced. 'It's true, it's all a seesaw – buy and sell, rich and poor, intelligence or success – there is a rhythm. The tourists come to see the painted forts – once they were churches, local people hid inside – and now... They're something else, a wonder, pictures in a wood ... a mystery, revealed to ticketholders only...'

The landscape ... it no longer flows past, constantly. Maybe the bus has broken down.

'George'll fix it,' says Beata. 'It takes time – he's binary, so it's either–or. Making the robots – of course, you feel inferior. But he's a sex-machine...'

Flavio half unlocks George, half-shoots his bolt. His mechanism breaks, George thinks, he stutters and reflects.

'We'll dump George here,' says Flavio. 'They're hostile, but...'

Beata sighs – 'He was my love, my mascot,' she declares.

They push him out the door.

'There,' she says: 'Now, I'll concentrate on you, dear Flavio, and thrust you to the top. There, everything is free, the transport and the food. Don't steal and stash away – you're made for life...'

'Yes,' Flavio says, 'and is that life we've found?'

'Oh twiddle,' says Beata. 'Life isn't you, it's all the cloud of nullities like me, who fasten to your tail. We don't have wisdom, we don't speak, but oh! the living's good.'

'It's futile,' Flavio says, and Beata pummels him:

'No! I told you, Flavio,' she says. 'Way back, there was the journey, hell and paradise, the grimy child who's cleansed of poverty and drives a pony cart, has pony-skin accoutrements. Then came the quest – somewhat selfish, but you had your arts and tarts, your cabinet of curiosities – remember, Flavio: Dickens and Proust. Once, improvement, degradation. Then – gay scenes and trenches. Lots of guys around, sweating and real. Now – it's not like that. It's all sequential, lengths of track. You do a distance with a friend – they disappear. There comes an oldster, hooves and tail – you end up in the ditch. Then you reflect, and sort it out, supine: sometimes a *horizontale*, sometimes on a medic's couch. You choose, my dear: fine writing, or in dialect and highfalutes...'

The back seat of the bus ... it's made for intercourse and making friends. It's not a great success, thinks Flavio: Beata's like a thistle, with procedures long and intricate – and he's agnostic. Sex is the fence that they must overcome, but then comes the grassy field of circumstance, lust, and the climbing leg that's out of place.

'What can be made of you, Flavio?' asks Beata. 'With all your talents. Remember, nothing is of nothing made.'

'Nothing is best, that's what you said,' says Flavio.

'That's what there is, Flavio: I told you that,' she says. 'It's all new, I told you so. Friends, jokes, your so-called loved-ones, it's all last century. The new's the old refurbished. Think, Flavio: those fortresses, the marcher churches: now, they're simple attractions. Could be Mickey Mouse. You gawp, move on, you and your girl, your guy, the tiny toddling clone you drag along, all ignorant as vice or virtue: your group is standard, like them all – its joker, those that moan, the anguished guide; it melts like chocolate when the plane arrives back home. You move away. Back to the nest. What was there, holds you? Glue of your life. A decision: yes! Some soldiers, bank drafts, those horsemen – not those Dickens people, though, dear Flavio. Not Marcel, his chiffon friends. People are not needed, they're an embarrassment – too loud, too hard, too self-obsessed. The more you think you're progress – the more those horsemen dream of drinking from your skull. Where do you fit, my dear?'

'It's all quite inconsequential,' Flavio says. 'If you are right – it's just reality. And if you're wrong – the same.'

'Nothing's inconsequential,' says Beata. 'You can't poke a hole in what is real to see what's on the other side. That's why they made the Web – there's the spider, we're the fly. Every thought and every deed...'

'It's true,' says Flavio. 'But also inconsequential: some causes matter more than who's to boil the egg. Take Rascoala – your epic, the Uprising – that's a thing you go on practising ... those peasants stamping in a ring, quite unforgettable, although for me the dance means everything: the calm, the question, not just rising up and falling back...'

'Forget all that,' says Beata. 'Power over other humans – not your thing. You're not one who spends his time staring in mirrors, looking stern.'

She pushes Flavio towards a buzz – a buzzing, some guy with a drill, making stone blocks look like heads. Not exactly heads with faces. If we were born of stone, that's what we'd look like in some mamma's stony womb. And if we were just heads of tufo or of basalt – there's no hollow, so no sound, no breath, no brain to jiggle round, no eyes wired up, no wink, no sneeze, no spit.

'This is the man, the foot man, Bethlen,' says Beata, pushing Flavio in. 'Who makes the heads.'

'I'm terrified, Beata,' Flavio says. 'Those hateful sculptures – what a dread! To see them in their rows, immortal, amputees, gouged thoroughly, polished with a disc – our ideal thoughtless sightless selves, our totems staring at the sea, the wall, the heath, the polygon...'

'Bethlen wants a person who will tramp the world, and make a catalogue,' Beata says. 'You get no criticism, make no judgments – just find and snap, and write it down.'

'It could be the best job ever,' Flavio says, 'except you might find these awful things...'

'Of course you will, you must,' Beata says. 'An archive gives a lustre to the works, and raises up the prices too.'

'It seems, well, nothing,' Flavio says.

'Fame and travel?' says Bethlen.

'They're all bald,' Flavio objects. 'You shouldn't mock creation – it quite disgusts.'

'Oh,' says Bethlen. 'That'll be your religion, coming out.'

'It didn't go in,' says Flavio.

'So,' says Beata. 'Those little churches – made us like sculpture. We're Christians then? Well!'

She raps her knuckles on a head. 'I heard about that messy death, nailed up – what happens when you cut that out? We all end the same, wherever it takes place and who's around...' she says.

'It's just heads?' asks Flavio. 'They could be in attics anywhere. Or used in walls – some keeping out the seas...'

'Ramparts: talking heads... Go find them, Flavio,' says Beata. 'You're the Roman, Romanian, roamer, the Rom, the poor wanderer who'll leave no mark. You need be a group so's to be properly discriminated and written down...You'll slip through whatever is, like water between rocks... If they find your body, they'll rebury it without a word in that same spot ... otherwise, those forms, police! You haven't understood, Flavio: find the heads, make them commodities, a price upon each one. It's bounty – you're a hunter. You get expenses, the heads are counted, the owners get the prize when the heads go on the roundabout.'

'They sell, they lose their head,' says Flavio, trying to keep up.

'No, they had stuff,' Beata says. 'More than stone – art! An item. Tease it up from hell. Throw it in the stream – it's culture.'

'I feel I'm locked in,' says Flavio. 'Locked out.'

'That's exactly how it goes,' Beata says. 'You're a Dacian, Flavius. A homeless child of ancient empires. We weren't innocent, when the punishment came, after the war, smelling of war. Then, there were those two old crows ... but they gave us all hot water. You had to stay, and think carefully of what you thought – that may be good. They shot those crows: Ceaucescus. Then, we had free choice, we chose the flock of magpies. You couldn't stay, you had to leave ... But, Flavio, it happens everywhere. You sit outside your hut, then, 'it's a camp for you'. You've nothing in your head – down comes a bomb... Our world is so, dear Flavio – it's not that we all die – that could be a good. It's that we haven't managed anything at all, not all the rest... You are the lucky one! In the service of the art – but needn't buy a sandstone block, a tube of paint, a risma or a tuning fork... You float, dear Flavio, you set a price upon a cube of air...'

'This old guy, Bethlen,' asks Flavio. 'Why's he need the cash?'

'Oh, he has family,' Beata says, 'but when he dies, his prices are his fame.'

'I know all that,' says Flavio. 'It seems banal.'

'Find something for me, Flavio,' Beata says. 'Find a second life, live it, and bring one home for me. If I'm still here... I'd give you a whistle, blow – and you would find me, no one else would know...'

'No, Beata,' Flavio says. 'The panorama. It used to be on celluloid. Now, it lasts for ever or a day – it was water, now it's air. Those heads – imagine, Beata – a sea wall of them, staring at the waves. Leave them, don't touch, or everything will flood...'

It's difficult, coming back to someone. Someone you don't like much: is that as hard, as someone you might miss?

'I promise, Beata,' Flavio says, 'if I come back, along with all the rest – there will be you.'

'I'm the instrument, Flavio,' Beata says. 'Learn to play me.'

'You need music, Beata,' Flavio says. 'When you start.'

Thinking of learning – an oboe, say, like a language, only worse – it repels.

'That's what I say,' Beata says. 'Bring back the music.'

'That too?' Flavio asks. 'Along with the head count?'

'Oh, he's not just an old guy,' Beata points to Bethlen, bent over, his wheel sparking out, 'he's a genius, and if you don't make an inventory – he'll disappear.'

*

Heads – they pop up everywhere you go. Flavio does not intend to look for them – they're there. They are not lost, they are unfound. He thinks – the fewer heads you find, the higher is the price. That's the curiosity of here – the people's poor, the prices low. Too many people – maybe that is why...

'Why are you doing all this, Beata?' Flavius the Dacian asks. She makes an inventory of those dire cut-off things – multiples, pop, the minimal, a satire, a chronicle –

'You mean who am I doing this for?' Beata asks. 'Money *is* posterity, Flavio. Find lots of heads. Keep the prices down, make everybody rich,' she says.

'We don't know how that works,' says Flavio. 'Some old guys went on producing, and people can't get enough, and up the prices go. Is it a mystery or a con?'

'Get moving,' says Beata. 'Leave. Thanks for the ride. Don't bother coming back if you don't love me.'

'I'm not from here,' says Flavio. 'It sounds like Slavs against Romans. There could be wars without casualties.'

'No one would give us weapons,' says Beata. 'Anyway, we're all on the same side. We're lucky, wars without explosions, low prices. I'm an idiot to want a ride from you.'

'You had the ride, Beata, maybe you took me for a ride as well,' says Flavio, starting to feel affection – after all, the person conning you knows you as well as anyone... love's supposed to have a pinch of knowledge in it, like pimento, 'Could this be love?' he hums...

'There's no harshness in you,' Beata says. 'Till you get that, everyone will jump on to your back, and spur you to the bone. Then, you'll be like us, tough, thinking of nothing else but doing down. You're not free, Flavio, but to see your silly face, looking as if you are – it makes you look a clown.'

'Clowns hit each other – so, you'd be stupid to hit a clown,' says Flavio.

'There's lots of places I might come from,' says Beata. 'All of them need sex clinics – some open on the street, others you need a parchment to cover up. I'd be by the side, an escort, a doppelgänger. Big money, Flavio: but the therapy, it's cheap and nasty too. How strange – most doctors give injections, this way – I'd get them: make me sore, and maybe catch a rash as well.'

'Saving you – from sacrifice or quackery, would that be another con you lay on me?' asks Flavio. 'You harsh people – just sound like poor and losers, poor losers, maybe.'

'You philosophers!' Beata says. 'You always leave the cash part out.'

'Don't cling, Beata,' Flavio says. 'My usefulness is done. Subtraction – that's my big idea. Subtract and what is left is precious. It's my message. Even if it's only what you leave – your body, made into a brick, perhaps. Subtract. And – do no harm. I'd add to that – "and do no good". Even if you took the course – be very very prudent. Of course, there's everybody all around, while you're retreating – not just the bunkies, squaddies you might have had a leg up from, over the obstacle, your countrymen, just anyone at all... It's their leavings, their memento, that you value. If you don't, still, it was all they had to drop, into your head, a head in the seawall – watching the sea dry up, the odd fish, in with the tide. Beata, do you understand?'

Why is what's left so valuable? Beata's capricious, doesn't listen to long spiels. Flavio is one who doesn't cling to money, she thinks: that's the best kind to kept acquaintance with.

'The bus has left,' Beata says.

'Those heads,' says Flavio. 'I know the trick. The sculptor Bethlen thinks he gives an immortality. The kings and queens of Ur – once up, it gave them another chance at life...'

'No, no,' says Beata. 'Let's not go there again. Eternity, not immortality.'

'Well,' says Flavio, 'another turn. Another life, although you're dead – all nature came within Ur's realm ... the moon was god, the ass played music, and the lion used his butcher's knife, prepared the flesh... The heads – they're over the whole world. Anonymous, like men and women now. You make an inventory – they serve you, they're your retainers. Stone heads, bone heads – some down in the death pit, the rest just scattered over. The sculptor Bethlen, he will try to be the biggest king there's been, Beata...'

'Not king,' Beata says. 'I'm sure he doesn't believe in kings. That's just what you do. It's art, not power, is what he does right now. When you die, your good, your bad, are cancelled out. Only your art remains – that's power. The power that remains – is in those stone heads. That, and your bones, if you can find them, and they're not given to the dogs.'

'I won't go with that,' says Flavio. 'The world, its story, is not all us; the globe is not a seal, a cyst, a flowerless bulb. The past is not the future, the world is not ours that we shall lose it. Into the death pit, maybe, we shall go – we'll not be dug up. No one will mourn. The lions – we've done for them, the donkeys that played lyres – they're gone... Those heads – they are not all of us, they don't make Bethlen here a king, a presence in the line, who passes on the power...'

'Oh yes they are, exactly that,' Beata says. 'You're wrong, poor Flavio. That's what there is. They're what remains, are visible. If you don't obey, Flavio, you're wafted like a leaf, no one will dig a pit for you, you'll lie there in the sun, along with donkeys, sheep and all the rest, dried out: you'll not figure in the tale, not in the monkey army, won't go in the pattern book, the chart of moulds, the catalogue. At best – indifference. At worst – just disbelief – that's what you'll get, dear Flavio. Obey. Follow along!'

'It's good,' he says. 'That's maybe what I want, now you've explained it so. A project... You, Beata...'

'Oh,' she says. 'I don't have the fare. I have to sell what I have got to pass along the road.'

'What's left is pictures,' Flavio says. 'Parchments, tumbled mosques. The epic, songs for camel trains, and tales of miracles, all jumbled up, baroqueries, one step forward and one back, the wave corrected by the line, the dangling foot is caught, the pointing finger never writes, it indicates angelic bums – the discipline of frescoes, dear Beata, means you have to work in lizard sneaks...'

'I told you,' says Beata. 'That's where power is, in the symbols, leaching out and fading. We don't add to that, we just collect. I collected you, dear Flavio, and you collected me – now, do your task. Heads! Pass them on! Accept mortality, accept it's futile, reconcile to death without a marker or a plaque, ordained by cretins in a cretinous cause – and don't complain. You are the same as all the rest... I must ask, though, still – where's my voice? My point of view? Lots of them? A magician's – now you hear the oracles, now she's fallen off the screen...'

'If I unlocked them, all those heads – what a babble!' Flavio says. 'Whoa! Beata – keep that fox from out the field of hares. Language, writing – stringing them together, making a structure – that's not power! Everything is structured – snowflakes and centipedes – but you don't believe there is a mind, a Christian, a Coco or an Yves, sitting somewhere, deciding everything, how it should look and might endure... No, what remains is ramparts, silos, dynamite, cages for the rhinos and the peacocks... The big cage...'

'Wait, Flavio,' Beata shouts, 'there's a bus that might be mine...!'

'There!' thinks Flavio. 'Out comes a sentence, perfect, ephemeral, just like anybody might have said – and look! The bus goes back to Bucharest – the words are right, the bus is wrong...

Language is structured like a peacock – when it's hungry or it's mating time, it screams.'

Beata sits on her big red case: it ought to show that you have lots – instead, it shows you've almost nothing. It bursts.

'The dead can have no interests, Beata,' Flavio says.

'Quiet, Flavio,' says Beata, weeping. 'Help me pack.'

'You can't pack, Beata,' Flavio says. 'If you don't know where you're going. Remember, language is an open book – no one can have an interest in a word, a formula, a necklace of them – the string breaks, the beads explode – all over the floor... Everything is up to us, the living...'

'I'm not alive, not without a bus. A destination,' Beata says, standing in the road, trying to stop traffic. 'And I know – a bus is not a destination – but it might do, for now – sit still and move – that's what I need.'

The fastener's broken – you zip – as it closes, it unzips where it was closed.

'I won't ride with you,' Beata says. 'I wanted to – but you say dreadful things – it's chance, it ends up in a pit. You are a crow – or worse...'

'Chance is our chance,' says Flavio, who's lived on it. 'The pit is our identity confirmed – there's no dissembling after, no lies, false monickers.'

There's a bus – to Budapest – 'No, no,' the driver says to Beata. 'All must be baggaged up – us Hungarians are neat...'

He won't take her. She's no money anyway. 'See,' says Flavio. 'Me? I've no case. The prophet says – "Don't carry gold, smoked fish or underwear – notes and plastic is the best..."'

'I'm sure the quote is wrong,' Beata sobs.

'That's just my point,' says Flavio. 'He didn't take you – I didn't even try to board.'

'That's you, Flavio,' says Beata, with a touch of evil. 'Your stony face. Fixed, impeturbable. Don't reflect, don't double back: take it all lightly, history's your spear – "forward!" Disasters – just pebbles in the hero's path. Oedipus sums it, at the end, "Well, I've had a funny old life..." That's you.'

'I don't see it,' Flavio says.

'Help me with my knickers,' says Beata. 'They're all over.'

Flavio helps her gather them – towelling, with stripes. He says:

'The philosophers, the scientists – now, they're trying to save the world. It's so reduced? It's being killed? Help it to stagger on, a clinker, even the worms all eaten in a pie. The scientists, philosophers, are looking for an exit. Hope's lost. The option's suicide, and call it starting over... Colonise the distant rocks: you're dead, years before you can arrive. Who'd want return tickets anyway – farewell, farewell, goodbye earth, your time is up. Lots of interpreting, try to re-animate...

'We're the bright ones, Beata, the monkeys with big heads. We want more, surely? Something more than cooling down the world, or leaving it. A plan, Beata. Not random culling. Not talking more about the less. A failure, Beata. What we need's – the species project...'

'Fulvio, you're snide,' Beata says. 'This species project. We're all a part of it. Going to the gym and eating kakis... The good life – choose the regular guy, and if you can't, then masturbate. You'd laugh at that – you're right. The species project must be more... Beyond you, though, dear Flavio. And – right now – the project is a bus to Budapest.'

THE SPECIES PROJECT

They keep on sitting, fussing about. Beata floats a project, Flavio tries to catch it in his net. There's traffic – no one stops.

'See,' says Beata, 'no one protects us. No state – it made the roads – we didn't pay. The roads go in and out, like you – free will. Somehow they'll find a way to have us make a contribution.'

'You'd fit into a uniform, Beata,' Flavio says. 'I'm too lumpy. My feet are different sizes – a pack would slide from my uneven shoulders – each eye sees different things.'

'You could clip tickets on the fucking bus,' Beata says. 'That needs a uniform.'

'We could catch,' says Flavio, 'something that goes back empty to where it's empty, empty of everything, but full of folk. 'We could go to Kosova. This year – they need a species project, that's for sure.'

'We can't,' Beata says, looking like she's going to cry. 'It's been written down. We have a limit. Even the rules that let us fly are those that tie us to our eggs, that make us feed on carrion, and fall down perfect from the skies. We reach the top – then have to start again. All you'd find out, dear Flavio, is how we're flawed.'

'Well,' says Flavio, 'I'm not flawed at all. But I shan't boast, or force myself on anyone.'

'That's good,' Beata says. 'And bad. It's all locked up in you, all you need to know, all you can know. God too, they used to say, inside. Now – it's just you. Everything within. And whatever rules you make, and hope the others see ... those too. Do as you will – and take the punishment.'

'That's – nothing,' Flavio says. 'Beata, there's leaflets where the buses start that tell you that. Go anywhere, be anyone. Buy tickets.'

'Forget it all,' Beata says. 'It'll all go wrong. Look! Look at us – it already has. We can't beg, even – the culture's wrong for that: here, the poor spit in each other's eye.'

'Lose everything,' says Flavio. 'You're free to aspire to what you really want, they say.'

'Oh Flavio,' Beata says. 'You're nowhere near the bottom – your body's slumping, but your eye's still up, still high. I'm nearly there. I don't come from anywhere they give you documents. I wasn't even colonised. No one's to blame, no one's responsible. I'm not even black, my people – they have nothing, can't be conned, wait here for paradise ... not like Biafrans, or the Delta folk. Riches that bring misery ... not us, just misery. That's the truth, that's being honest. That's what the philosophers know, Flavio: you have forefathers, built the stadia where they killed the animals: we don't. Your scientists, once the philosophers – they see we're at the limit. Everybody knows that, and no one knows what to do. You'll never fly like your canary, love someone as your cat loves you, run like a leopard... So? Kill them, stuff them, cage them? Maybe you're sick because of them, their plagues... You can fiddle the limits, unlock some people, lock others – the bad guys – lock them up! Turn into other people, as many as you like – you reach the end, and there is your beginning, like the guy who pushed the rolling stone.'

'Here's something!' Flavio shouts, pointing and running. 'Our side of the road! Up we go!'

It's a coach – no horses. Inside, though, you can take a crap – the journey must be going on for ever. They've thought, prepared! 'Our ride awaits!'

*

Flavio sits by a guy: the guy points, 'Saint Lawrence was griddled here. They drew his soul out through his nose, cool as a lemon-flavoured popsicle. It became the river that now bears his name, sometimes it melts again: on those islands, each a droplet of his blood – there you feel free.'

'I'd never heard that,' Flavio says: then, to ingratiate and soothe. 'We've not been anywhere long enough to be terrorists.'

The greeny-grey of the mosque roofs in Prizren, the slates come from afar, not this mottled river bed, not Iskander's marble roads, but surely his steatite from Bactria... 'We're here, Beata,' Flavio says. 'Quick! We've not much time – too bad, the river's not in spate. A wonder! You know, there's people here,' they push among the crowds. 'Of an extraordinary beauty, and wisdom too. Alas, our time here is so short...'

Beata pulls at him, to stay. 'Looking at beauty won't make you beautiful,' says Flavio. 'Wisdom, they say, is catching. You get it through the breath, or through the blood. I'm telling you, so's you'll know to come again. Remember – wisdom's not always of the kind that we might want...'

'Oh Flavio,' she says. 'How I understand! Where? What? Next?'

'We could walk up: up these low mountains to the trees,' says Flavio.

'I know all about trees,' Beata says, trotting along. 'Everybody does. All written.'

'You can make furniture from them,' Flavio says. 'They used to, when I first came here.'

'I don't see anything that's special,' Beata says. 'Nature, clouds.' They look down on the little town – the stalls, cheap stuff, people wandering up and down.

'They say the soldiers used this route,' Flavio says. 'I don't believe it.'

'Oh no,' Beata says. 'There's always soldiers down below, already there. But – what's so special here? Pitchblend? Silver? Lead? It glows?'

'Nothing like that,' says Flavio. 'It's just a special place for me. I expect we all have a settlement like this – the beginning of our universe. Quite particular, but nothing really extraordinary, starting from anywhere is the same.'

She doesn't understand. It's irritating, she might say – coming all this way to someone else's place, and then you have to find a way to go on somewhere else, someone's mystery, you've seen it, many like: Flavio too – he can't explain.

'Dacia?' Beata asks. 'Your place? Not here.'

'I hadn't thought of that,' says Flavio. 'No one knows where these people came from, who they are – nothing to do with me, or you. Just a place you end up in, like everywhere, a place you'd want to leave, or else to stay.'

'Well,' Beata says, 'it seems we're leaving now...'

'Yes,' says Flavio. 'The project needs a place that's in between. A border, a state unformed, a crossing-point. Where people know they need a project, and it will fail, but maybe not tomorrow, nor for a million years.'

'It makes me tremble, Flavio. I'm afraid,' Beate says. 'Better do nothing than uncork the vase...'

*

It's dark. They see four dark-faced guys sat round a fire, a dark car in the shadow just behind.

'They'd take us,' Fulvio says, 'but they might roast us first.'

'Oh – a delight,' says Beata, wriggling in beside. 'I could eat one of my thighs entire, on the bone, with sauerkraut.'

There's no eats on the fire. 'I hope you'd not traffic us,' says Flavio. 'Buried alive – that would be your fate.'

'Oh,' says the head dark-face, 'we're that already. But have no fear. It isn't cash, nor even violence, that's the root. Erotic love. That's what drives the ship, my friend, no docking, broadside on to every storm and wave. That's the spur, the prick, that's the wound you'll bleed out from.'

The other three: they nod – one – Felician? holds ... maybe a mandolin? A ukelele? Specially small, for whiling time away – music from the back seat of a car, the springs are shot.

'These guys,' Flavio whispers, 'Create. They dredge, erect, they bolt and screw. The sacred, dear Beata, is guaranteed by work, not an idea, not art... What's the sacred, then, you ask? What's it worth? Will these guys let us in to it – the secret, how some guys rise – and fall – by work, arise from nature, drop back into it as falling leaves, or algae in the stream...'

'Look, Fulvio,' says the guy, Bik he's called. 'We've been old-fashioned thugs. Now, we're off to find our place. A site, a project ... we shall raise it up, a structure lifted from the mud ... a road, a dike … a drain...'

'These guys have it figured out,' Beata says, entranced. 'They're Faust with boots. I'd go with them,' he says to Bik. 'No confidences, no biogs – I'd avoid you guys telling of your past, your present suffering, the vengeance you might take...'

'Oh no,' says Bik, 'we take that into our account. Between us, we're Siegfried, Faust, and Wozzeck too. Don't wait to eat,' he says. 'You'll fall asleep.'

They fly along. 'We're off to work, raising up from nature, till, alas, we fall back in,' Bik tells the guys at checkpoints. 'Erotic love? Later, perhaps: now, it's destiny – ours, we're following. It will be your panorama, when we're done. Men and women – make their mark, those are the guides they leave when they have gone to ruinous ends... Structures. The domes, spherical triangles, the ovoid sewerage...'

'Goodspeed,' shout the cops, waving them through. 'Work is sacred ... you are the blessed ones,' and on and on they drive.

'Don't be swept away, Flavio,' Beata says. 'Stick to your compulsions. Stick to principles.'

*

Remember blacksmithing: you didn't even make built space. Just trinketing. These guys are free – except they're poor. Don't follow them!

*

Flavio says, 'Erotic love, Beata – that ends bad too, remember. We haven't even tried it yet.'

She's in the back – Alois, Ilya, they try feeding her. Cold fried stuff from a pack.

'We could try the erotic route, Beata,' Bik says, swooping the car along. 'But you've all kinds of gender hangups. Hanging on that guy, Flavio – his schemes, his hesitations ... sticking to him.'

'Oh dear,' Beata says. 'It's stomach hunger that I feel. It's true – there was a George the Greek – was he erotic? He didn't speak too much – maybe he felt passion, maybe I did – but was it for each other? There's no bridge from me to thee.'

The big bouncy car ploughs on, melding the occupants, blessed by security all the way.

'We're all promiscuous in here,' says Felician. 'Sex and ideas. Each a free-float. Let's get the sex part sorted out – everybody equal, no prejudice – then we can move on, to Flavio's projects, the ideas.'

'What is proposed?' Beata asks, nervously. 'Sex? A gift unwanted? Or an exchange between unequals...? Sex – if it has a meaning, it's before the words were made for it – even the bugs, the crabs...' No one bothers to respond: then. 'My case!' she shouts, 'All that I own... Left somewhere...'

'Here's the answer,' Ilya says, handing round some rubber boots. 'Sex – a transaction we can't say it adds or it subtracts... A case? I remember, a tall russet shape, standing abandoned in a forest clearing... I thought, "No room, no room... The colour shouted. Was it abandoned, or in wait?"'

'And Tristan here,' says Bik, laughing, punching Flavio's arm. 'All unaware. Watching the parade go round inside his skull...'

'I expect it's ancestors,' says Flavio, embarrassed. 'There was this Dacian, Flavius – when they were escaping from the Goths... A nation, evacuated, the next bunch takes the names...'

'Ah yes,' says Alois, 'these writers – tell you what it was, but when it comes to "will be" – it's a nightmare...'

'So, you, Bik,' Flavio goes on. 'The name means "Prince" – maybe you're in the singer's line as well. Bik's "Beg": like Iskanderbeg...'

They laugh. Erotic dreams are spun away. Where Beata's case should be, in the trunk, there's shovels. 'Here, we go down,' Felician says. 'Dig for a better world.'

'Escape the heat?' Beata asks. 'Or maybe there is water there...'

'No, no,' says Bik, still laughing. 'It's for the new people. First, the tunnels, under everywhere, and then the cities. We make little tracks, too small for tanks: runnels: they thought that way the undergrounders wouldn't go to war – but they'd have machetes, two-by-fours...'

'I knew there was some tunnelling between Russia and the States,' says Flavio. 'But – under everywhere?'

'Oh, there's no room on top, and they're not loved, those undergrounders,' Ilya says. 'Those Russian tunnels – they were for the bosses, Yanks and Russkies, when they have to run. This is much bigger.'

'What'll they do?' Beata asks. 'The new people, they're called barbarians, in from the East...'

'Oh,' Ilya says. 'I expect they'll print those Plutarch sonnets, using movable type. Something sophistic, that's for sure...' and the four all laugh again, a little reluctant, maybe, to go down the hole that faces them.

'In those old days,' says Bik. 'They moved the peoples round: the old, the ancient Romanised evacuated, then – the new came in – the Vandals, Huns, and nameless ones. There was a crush, and darkness too. Now – to avoid the clash, the new ones go straight down.'

'Well, for certain,' Flavio says, 'we all had famous relatives, unknown and distant now. Riding those ponies, drinking kvass from skulls. The distant clans – they meld in bed, or in the hay – the customs stir together: out the omelettes come... But – my friends: all the erotic stuff, it ends up bad. It's narcissism, reconciliation; starts with the featherbed and ends with two's and sometimes three's, shut moody in the bedroom, then impotence and being carried in a canvas shroud down narrow stairs... These diggings – free space, or a tomb?'

'We must conserve our strength,' says Alois. 'Forget equality and love. Those leave us nowhere – or, better, that's what we start with. That's what babies are. Equal, dependent. Your project, Flavio, must be different, ramped up...'

'Oh yes!' says Flavio, much cheered. Perhaps Beata should go on her separate way...? 'I'll look around ... for someone else.'

'No, no,' Beata says, 'All my possessions lost, from being with you, Flavio. This here – it must be Danube land. That's a place where peoples cluster, get moved on and herded through...I'll stay with you until we find our place – above ground, please, despite the disadvantages...'

'Even if we dug,' says Flavio, seeing Beata would quite like to stay with these four guys, since they have plans and work – and she has nothing much... 'We don't fit in with them. The task is so immense – for workers, for revolutionaries, for all people who go tunnelling and making space down there, the rat-tracks, damp refuges in the dark. The roof can fall on you, you never know if there's rain or snow above... Some of the guys live by the rules, thinking – if you submit, mercy is shown whatever else you do. You show some willing, like you and yours have always done. The others, well, they have intelligence, they do what seems best. Best for them, best in the moment. I'd be out of place entirely there, Beata, with those guys, masculine as they seem to you. Maybe that sounds arrogant...'

'Yes, and stupid too,' Beata says. 'I don't respect you, Flavio. Not a bit.'

'Well,' says Flavio, 'think round this. All the dirty work there's been done to guys in Kosova – accidents and aspirations, you might say ... those four, digging in the mud – how many will be still alive in two years time? Four years, four guys still? Not taking care, that's them. They'll all be gone before I've started up the process, like a scientist, with trial and error. Philosophy by slot machine. Try everything, what's left is not the truth, it's just what you can't eliminate. Maybe a legless beetle that got left behind, a snot left in a petrie dish. They'll all be gone, our friends: we shan't, Beata. We'll be fumbling on, doing the ghost-walk through the trees. Life! Yum-yum, Beata – no waiter and no tips. Erotic love? Lick the plate, and no one sees.'

'Oh Flavio,' Beata says, 'I have to baby you along! Those guys – won't tell you what they've done; don't understand what they are going to do. Shovels! The scheme's immense – you don't expect each little creature with a sting can have conspectus of the whole – the whole, unbuilt, a project in the blue ... an *idea* of a whole that's modified as soon as thought of. Another world laid underground: say no one comes, it's vulnerable to *plastique* bombs, a grader uncontrolled; or those giant nautilus screws they use to dig a metropolitan. All are projects – like the greater Albania Bik talks about: – they never happen; or they do and it's banal, you have to borrow everything, you never pay it back, they don't let you forget the cash, ever. Dream of an underground much bigger, livelier, than what's above: the tourists naked in the fountains, ostriches decapitated by the score in Olympian games – the emperors in some ticket scam, and off to court and jail with all of them – they're lucky ones, shut up for life with spruce chairs and a spotless crapper from the Netherlands...'

'You seem to know it all,' says Flavio, 'The projects...'

'Yes,' Beata says, 'I do.'

'Watch it,' says Flavio. 'The guys are over there still, sussing us, they've not gone down the shaft where they will chance their lives all day.'

'They'll take a note of us,' Beata says. 'Will someone take them seriously, if they report? I wonder – who do they tittle-tattle to?'

*

The cops – they deal with losers all the time. That's all they ever do. They are the losers' hope – redemption. Redemption through punishment, on and on, no tenderness for sure. Who then redeems the cops?

*

'Don't be misled,' says Flavio. 'I haven't won yet – it doesn't mean I've lost, that I'm a loser.'

'Certainly,' Beata says. 'Put like that – you're not.'

'I always think,' says Flavio. 'How the cops are always walking just a pace behind you, the soldiers, the militiamen as well: when they take you off, they're always just a step behind, but you are always just a step ahead.'

'You said it first, the right way,' Beata says. 'It's not redemption, it is punishment.'

'Well,' Flavio says, 'we'll not go into that. We've done no wrong – I've done much right. We're on the good side. Credit's good.'

'Maybe,' says Beata, 'But your "special places" – that rather lets you down. The travelling: necessity, not counting good nor bad. There's no use being anxious, foresightful – everything will happen as it does. Almost all the projects – they are perfect. Not one has ever been realised, not perfectly. Most – never, not at all. They're all different anyway – that's their point. No one has a clue... Potatoes look and taste the same – but each is special and unique. There's nothing wrong: so there is no redemption.'

'Why doesn't it thrill me, then,' asks Flavio, 'What you say?'

*

There's a plan: look! the project. 'Yes!' says Flavio. 'There's Dacia. Bessarabia, the Banat, Vlachs and Moschopolitans, Sarmatians – occupiers, occupied – but all in the provinces underneath, as they ought to be. The Khmer empire, now installed, perfect, under where the Bavarians were, they're all off to Italy, where almost everybody passed, and there was traffic and traffickers for centuries, and wedding feasts that lasted months and some that lasted seconds, or even ... not at all.'

'You see?' Beata says. 'A project. All settled, all down in the subsoil – those Albanians ... where did they come from? – almost all have moved again... Thracians, perhaps? Normans from Italy. Here, they have a place below the crust. I don't come from anywhere that's listed here... Nor you, Flavio, you just read a book, chose the bits you liked...'

'The African empires – hardly room,' says Flavio, entranced. 'Look – there's Ethiopians beneath Ukraine, some many sorts of them; there's Luo spilled into Kamchatka, Hereros in Manchuria

– all climate is controlled, of course. What do they eat – can't all be mushrooms and worm stew...?'

'Oh, there on the upper crust,' Beata says. 'It's hot as hell – there's peppers and dried fish, bay trees for flavour, and some plums... There can't be too much else. All's written down – but there's no place for us... Unless – "the residue". That's us?' she asks.

'You're right,' says Flavio. 'It is a plan. Just – only – that. Bik and the rest must dig it out – new people, driven from their huts and palaces... A project known for centuries – now it's matured.'

'But, Flavio,' Beata says, 'it's not a species project. It's just housing. There's no system, no intelligence. No achievement for us all... A hole, is all. With prefabs, bat-hanging roofs, catacombs of bunks...'

'I can't be bothered with all that,' says Flavio. 'That's only the beginning. People coming, people going, believing this, speaking that, wanting ... and all to be done by four guys with shovels... It's not possible. Ethnic? It's an adjective. Countries – that's land: – these guys have none. Fresh classifications... Gods? Languages? – a basketful, all moribund, worshipped and invoked by grannies...'

'Put it to them like that,' says Beata. 'Bik seems a bright sort, the others follow him. Maybe they'll see...'

'But, of course,' Flavio says. 'They're being paid not to.'

'Talking of work, Flavio,' says Beata. 'What about those stone heads?... The catalogue.'

'You must see, Beata,' Flavio says. 'There's millions of heads, all talking, all more or less locked in. What did we learn from Bik, for instance? See – the four are going down the slope, then there are steps, and then a cage... There's galleries, but there's no art; wooden props – no stage: dynamite – no revelation. Music – you bring your radio down, and have it joust with all the rest?'

'Be careful, Flavio,' Beata says. 'Don't fixate. Above – below? It doesn't seem a plan that lasts, or even one thought out... You improvise...'

'Don't raise irrelevancies,' Flavio says. 'You could watch the people that arrive – many already armed, in thought and books, others will learn, be weaponised... As for those above – their being up on top means they can see the space they want to occupy... Below – it's dark and dusty, when it rains, there's mud. Those who think they make the plan, they have designed the roads so tight and wriggly there'll be no room for conflict, but – determination finds a way... That's not all. Poverty, dear Beata, and all hugged hugger-mugger in the dusk, nostalgia and fellowship, passion and revelation, not fine feelings ... up top, a suburb, down below, a slum.'

'Come on, Flavio – the rich can do more damage than some guys with sticks,' Beata says. 'Besides – ignore all that – your species project's not about the peace or some affinities. That's quietism and flaccid thinking. You wander down the path, and "oh", you think, "the project's about peace and feeling good". Rubbish, Flavio. Don't be misled, dear Flavio: being bien-pensant is the route to nowhere – to the pamphlet, or the speech, or gazing into eyes.'

'Of course,' says Flavio. 'The species project: doesn't try to make you happy, ease conflict, hone your mind, discover cures, places of settlement, all that... live long, die stupid. Quite the contrary. And, it's not intelligence, it's inspiration that must drive.'

*

'Give me a shovel,' Flavio says. 'Leave Beata here on top. She's nothing more to tell.'

'Another shovel?' Ilya laughs. 'You have to earn it, Flavio.'

'To be saved, my friends, what must I do?' asks Flavio. 'My past ... mere pretensions to empire, truth and tenderness. What now? Strong with the strong, weak with the weak?'

'Forget it, Flavio,' Ilya says: 'Till now, every project starts by promising – a realm, a continent, a world, poems to go with, and dances too – and then... It all becomes a quest to keep the others out. They'd keep us out as well – but we have shovels, and a plan...'

'You'd need centuries to dig it out, the undersoil – and then the lodgings are still mediocre,' says Flavio.

'Oh,' Bik says, 'we'd do it in a day or two. These shovels – they have a scientific curl – better than everything that's gone before. But – our interest is not that way inclined. Survival can't be rushed.'

'It's true,' says Flavio. 'There is no project here. It's all free will, when there's no freedom and no will. What's left? What can the species do? The old guys: they left ruins – the even older ones, they left titanic boulders stacked as walls. These guys leave a dugout and some tents... And if instead of settlement, they decide to have a cull...'

'Exactly,' Ilya says. 'That's why hurry isn't indicated. But don't get sentimental about big stones...'

They all laugh, and Flavio hears the whisper 'stone heads...'

'You must come down with us,' Felician says. 'It all will happen here, beneath your feet.'

*

Of course, Flavio stays on top. Anybody would. Digging's a bore, and in the dark – everything's the same, and yet – that's no resolution. It's mysticism too, to say that all is one, the same...

'Besides,' says Flavio, 'everything will happen where the people – the most people – are. Where the ground's not good for excavation. Only Europe has the rocks – what will happen, what we don't know about – it's all in Asia...'

'Down in the dark,' says Alois, 'you don't age. Like you, Flavio, we're all last century. Remember – the fascination with the atom. That was the new thing – the universe, made of it... Dropping it – letting it indoors. And now – big shelters everywhere. A great delusion.'

'There's time, Alois,' says Flavio. 'I've started. I'll solve it all.'

'No, Flavio,' says Alois. 'No time. What's your progress up till now...? The legacy? A building? A temple to forgotten deities who still demand their milk? The golden bowls of blood?

'Some guy's palace? Well, some architect would like that, naturally. A rocket? A book you can refute?... That wasn't what you meant, I'm sure. Something to make it all worthwhile. Maybe some other species, with a bigger head, would be impressed? Think, think quickly, Flavio – or else it's vanity. Man leaving heaps of uninhabitable stones – like termites or the bower-bird, the rabbit and the stoat.'

'Help me, Alois,' says Flavio, quite desperate.

Alois is binding up his pants, knee-level – 'Rats,' he says: 'They're curious. Much more than me. No, Flavio. The idea's precious, and it's yours... You're right. Be satisfied with that.'

'It's for everyone,' says Flavio. 'Not just survival, something to show...'

'Don't wait!' says Alois. 'Do it yourself. With others – there's arguments. Come on – what will it be? A song – for all the universe to whistle? A piece of advice for every rock twinkling up there: diamonds in the sky? You unlocked Célestine – you could try it on a bigger scale...'

'Half unlocked,' says Flavio. 'So she'd live, without the suffering. Thinking it was happy land ... happy like her.'

'Well, we're off,' says Ilya. 'True – you've seen it all before: first, old people, laden with menace, knitting comforters, and now – it's us. Shovellers.'

'I want part of this,' Beata says, hugging the four diggers. 'Action!'

'Escape! That's all it is, Beata,' Flavio says. 'Ludivine – she loved me – but for her, it was survival. Valentino's truck broke down. Somewhere, it's menaced... It's up to me.'

THE SAGE

'I've come a long way to be here,' Flavio says. 'I left many people behind. Here I am, Dulip! "Bury them or bomb them" – that's what they say. Help me sort them, Dulip, the unspeakables!'

'I don't feel the need to travel,' says the sage: 'What did you expect it all to do for you? Cash? We're already moving at a lick, all of us. The people left behind – is that their wailing I can hear? Or is that music of the spheres, a new top song each week?'

'I'm rather stuck,' says Flavio. 'The project...'

'Yes, that is genius,' the sage, Dulip, says. 'But you can't take it further. You're finished. Coming to see me makes it worse. You found a hole. A hole in everything. What can fill it? You, jumping in? A march? The human species, labelling every other living thing as "species", flushing them down the pipe, or eating them?'

'I've asked myself the same,' says Flavio. 'You're a wise type, Dulip. Bomb them, those that disagree and threaten? Others similar – they're always mustering... Survival? – you're right, there is no goal, no aim, in that: nothing that has you pass the time at ease. It's the primary condition – what comes next?'

'You're stuck,' Dulip repeats. 'So – I'm to take it over? Your revelation?'

'No!' says Flavio.

Dulip stands, unfurls his black cloak, his academic gown, maybe – and stands, his faded transparent frame, see-through rosy as the dawn, on the tower's highest sill. 'You see,' he says, stretching out his hoopoe wings – 'I made this all for me, this tower of every wind, that lets in every sound and lets it out again, scrubbed silent, without an inadvertent noise, leaving no crust, no scab, behind. Cleanliness – enough in itself. Forget the godliness...'

'Master,' Flavio says, 'I fear this is only whimsical.'

'But – if I flew,' says Dulip, 'it would be something, surely, something more.'

'Prometheus?' Flavio asks. 'Isn't that sacrifice? That seems self-defeating...'

'No, cretin,' says Dulip, wavering on the narrow band of stone. 'Crossing the bounds! With a little concentration, you can cross from one part of nature to the next. The hoopoe...'

'Even if you don't succeed, the point is made,' says Flavio, fearing for his latest friend.

'I don't agree,' says Dulip, flapping hard. 'Saying's not doing. A hypothesis is worth something only if applied to something not worth much at all.'

He bends, Flavio sees his face purple with the strain, the conviction – and he's gone!

He falls swiftly to the ground. Thud! You would expect it so. Even hoopoes find it difficult...

This is – has been – a project too. What a lesson! What a demonstration, what a loss!

*

Dulip's lover, Fatimah, says, 'What a teacher! All his wisdom, curled tight, like a nut inside its shell... How terrible – and yet, it's formulaic, don't you think? And, Flavio – did you learn?'

'I confess,' says Flavio, 'I learned nothing I didn't know before. They say, it is God's gift, the birds: – they're quite inscrutable. What did they do, what have they ever done? Those distances immense they trek – the threat from winds, precarious heights above precarious lands... The flightlessness that threatens – dodoism ... the nets awaiting those that cross the seas... No rest, no peace ... the flight of angels and the appetites of pigs...'

'You miss the point,' Fatimah says, helping Flavio put Dulip in his hole. 'Your project. And its limit. He'll have thought you'd understand and learn.'

'Well,' says Flavio, 'there's learning to repeat, and learning so's to change.'

'Tell me,' says Fatimah, 'did he still flap his wings as he went down?'

'I missed that part,' says Flavio.

'He was still learning,' says Fatimah. 'He learned so quick. I see you smirk, Flavio, beneath your tears. Remember, aeroplanes began this way – through honoured pioneers. Error and trial. That's science, as you know. Nature too.'

'I couldn't stop him, Fatimah,' says Flavio. 'Now you say I shouldn't have.'

'Starting him, you mean?' says Fatimah. 'Everything starts off with a heave, a bang. It's risky – that might go on and on. We're always close to killing, naturally; it's an option, even when we give the doing of it up to others. There was just you and him – classic: heroes of our time. Maybe a push? Not physical, of course. Just from being curious. A self-protective shove? We all have projects: mostly there's a clause that says – if someone goes too far – they run the risk...'

'We're back to that?' asks Flavio. 'What's left? – after the tumulation ceremony, amazing graciousness – the inquest. The right and wrong? That could be the easy one to answer...'

'Maybe you'd like some memento, Flavio, of dear Dulip? A disc? Coltrane? A book? A mat?' she asks.

'"Always ready to kill. Less often, ready to die..." That's what he meant,' says Flavio. 'Mankind. Worth knowing – but no discovery.'

'It only makes its point if it gets shown,' says Fatimah. 'I needn't tell you, Flavio: your future? – you're abandoned to a sudden death: falling off trucks, sleep-vomiting in a bunk; a mine-shaft where you weren't supposed... a battle for some boots – that's your world, you chose it.'

'It's Beata's,' Flavio says. 'But she knows the way around.'

'Easy,' says Fatimah. 'It's judo – let your enemy do the work.'

'Destiny, Fatimah,' Flavio says. 'See how it points! So – come with me.'

'Never!' says Fatimah. 'You're a deep reactionary. You mock the good things, the hopeful ones, wait for them to drop from fashion, then find fault with what next comes along.'

'How should I be?' asks Flavio.

'Utterly different,' Fatimah says. 'Analytical, organic, for a start. Belonging above, below as well – a persecuted law-giver.'

'People underground...' says Flavio. 'I saw the scheme...'

'Terrible,' says Fatimah. 'But the unlucky ones who aren't? Aren't under? Not that it's luck... Not anywhere?'

'There's something not right about everyone, Fatimah,' Flavio says.

'Dulip had enemies, Flavio. The best people – that's how you tell them: they have lots of foes,' she says. 'I could get you into trouble, Flavio.You could have saved him...'

'Fatimah,' says Flavio. 'There is a plan, it's evident. And you accept it, or you don't. I'm not there, not on either, any, side.' He pauses, turns. 'There is no plan – though there are sides: it's everything, a chain; it's terrible. My project – goes beyond...'

'You don't have one, dear Flavio,' says Fatimah. 'And there's nowhere else beyond.'

'It's not a place,' Flavio begins. 'And it's not found by chatting with people you might know...'

'Well,' Fatimah says. 'Who do you know? Do you always eat alone? Do you know ministers? Dictators? Who offers you a job? Where do you lecture? Have you sold arms? Legs too? Whole people?'

'I usually eat alone,' says Flavio. 'I was in the trade. And – I know no one,' he lies. 'I don't do journalism, and students are a bore... Maybe I'm not your type, Fatimah, after all?'

'Dulip thought you were his type,' says Fatimah. 'It seems he planned it all. You were the last person in the world that he would want to see: and lo! – it all came true. People are keys, Flavio, keys to other keys. It's not they open you to nowhere, through the glass, nor do they unlock empty rooms: people are keys to more keys.'

'Oh,' says Flavio, rushing in. 'I know all about locks...'

'That's just it,' says Fatimah. 'Locks enclose. The special room where porno's kept – that has a lock, the only one. People are the infinite here, Flavio. Chat with them; drink – they'll tell you all you need to know, they pass you to the next, drop names, and soon you'll have a chatelaine, more keys than there'd be doors or trunks... That's how you get to have a project, Flavio. Influential people, doing their act, passing you on and up, flattering, defaming – not guys with shovels...'

'I'm sure you're right,' says Flavio, preparing to leave. 'For me, it's too late now.'

'Of course,' says Fatimah. 'You have to start at the beginning.'

'Dulip was great,' says Flavio. 'I wouldn't aspire... A great death – will be remembered. And the rest ... meetings, exhortations, the pamphlets – his name for sure, high on the wall; too bad it's where the black birds perch...'

'You've no deference, Flavio,' says Fatimah. 'You don't kneel ... it doesn't matter, no one would notice if you did – you are too small. The repugnance that he felt! – that it should be you. And you, for all and ever, to decide what was worthwhile... Your project, announced and absent, eternal legacy without an heir. You had a project, Flavio: Dulip was jealous. And – the idea's wrong. So, he was contemptuous. But – your project filled his space, left just his hole.'

'Oh come,' says Flavio. 'If you've a philosophy – you let it swallow what you feel. Even the nausea.'

'That's what your "criticising after dinner" gives you, then?' says Fatimah. 'Total confusion. What's a project? What's a species? How could it act? Mistaken words. Objectification, Flavio: guesswork, speculation. It's all down in the book: you make a kind of ford, where the knowable and trite, the formulaic, philosophical, crosses over to what's unknowable. Strip off the rhetoric. Behold! There's the true, the free, unpredicted, unpredictable...'

'I know, Fatimah,' Flavio says. 'Be patient. You have to think like I have thought to get to what I don't yet know.'

'When we are free,' says Fatimah. 'Each is their own: so, that's the end of projects. The human species too.'

'That's immortality, Fatimah,' says Flavio. 'We don't get there. The sun eats us all up long before.'

'It's immortality, Flavio: that's what you're after, and you did it wrong. When we all go in the sun – we are immortal,' Fatimah says. 'It's how it is and will be. There's nothing more, and nothing else.'

'I shiver, Fatimah,' says Flavio, doing just that.

*

'If I don't like the underground,' Flavio tells Beata. 'There's not much left but being critical. Like where I started out. Hunting and fishing – they're free, essential. Your day in nature. Otherwise you dig. And plough. But I have this sentiment – it's wrong to have these species wars... The fish, the deer, poor things ... on your plate... That diet isn't good. Besides – there's not much game around. An awful waste of time as well. I could do the criticism – but it didn't work before. It's a slog, and they don't pay you, you have dependents on your back. It's scavenging, you carry corpses up the slope forever. It's just, that – right now, my broader purposes, they hit an obstacle.'

'Come and watch, for free,' says Bik, 'our old-style work. No unions, the wars are far away – we never criticise what we are paid to do.'

Flavio peers down the shaft, into the gloom. 'There's people down there,' he says, 'in running shoes. Spooning giant haricots from cans.'

'Of course,' says Ilya, 'what did you expect? There's refugees already in every refuge, hence the name. They'll be sent onward – we ignore them, naturally.'

'I see lumpy bodies jigging round a flame,' says Flavio, much disturbed. 'There's a kazoo.'

'That,' says Bik, 'is the beginning. If it isn't civilisation, civilisation springs from that. Those guys will be moved on. Their song and dance remain.'

'They are your – maybe my – countrymen,' says Flavio, searching for a hook to hang on to.

'Dancing men – they have no country,' says Felician. 'The tune is always similar. They go no further – their beginning takes up too much space.'

*

'Listen carefully, Flavio,' Beata says. 'This is how it went. Bik is a monster – he'll drive these poor people out. Felician's the one who will protest – his comrades will go after him. Oh no! No one deserves that! – but put yourself at the front, what do you expect...? And Alois tries to mediate – that's a mistake; and Ilya ingratiates with Bik who doesn't trust him, hates a flatterer... There! It's done. The few: a worthy sacrifice to install the many – there! – see the dust rising, here they come! More wretched of the earth... Now – is that enough to make you decide where you go next, dear Flavio?' she asks. 'I know these guys. It's all in their interpretation of their job. "What's to be built?" they ask. "Where are people to be settled down?" Build strong. Remember Alamut – no sex, no drugs, a fortress. The best society you'd hope to have – a rock. Astronomers and sages. Immune to siege and tunnelling ... but oh! it fell. This place – for sure, it will collapse, the paradises always do. New armies – find the soft spot in the stone. Those who are left will climb up, up into the sunlight, start again ... forcing a space. Forget that! Build as if for ever. Bik is right – the job's there to be done, though he won't see it through.'

'You're right, Beata,' Flavio says. 'It is not my thing.'

'Every kind of extravagance, Flavio,' says Beata. 'Atrocities. Even if you read about it, it won't match. Believe me – it's too terrible to take it in. For years, your psyche will be radiated by all the horror here... When you're at the limit, any one of you – it's all extreme, everyone succumbs, turns savage – nothing's too outré. It's the top, the limit: no surprise you don't want to go there again, to risk. Slavery and immolation – that would be the best of options. It means you keep the masters going longer than they should, jolly along and smarm and cosset ... gather narcissus for the vase each day, forget the guys who dig the funeral pit, the fine horses mustered, the optimistic sheep...'

'They said only the passeurs would be buried alive, I didn't much think about it.' Flavio says.

'Well, of course it happens naturally,' Beata says. 'It's just a happenstance. Sometimes it comes together with the job.'

'You can't say the diggers are great men,' says Flavio. 'What they did when they were all alive. At any rate, greatness isn't an excuse for what they did...'

He does wonder if Beata's telling it quite right – the guilt where it should be, the plan like they all say.

'None of them is dead,' says Beata. 'The diggers. And we're all great. All around is great, and greatness; we contribute, everyone.'

'That's not the story,' Flavio says. 'Not all of it, anyway. I survived, I came through – I saw much much more than all the rest. I have a perspective, a judgment for the petty ones, the monsters, the divine ... the sacredness – don't forget that, Beata. The flame, the spark – us, all Zippo lighters in the dark.'

'Oh, I shan't, of course,' she says. 'Without that, where would we be... You must always look for that.'

She goes down the hole – that's where she has to live. Will she survive? Maybe she has.

'You have Dulip, of course,' she says. 'Remember that.'

It's vague, all vague, but plausible.

UNDERGROUND

Flavio visits the mensa – just once or twice, he doesn't want to, and they don't want to feed him.

'Slave quarters', the guys say. 'Slave food': they don't want to be freed. That's another fear. The work is hard, they're bruised all over, sleepless and sick. Bathing constantly – new grime sticks on.

'The guys who do the dirty work in the pit – of course, they get dirty,' Flavio tells Yann. 'Think of clearing the underground as, well, farming. You clear the land, and in the end you eat what you have put upon it – it must be fairly healthy, or you too will die. You must find room – people are sacred, you can find a use for some of them. Beata's strong – a reporter. I trust her wholly, though she's dead to me by now... She'll remember everything, keep quiet – or else you start forgetting, making it all up.

'Of course – it's not who gives the orders, it's the ones who chased the squatters out... That was the scandal.'

'Not slave food,' says Yann, standing next to Flavio in the line. 'It's world food. And we are world people. Everybody here's sceptical about freedom: it's the void. You're out, Flavio, outside the crowd: you've betrayed your big idea... You're suspect because you ran from it: maybe it slipped your leash.'

'I can't hold all your thoughts together, Yann,' says Flavio. 'One day at a time ... just one impulse. Try that! Is that a thought? Or a wind? A breeze?'

'You have to wear all your clothes at once,' says Yann, 'or they'll get taken. All your finery, all the watches up your arms and legs. Always ready, like a soldier – over the top!'

'People get moved on,' says Flavio. 'The lucky ones. Mostly it's up to you.'

'It's hard keeping an eye on everything,' says Yann. 'All the time. Quotations, secessions – if you miss the discussion, for sure your side is in the wrong.'

When you've not much to do but wait, you're always busy, always anxious.

'Flavio,' says Yann. 'You're not by chance a poet? work with marble? a speechwriter – *françafricain?* All the guys here, children of that idea... It's your kind of puzzle – paying off, controlling – those goddam nomads... The sand – no one can run in that.' His eyes are far far off. A tear? He puts his cheek against Flavio's. 'It's if I die. The news. How will they know?'

'Oh, you'll know,' says Flavio. 'That's enough.'

'We've rid ourselves of family,' says Yann. 'Children, wives, all that sticky stuff. Lovers ... they cost. It's baggage, Flavio: you have to shuck it off, so's you can move. It wears down your psychiatry as well – it becomes a fictive discourse, ghost to ghost. I'm free, myself, choose anything. But – you're still tied on. We still need someone round who'll say "he's dead". Here, they do shifts, no one will know.'

'I'll say it, then,' says Flavio, exasperated. 'If you're not hanging round the door one day, waiting for the time to start, I'll say it. But don't delude yourself – we're at the beginning, but if we stay here, it's a short trip. We're like the spawn and mayfly, uncounted and unnamed. The rest – the plump, the normal, the obese – the real beginners, hoping for a longer trip – they've all flown off, on a big turf, to start another moon. We're the clods that dropped as their rock flew off.'

Yann would argue several points, but Flavio says, 'Now, if *I* don't show up – don't say anything. I shan't be dead, besides, you've no memory of me, nothing to mourn.'

'It's true,' says Yann, quite satisfied. 'As for that Beata? Should I leave a note? Oh, that's too involved – she went off with Bik, the others. We're just idling here, black mould in the fridge.'

There's no more food, none handed out. Yann and Flavio's the only ones that's left outside the door, not knowing what to do.

*

He takes the bus. It's full.

At the manège, there's always work, and guys who give it up.

'Flavio,' says the head guy, Savarin. A boss. 'Take the troika out. It's difficult, I know – the two outside horses gallop, the central one – he trots. It takes a sense of rhythm. It's the driver who conducts.'

Flavio – it is his thing! He has the knack. It's like it was with Célestine! A project...

Célestine, though, was real – but there's only one troika, and one driver in the world who knows how it is done. Most people who work with horses start by saying it's rewarding. When they find it's not – they leave.

*

'There's a terrible smell of horse-shit,' says Savarin. 'They must be burying a soldier.'

No reply is needed. Flavio once talked of the Greeks and their 'rabbits' penises', and a Greek, he took offence. Best pretend you haven't noticed.

If it's not a question, better not reply.

Savarin sits, twiddles his screen, like all the rest.

'You see them on their statues,' Flavio says.

'Well,' says Savarin, 'you won't get far with me, if that's an overture. I'm straight as a stick, you understand...'

'Nothing like that,' says Flavio. 'Though I might ask you to pay my fare, since I'm without.'

'Why not?' asks Savarin, looking reluctant, but no one asks them if they'd paid.

'I'm set up well,' says Savarin, as the bus empties itself out, and they get off. 'I have three rooms – I need them all to do my stuff...'

'Oh, I need six at least,' says Flavio, reassuring Savarin he's a large-minded, independent sort.

'It's terrible,' says Savarin, as a group of strangers scurries past. 'Imprisoned underground. Of course – they've every kind of luxury...'

'Oh no!' says Flavio. 'There is my friend, Yann. I thought he'd be moving on, or even died.'

'I'm a keeper, Flavio,' says Savarin, relentlessly. 'In olden times, they used to have a cabinet, of stuff they found in graves – all bitty things, coins, keys, empty lipsticks, bangs and bangles and the like. My cabinet is up-to-date. I keep the old machines: so if you find an old-time disc, I find a player that can play. Makes you happy. An old song, a will, a lamentation. Document it all.'

Yann leaps in. 'That's what I need! I'll make a record that will tell my life, its end – that I am dead. That way, the world will know...'

'Oh no,' says Savarin. 'You cannot be alive and send a message as if it's from the past. Or is it future? You see – you muddle up the temporal line – we have to keep a check. There's people moving in and out, displaced, converting, changing names. The past must be the past. You must die in present time, not in a past, and obviously, the future's blocked. It has to be that way.'

'Suppose I have another skin,' says Yann. 'Just like the earth, which has a top with trees, and then beneath there is another world, that's dry and sunless, drab but safe, with many millions improvising there, and tiny animals that eat the soil and made no friends – suppose I have another person underneath, I peel it off, my mottled skin, just like a snake, and maybe underneath I'm black, or green, or maybe give out light...'

'No, my friend,' says Savarin. 'I'm sure that you don't give out light.'

'There's cobalt underground,' says Yann. 'And we have all been radiated...'

'Your friend's psychotic,' says Savarin to Flavio.

'He's been unlocked,' says Flavio. 'Quite thoroughly. He is a poet. Just let him make his disc and store it in your room. He wants to show that he was here, and then was not. It is the smallest thing...'

'Oh well,' says Savarin. 'Some think they are in paradise, and almost all think they are getting there, if only things were different. Yann is sure: it is a passage one is in, a canyon with dark sides; on a moving rail, you cling on and it takes you for a distance till you drop... It's not a humanism, that's for sure. It makes me weep, to think of such a lack of enterprise and fantasy, your dreary friend ... cosmology without the eagle eye...'

'I have to get away,' thinks Flavio. 'These guys...'

Beata – up she pops again and says, 'You're wrong.' 'They're narrative. The life you make in solitude yourself – it has no sense. Sonority arrives from all the rest. Media sources, Flavio: they give continuity, repeat repeat the names. It gives a sense, an echo. Something moves on, flows past. Then you have kids, they grow old and you are on the bridge – they are the river, and you watch until the bridge falls in...'

'No, no,' says Flavio, 'bridges are made so's they don't fall...'

'Well, Savarin,' Beata says, 'is the big cheese – he decides what work you do, which machines; the fonts, the pay, and if you stand to do it or you crawl, and if it's hours or days it takes, and if you leave a print, a password, or a smear... He has two cabinets: one – with doors and locks. The other, just guys in suits. And Yann – he's into countries that you're friendly with, and those instead you fight, and where do all the extra guys that get displaced, invited in, or driven out – where they all go... And in the end, he says, besides – they die, the people, many countries too, they leave no trace at all, their kids grow up all speaking different and some don't speak at all, the clothes get short and hot, the songs lose quarter tones and goddam drums take over, drive the whole parade ... and so, perhaps there are some Folklore Discs – a label that gives immortality, except the artists are anonymous. And Yann's in charge of everything – when it starts, the precariousness, and then the death.'

'I'm sure that's rubbish,' Flavio says. 'They're boring losers, both of them – one is picayune, the other an obsessive – nonentities...'

'Remember, media sources, Flavio,' Beata says. 'Trust me. Remember them. Yann and Savarin – the biggest, roundest, kind of cheese. Both big politicos – ministers who minister.'

'The guys who dig,' Beata says. 'they've made a hall of wonders. Columns of organ pipes, holes that run down to the red, the white, that heat it all, giant mushrooms, thrones for millipedes – the sulphur blinds you, naturally, it's toxic and it's marvellous – to live there for a day's enough, your sky is black, it never rains or snows, and everyone grows white, white as the angelic host, though you can't see a thing, this civilisation needs no eyes or ears, there's no acoustic, no one sings – but dance! They're experts, whirling, twirling in their heavy boots and capes thick brown as potato skins, but ... lightness on their feet! The movements – navigating like a crowd of bats, no bumping in the silence...'

'I take your word,' says Flavio. 'I'll do my best to stay away.'

'It's dark,' Beata says. 'But there's the red, the magma down below, heat without light. We can't see who is who ... when they arrive, they're all a folk – they bring their salted stuff, the pickles, the nougat, and they wear cork hats, the skirts ... and then we dance. We don't see anyone – we pass like owls or neutrons, we hum a roundalay, but no one hears a word, there's no echo, it's like chanting in a sack, and we don't speak to one another... It's as Yann says, only when you die do you know you've lived, and who you were if you were anyone.'

'It's my project!' Flavio says. 'In its nutshell. I think. But aimless...'

'We could think about it, our "something more". It's not so different,' Beata says, 'from what existence there was before, except down there we have no cemetery, and, obviously, no photograph, no album ... and we've no memories ... of ourselves or others. Underground, it always it is the same. It doesn't matter, Flavio. You were wrong, for sure. We're quite indifferent to what a species might produce. It is itself, and that's enough, the greatest thing...'

'I'm disappointed,' Flavio says. 'But – Beata, now, you're settled underground. You might one day – come to the surface, up to the light...'

'I shouldn't envy them, up there,' Beata says. 'Down there, we're friends, we toil, but there's an end to it, and then we dance. If there's a future – those on top will be the first to find the way, shout down to us ... and be the first to take the blame...'

'Beata,' Flavio says, 'you don't need to live below. It isn't settled. There's the atrocities to rid the place of those who started off down there. Then, atrocities to get the new ones in. Making them anonymous, and then ... there's moving them around, and ever with the hope of moving upward... Why wait it out? You could take the bus, be out of that...'

'Oh Flavio,' Beata laughs. 'Remember old Copernicus – what fun his name has given us at school! – he went round Europe, because, a Pole, he had no country then at all – contacting the heretics, then moving out, and they got burnt and he went on to university... Well, remember, it was him who saw the time as simultaneous. Past and future happening together, always – how could it be otherwise? If it's not so, there'd be no time. It's so, everywhere, to come, has been and is. Time must have constant properties all over: that cat, it's living somewhere, having its kittens, showing no passport, doesn't speak our language, isn't *our* old national moggy crying for its food... I live down there because it's fun, despite the fights, the knowing what comes next...'

'It isn't true, Beata,' Flavio says.

'Of course,' says Beata, wrinkling up, then weeping. 'It isn't so. I'm there because it has become my home, I belong there, I am someone's girl. If that's not so, then...'

'That work, Beata?' Flavio asks. 'Hi-tech, I guess?'

'Shoring the roof. Sorting castoffs. Order,' she says. 'There'll always be that – it's not everyone it suits...'

'Love, hate, indifference – all that too?' Flavio asks.

'Love's like arms and legs – they're yours, you avoid the amputations – but no one enjoys gangrene...' Beata says, shoving Flavio away.

'They say us Dacians, Southerners – we have a natural bent to criminality,' Flavio says. 'Perhaps I should let that side out.'

'Go with your own,' says Beata, scrabbling a hole, in a hurry to get down.

'Are you excavating?' Flavio asks. 'Or do you have something, some part of me, you want to bury? To eat later, when it's ripe? Or to hide? Is that what foxes do?'

'Oh, something you won't miss now,' says Beata, laughing. 'And it'll rot, for sure. Our time together ... what there's left...'

'You dig to get somewhere,' Flavio says. 'Hiding a treasure. Getting rid of something – a secret, the work you do, don't own up to...'

'Maybe all of those,' Beata says. 'It's time. That's what you bury. Time spent, thoughts squirreled down ... thoughts for due seasons never seen again, everything disappearing into heat...'

'Stolen,' says Flavio. 'Time subtracted. Forgotten, except when they start to smell, those spent hours, afternoons becoming graffiti inside another's skin. Yes – how I resent all that. "Time forgotten, time wasted, and time stolen." Great tales.'

'Some are hoarders,' Beata says, scuffing away at the topsoil. 'Some do a record and forget, some see their time like frost and storm rings in a tree, irrecoverable, gone, gone, hard times, bad times – what did those accomplish, what if those hours had passed asleep – spared you struggling to keep the lantern lit and shining outward...?'

'Yes,' says Flavio. 'It's that. All you say. Life is time, not breathing – you don't remember breathing. The time spent well or bad – it's buried in a hole – it rots, or else ... you've forgotten where, and what it was. Skeletons or nuts.'

'You've rid yourself of context, Flavio,' Beata says. 'You think it's creative – but you've built nothing, have no friends... Duration – too dry, Flavio: no battles, no harangues, no mambo. Down there, some are poor and some are very poor – to you, we're all alike. We do what we are told even making secret stuff, stuff with no face – but it grows, it becomes much more ... what we make is ours...'

'No, Beata,' Flavio says. 'That last part's not true. Besides – it's invisible. If it exists at all, what you make new has no track, no trace.'

'I'm late,' says Beata, at last locating her way down.

Flavio shouts, 'Too bad, Beata! I'm one of you – you're animals who live in a hole. I prowl. I fall down, no one picks me up but me. I look like you, like all of you.'

MAX

'It was what you'd call a relationship – it covered everything. There must be something more ... it seems a stream that runs, indifferent to you if you look at it. Love, affection, friendship – to experience any one of these as deeply as they say, as you're supposed, you need to read many books – a load – or none. That's what the book says, anyway,' says Flavio. 'Everyone who's been to school has read at least one. Bits of one.'

The guy beside him, Max, says, 'You weren't in that place for love or passion, though?'

'I couldn't hook myself on,' says Flavio. 'It wasn't my scene at all, not my past or future. They knew where they were going, and I didn't want to. I didn't have to.'

The bus stops in a square. There's a tall statue: 'There!' says Max. 'That's Maximilian, my namesake. He was modern. He acquired sages, books: but – paradises fall. They left me nothing but the hogmouth,' and Flavio peers at him. 'Yes,' he says. 'The overslung jaw, that's all they left you? It must be tough eating.'

Max the first, says the plinth. This guy is covered up, no Greek problem for him, it's a whole protective coppery suit, as if he's been to the moon and back.

'I'm a copper engraver,' says Max. 'My father was one and he wanted me the same ... so I'm not only the last, I'm the one after the last.'

Nothing to say to that. 'We have this problem,' Max says. 'These wars, the instability – it's the pre-moderns. They pull you in – it's like you clamber out the pit, and these guys fasten on your pantlegs, and there's carnage, survivors knocking on your door and camping in your orchard.'

'I've heard that,' says Flavio. 'There must be more to it all...'

'Oh yes,' says Max. 'There's much more.'

The border's closed ahead. Flavio and Max – neither has a document to get them through. The driver lets them down. 'Don't stray,' he says. 'Stay where I can see you.'

'You won't believe this,' Max says laughing. 'The only Inn round here's a river! We'd better run and find a place to sleep.'

They do just that.

Missing Beata is no use at all.

'See where we have landed,' Max says, reading from a tattered book. '"Primitive hill-tribe...they are short, brown, straight-eyed, lank-haired and medium-headed, cultivators of Austro-asiatic type, speaking a Non-Khmer dialect." Well! I bet the author didn't expect they'd read about themselves. My ancestor, Max, he put them all together – Dutch and Czechs – bequeathed our tolerance. Though – with all the sun we get, these Austro types'll be more black than brown. I told you – it's the pre-modern legacy, can't shog it off. Now – let's eat some apples, they're the best, second to pomegranates only ... and sleep, and hope the primitives don't chase us off...'

He eats some apples without difficulty, sliding his hogmouth from side to side.

'Didn't your family leave you anything else?' asks Flavio. 'Besides your mouth? I know that lots of you were, as they say, quite natural children...'

'It's not an insult, Flavio,' says Max, offended. He takes white silk pyjamas from his pouch and puts them on behind a bush. 'Sleep!' he says. '"The peoples are all one."'

'Maybe the book is out-of-date,' says Flavio.

'Books aren't like eggs,' says Max sleepily. 'They don't go bad.'

'This could be Eden...' Flavio says.

'Right! Let's get out quick,' says Max, cramming apples in his mouth. 'Before the alarm goes off. Good and evil? No – the evil part is stealing. That's what pissed off God. "Ignorance of the Law is no excuse." That's what's supposed to be written down, tacked up – but if you can't read, just speaking Hebrew is no good. Not knowing – it's no excuse for anything, Flavio. Suppose you know it all? And go out scrumping just the same? Pomegranates – they're the best, of course...'

He talks hot, strong. 'I have the answer, Flavio,' he says. 'Like the first Max – it's marriage. Better than a war, and just as risky. Make them intermarry, have a flock of kids. Even if they all have hogmouths... All the land is yours – you don't need dig, just raise the tax... God wanted everyone, the stupid sinners, to be married, middle class and moderate: ignorant too. And not too brightly coloured. I don't believe in any gods – forget the colour part, it's quite irrelevant. But now – it's me. I have the answer. The answer – it's for me as well! Or rather – I don't care.'

'I too had a big idea,' says Flavio, quite forlorn. 'Bigger than yours – didn't require apples, nor a god and law. My fortune would have been assured – though that's irrelevant as well. But you, Max – have taken convention to new heights. It's a bit old-fashioned...'

'Oh no,' says Max. 'You can have bastards. You don't pay a cent to anyone, don't remember birthdays – indeed, births and deaths don't count. You know it all goes on, there's no call for you to intervene, it's all as it was with Max the first, except... forget the family name. You understand, my friend. You're a smith, Flavio. Call them all "Kuznets". Everyone. None of this dynastic crap. All Russians from the steppe, heating the furnaces, shoeing the local breeds... Now! That's the thought: dynasties! – the horses, they will bear the names. They are the thoroughbreds... I fancy those Bashkirs...'

'I'm not sure,' says Flavio. 'My idea, it seems, was extravagant, but yours – so homely, yet – so strange. I don't know if I can keep in step with you...'

'Oh Flavio,' says Max. 'The palace of the mind! Only ever room for one, it seems. Those ladders – rickety. The dark storerooms full of mice and sacks. We must climb up, it gets windier, you see the bones of those who forgot to bring their food, the bottles the drinkers left, the wormy beams, the panels flapping off ... must we go higher, when there's cellars underground, musty, racks of good Bourgogne, Spohr playing on the systems...? No, we must climb up, lift more doors off the single rusty hinge – and, at the top, what, Flavio? The sky? Was it for that we climbed? You see it from the ground... The wind? The carpenter who stands above you? He swings his lead, saws at your hands, you cling, you scream, there's the drop, the fall, the void – and then, as you go down, your hands still cling to the top beam, and then you see there's rows of them, the severed hands...still clinging on...'

'Yes, Max,' says Flavio. 'That's it! That's the lofty palace. That's what Beata didn't want to see...'

'She's the clever one,' says Max, leaning against the bus-stop. 'She saw.'

*

'It could be a day the bus doesn't run,' says Max. 'Everyone who is awake would know. Most aren't, don't want to wake, not today, when maybe nothing runs – after all, after five hundred years, it's much the same – the clock, the sun, the earth, the day – all circular. The others, our sisters, brothers – they're afraid. They're right. It doesn't help. When you're afraid, vindictiveness results. You see, Flavio, the couple is the rule. Resentment at the threat is commonplace. The human domino – has two spots: it's useless except when there's another couple ... a Jack for a Jill, David – a Goliath. To make a six.' He contemplates.

'My idea – a sea, calmed under its sheath of oil.'

'That doesn't work,' says Flavio. 'I'm always afraid, but I've no enemy. I don't adhere, not for a day.'

'Yes,' Max says, 'I see you anxious to move on. Thinking you'll change – but you are just the same, always. Variations on one note.'

'I see the whole world, everyone. As if I'd climbed the tower. Me transforming – what would that accomplish?' Flavio asks.

'You guys – it must occur to you. No bus today.' Max and Flavio turn, a bit resentful. The new guy's obviously right, and helpful, up to an irritating point. There's no bus, and no one to know where it might be going to.

The new guy's tall and worn – most people with not much carry it in a bag, a big supermarket one, but this guy doesn't carry anything.

'I hear you chatting philosophically,' he says. 'Waiting for something that doesn't come. Expecting it, or to find a reason for it not... No – that's wrong. Something that won't come because it's not anticipated, not chance, not accident or strike or summer timetable – what's not there, requires no explanation, can't have one. Something not foreseen, negative or positive, might turn up – this one, it won't. Out of the world.'

'It says "bus stop",' says Max.

'Suppose it said "genocide",' says the guy. 'That ends up quiet, there's no one to complain. No one waits around. It's a one-off service.'

'That's extreme,' says Flavio. 'For sure, speaking philosophically, genocide will come along, wait long enough. Another stop... But – by definition – it's not like a bus, you can't get on it.'

'You could start,' the guy says, 'to redress. The thorough genocides – are unknown, save to the experts. Someone remains – even because of the classification...'

'There's no redress,' says Max. 'Once done, it's finished, over.'

'No one survives,' the guy says, 'so there's no one who has loss. Do you think there's no one?'

'That's how you're saying it,' Flavio says. 'You pollute the stream of discourse. The loss is there, even when particular people – they are not.'

'Yes,' says the guy. 'I think you're on it there. And even if it's not complete, but who's left, they can't, don't want, to have redress?'

'You mean punishment?' says Max. 'Other people taking up the cause? That's what may not happen, or you don't know what it means.'

The guy nods, 'The bus – not today,' and shambles off.

'Well,' says Max, looking at the pole, to be sure it just says 'bus stop', 'that was a good effort on our part.'

'I wonder, Max – you knew about the carpenter. D'you think that guy ... we should tell somebody?' asks Flavio. 'Perhaps – he knew about a genocide, and no one else, or else, that there'd be one... Well, everyone knows that... Is it worth reporting?'

'Maybe we should, if we could think what to say, to who,' says Max. 'It wasn't a confession. Just a statement. It's true – it leaves a space, a gap where he could do what he has done, or what he'll do, and tell us kindly too – how it's a waste of time, us standing here.'

*

'I must move on,' says Flavio. 'Hanging around here – it's quite whited out my head. You're primeval prejudice, Max...' he laughs, to show how he forgives. 'I'll take that little river boat...'

'That's it, the end,' says Max, laughing and looking relieved. 'I can't join you, the motion makes me nauseous.'

Shake hands? Hug? Smile? Adieu? – too pretentious?

'I didn't think it apposite to say when we were together,' says Max, 'but, Flavio, you've beautiful wrists ... harpist's wrists. If ever you should decide ... though it's a torment, hoisting up, scaling the heights, the weight if there's a fall ... you'll need special equipment... Oh! Your face! No, I'm not the carpenter!

It's only music, a compliment. The harp's no gift, it's leaden! I play the harmonium. We all did, at school.'

*

On a boat, you always meet some interesting people.

When you move around, there's threats, accusations, guilt – but less than if you had stayed put. Each comrade that you leave passes on – sometimes quite silently – part of their load of guilt, suspicion, and the rest. The good time had with them – that's done: now it's part of the kindling the storms leave on the ground... It's not a drama, usually.

*

A frontier – must have been crossed, or else it runs down the middle of the river.

There's a sign on both banks – 'Beware the People'.

EFFIE

He explains himself to Effie. The whole, the big, idea. She's not impressed, and Flavio's a crumpled presence. But – she's not unkind. She says,

'I see. A provocation. Species don't do things. They don't think and act – they evolve and disappear, that's all. But – you don't do anything, Flavio – there's lots you could. Stop being poor, that's the first step. Exploit your privilege. You think you have no side you can be on – maybe it's so. But – accept what you seem, and flourish it. Your plan though... All in the dark, you say, the species somehow exhorted to create the unknown: your big idea. You cretin! – it's globalism, I fear. The last, the highest stage of capitalism, imperialism without emperor. All together, producing the huge monument! More capital? A mausoleum? A kindergarten for the robots or the dinosaurs that come after us – a clinker desert?'

'I hadn't thought, Effie,' says Flavio. 'I thought I'd gone beyond all that, and was original. Now, I don't feel like joining anyone, besides, they wouldn't want me.'

'No,' Effie says. 'Your strongest point is being unreliable.'

'Liberation's occupation. The people's army puts you in a jail. And then there is religion. My unbelief ... is infinite. Unemployment too – I know about it...' Flavio says. 'I should have seen what's what.'

'Huh!' says Effie. 'You're a hard case. A Dacian? Roman? Dacians have a poor reputation – southerners!'

'Well,' says Flavio, 'that's what the northerners say.'

'My family has military men, religious ones as well,' says Effie. 'Commies and fachos, nats and internats. That's the advantage of having lots of kids.'

'I'm fascinated,' Flavio says. 'I knew on boats you met the interesting types.'

'You stand out, Flavio,' says Effie. 'Off-white, off-male. A natural visionary. I love you visionaries, hate your stupid visions: – all flawed, a bubble like a buboe in the glass, and of course, you all have peppermint bones, with "empire" printed through them. Me? I eat your brain, but I'm not sick with it – that's for the primitives. Those cells are fuel – you need the heat for making steel. You're a smith; you understand – that's good.

'I take you to a house, deep in the forest. It's all yours. Have a cookie! You'll love the taste of gingerbread – I coke it up a little, and you're hooked, you're mine. I fill your pockets with crinkly leaves, next day they're crispy dollars, printed in Lanzhou, good everywhere, and...' Flavio is looking anxious. 'There's no oven. Don't despair. Anyway, you have no little sister who'd join you in the tall baguettes I'd bake. The whole house is an oven, and you, my friend, you are the molecule that dances till it's all white hot. and when you're cooked, you sneak out, loving me, despising me but most of all yourself, and off you go: another forest, another house made of gingerbread, another visionary for me to bake ... to solve the problems we know all about...'

'I'm flattered,' Flavio says, appalled. 'Computers and stuff – I only work with things that's real: hammers, anvils, white horses and lost keys...'

'Suppose,' says Effie, digging her nails deep in his upper arm, 'some big poppy calls and says, "Effie! People are not wearing shoes – my profits ... help!"'

'But that's banal,' says Flavio. 'They do wear shoes, I don't care if everybody's naked anyway...!'

'Nor me!' says Effie, leaning over him, so he can see deep down her frock. 'But you might tell them, "When we ran through the grass, savannah time, we all wore wooden shoes with pointy heels, outran the antelopes..." so that's the message sent out to our fans ... there's happiness again, they all forget, and no one cares...'

'And you give people cash for doing that?' asks Flavio.

'Of course, there is more serious things,' says Effie. 'People write books about me – but my magic isn't what those guys believe. Not what I do, but what I am. It's all within me, here, on this boat, up and down between two continents, where one sea meets the other, the rivers join, the tigers swim – and guys like you give up your ghosts and I can put them in my safe, perhaps it's hid behind the arras, you'll not find it – with your documents, your IDs, and you search and search for where I've stashed your skimpy souls – but there is nothing, nothing more, only the cellophanes you yielded up, your useless doubles, exchanged for your real selves, sniff! sniff! – and off it flies, your animus, and up your nose it goes, stuck in your body where you hope it...' She chokes on the word... 'Nothing, Flavio. It does nothing. And when you die, back out it comes, and stands and howls with all the misty others on this bank or on that...'

'Well,' Flavio says, 'I need the cash, it's true... but I'd come with you only for the littlest while...'

The 'weight of a woman's dead body' he remembers. Best beware, like the sign says. Effie's a threat to him – and to herself as well. Not live nor definitely dead and walking round, managing the world...

'Of course, we deal with serious things,' says Effie. 'Take those Arabs – always undecided, always in a twist... Prayer or parliament, ammunition or astronomy ... a hundred years of war enforced, more to come, hotter still... The big mistake was bringing those black Turks in to do the dirty work … so, – ah! they forgot the fellowship of desert treks...! And Africans: the whiteys kept them poor so's when they'd had enough of killing one another, they'd sign up as mercenaries, off to somewhere far away...'

'You've a stark vision, Effie,' Flavio says.

'Maybe,' she says. 'But this is the soft part.'

'In general,' Flavio asks. 'What's the solution, then? What do you provide?'

'In one way or another,' Effie says, 'soldiers. That's the answer. When a thing is not resolved – you think first of technicality. I can't bear with that myself – all fiddly strings of ones and twos ... it's not for adults, that. I leave it to the littlest boys. No – as a smith, you know that if a frame goes out of true, you need employ the hammer and an iron bar. Soldiers – they are your pig's foot and the tongs. A few, then lots. It changes every shape, the next chapter starts from that: – the nationality is quite indifferent, though locals, naturally – those come cheap. But all in all, you off-white guys – you organise solutions best ... most thoroughly. Down the cellar steps, the oven in the forest, you show the way for Meister Death...You are the copy-book. Your robots, in their high-heeled wooden shoes – they'll stalk you in the desert, in the hills, and down main streets. It's smithing work, dear Flavio; and carpentry...'

'Oh, Effie,' Flavio says, 'I agree. The project stalled. My vision had a flaw: no one was interested. Who cared what it was all for; imperialism or eternal love...? The long term isn't interesting, not when the tram comes up behind, and down you go... Who wants their freedom when it's only on the bus you're free of party and of state, and someone you don't know is driving somewhere you might want to go...?'

'Yes, Flavio,' says Effie, 'we disagree on all the issues. You're my type. You get your pay each day you turn up, wherever that may be...'

'I'm unclear, Effie – though in all respects it's quite a deal – exactly what I have to do,' says Flavio.

'It's up to you,' says Effie, and she stops the boat, she takes him in her arms and jumps – on to the shore.

*

Solving problems – is easy. Effie comes round and takes away the answers. Flavio's house, deep in the forest, has everything he needs. Sometimes Effie is not satisfied. 'I'll see my other babes in the wood, what they suggest,' she says, and she is never irritated. She hugs Flavio, wears that loose dress, and never pushes him away.

The forest's dense, it's full of birds; small vegetarian creatures in their holes. 'It's better than a fantasy,' says Flavio, 'Because you know it ends.'

He can shout across to Lomeric – another guy who's solving problems: they're both paid each day, and – who knows – there's dozens, hundreds of other visionaries working in the trees, who've given up, gone mundane – their visions flawed, not followed, bearing encrustations, possibly, some reactionary pattern that must be scissored out.

Those big brown mushrooms, the marigolds, those red berries that cure anything, the bold wild pigs – my! they're tough ... It is a wonderland!

'I can't work this one through,' says Flavio sometimes: finding some contradiction, combination of opposites... and Effie hugs him then, and says, 'Hmmm. That one means soldiers, Flavio.'

'I wish you wouldn't tell me that,' says Flavio. 'It makes me think it's all my fault, although I know the cash comes from the soldier side...'

'All right, my dear,' says Effie. 'Puzzle yourself no more. No talk of soldiers. I'll keep schtum.'

*

'Let me ask you something, Effie,' Flavio says. 'We deal with problems medium to large. Suppose I pose one for myself – a Ukrainian lady, very willing, very poor. She struggled to keep three little jobs afloat. It's not exactly a problem, hers, but it always made me feel – not so much bad, as anxious. Like watching a conjurer, or a juggler who dares the air...'

'Yes, Flavio, seeing how you have this compulsion in yourself,' says Effie. 'Idling until the right job might come along for you – I understand your nervousness. But – suppose you had an acquaintance: in Niger, say, something bad to do with animals in his past, who has no cash at all. The drought, a sickness: contacts, family – all dead. That's even more extreme. And – no: it's not a problem we can solve. Your Russian lady – not a true problem. The other – it's so particular, it links to one much greater and more complicated... Maybe it's all just chance, like meteors. Consider, too – as a philosopher – the difference between "big problems", and "his" or "her" difficulties – which, frankly, you could remove or alleviate by some donation from yourself...'

There is a pause. Heavier and heavier... The birds are silent, there is thunder, even rain.

*

'You see,' says Effie, pushing Flavio out the house, 'your interest in the miniature – it does you credit, possibly. Take it, try and cash the credit somewhere else. You've switched your gaze. The mountain tops belong to me: to you, the swirls of dust below...'

She bundles up her papers: 'Soldiers', 'Disarm *those* soldiers...' you can see...

'The finish,' she says, 'this is it, poor Flavio. You're interested in the odds and ends, the questions not resolvable, eternal ones. The weight of your small mind, I fear, lies heavy on you. You've lost your sight, my dear.'

She buttons up her frock, stomps out: and Flavio will never see her, never more.

'Masochism, Flavio,' says Lomeric, and runs inside his house, double-locking windows, doors. 'That was the thing you shouldn't do – raise questions we are not contracted for. The everyday of slip and slide.'

'You're right,' says Flavio. 'I should have seen...'

'It's commonplace,' says Loméric. 'Life. Avoid the details. Everybody knows them ... all and every one.'

'Before you go,' Flavio shouts after him. 'Lomeric, I don't know any Ukrainians. There is no lady.'

'Effie says you want the soldiers, they'll come and set things as you'd like, then go away,' says Lomeric.

'All that's out of my hands,' says Flavio. 'It's not hypocrisy – you know my views on everything. That's it – they're views. They don't wear boots.'

*

'Species being...? Meaningless!' says Lomeric.

'All those problems ... some I solved,' says Flavio. 'But everything around seems much the same.'

'Your project, Flavio,' says Lomeric, 'gets closer and closer to fulfilment. But – you may not like at all how it turns out. It's not just you, who loses the perspective – Marx the democrat becomes the assayer of capital. Lenin does the most, the uttermost, so's to have anything at all to show. Some see, some cheer, and many suffer ... just so that something's left. A few years only... Suffering? Whoever told you that comes in – my! you were fooled, don't understand a thing about what makes what move... Suffer suffer, before and after – everybody suffers but some don't, and no one will, ever again, one day, the day when you eat goose, fat goose for lunch and breakfast, till there's no geese left. It's logic that deceives you, Flavio. We all appreciate your notion – building, all of us, the supreme masterpiece, maybe it remains when we have gone extinct ... a pyramid, great wall ... a Babel...

'Forget it, dig a hole, and share your bread.'

'Over and over – everybody sings that song...' says Flavio.

'No, no,' says Lomeric. 'I don't despair, I'm not without illusions. I'm Marx – all the Marxes. The harpist too. Lenin and Trotsky. It's just – I don't let on any more.'

'It makes your storytelling easy,' Flavio says, 'but it's not my tale. Anyway, people often get on well together, but mostly they can't get a grip on ideas. Or find new ones.'

'Let them have their heads, like Effie says, and guys like us will stop everything falling down at once,' says Lomeric. 'You didn't understand, Flavio – though I don't see you as a revolutionary, still less with a kind heart in reserve.'

'You empty out the context, Lomeric,' says Flavio. 'It's what you're good at...'

'I'm free, Flavio,' says Lomeric. 'Effie's in the past. I'm setting up my own. Come work for me, dear Flavio. Live in the forest, lock the door and listen to the wolves...'

'I see now,' Flavio says. 'I was wrong. My project – it was vainglory, a de Chirico landscape, quite *facho*. The high point – emerges as the end: where it all stops. Some achievement, that! But – yes, you're the past, dear Lomeric. Your problems, those you solve – it's snakes that eat their tail, turn inside out and then – they are the same but shiny, wrigglier still...'

'Of course,' says Lomeric, 'we're all immensely old. We've dino tufts sprout out our ears, our guts are full of nebulae – it's like they said, the journey of a thousand years starts with a single cell. Think millions, milliards of years. Of course I'm Hassan-i Sabbah, and I'm proud to be Queen Boran, Terken Khatun and Penthesilea too. It isn't dominoes, dear Flavio, two spots are not enough – those cells – they last, on and on, dividing through little bangs and parents various, back to the first big one, the copulation starting it all off, the orgasm that made the flying horse of Lanzhou, the bottomless Wall Street canyon...

'It will go on and on,' Lomeric pushes forward. 'It creates all sides. You choose your pals, but everything began at once, together, in the same instant, and goes on, every combination, option, contradiction… the same origin. The same end.'

'But,' says Flavio, 'we've already chosen, Lomeric, our side.'

'We engineer so it all sorts out and everything goes on,' says Lomeric. 'Like it would do anyway, though with more noise. You, Flavio, you're a smith: you know your piece of iron can end up as a shoe, an axle for the chariot, a prosthesis for the sage. If you stop, halfway, and leave it in suspense – you've half-unlocked it, like poor Célestine, still silent and garbled in the metal, an eye, a toe, winking, fluttering, waiting for the liberating blow ... making it complete, as someone had intended. That blow, you don't feel like delivering it ... the clang...!'

'I feel, you know,' says Flavio, angling for words, 'I do feel – contrasts. What you say is all a bit, well, odds and ends, Lomeric. Patching. Tailoring. It's how we'd not want to become.'

'Remember Effie's motto,' says Lomeric. '"Do no evil. Do no good." And then she wanted to put – "Sort things out", but the lawyer said that was too definitive. All she did, of course, was fruit of coming from a big family. You and I,' he says wistfully, 'we're at our peak, we contain everything, but ... we feel that – something lacks. Did I tell you, Flavio, you have beautiful hands...? Such a pity to spoil them, digging, as you'll be forced to do, unless...'

'I know about my hands,' says Flavio, 'smithing has coarsened them.'

'Ah!' says Loméric, 'smithing days are done. A step back – now, it's printers do it all.'

'You're really not my thing,' says Flavio, embarrassed. 'But – you know everything ... my friends, what's happened to them...?'

'Friends you don't know,' Lomeric says and laughs. 'That's idealism! A wish! Yet, you could be a new man, Flavio. People formed on the old schoolroom globe – born in the countries, now needed for the world, but gruff and greedy, crude and competent.

'The diggers? Oh, they're all gone. It's the new men – guys like Yann and Savarin, now sleek, well-oiled, they're on the rise. Effie's the passeur, she ferries people from the dead to life, life in the new, knowing how to spend and despise the useless stuff that's then delivered...'

'So,' says Flavio, 'the diggers...' And he recalls the dark muscular ghosts around a timid fire, 'Gone.'

'Maybe you don't value life,' says Lomeric, 'but I fear you need the numbers – not useful guys, but lots, quite indiscriminate. It all sorts out.'

'Oh yes,' says Flavio, 'I'm not a humanist, but I'm not *facho* either. There must be space for that ... a crowd...'

'If there is that space,' says Lomeric, 'you need to pep it up.'

Flavio doesn't ask about Beata – she's white phosophorus – your bone burns and tells you if she's near.

'Oh,' says Lomeric, 'she made her stand. And she was swept away.'

'That's it?' asks Flavio. 'That's enough, you think?'

'That's what you get. She was a martyr, not a virgin,' says Lomeric. 'If Effie wants an epitaph – well, "Neither virgin nor martyr she." A lie? You mourn her, but it's for an absence, void, so what you really say is: "It should all be different. The system's crap." A quiet cry of rage, that this is what there is. Everybody disappears. That's how everything can last so long. If they didn't, it'd be stuck: the eternal moment. No opera, no novels and no movies. Think of that, Flavio, what desolation! What else can you expect? Don't let it haunt you.

'Now, Flavio: think of yourself. Think gonzo. Think apotheosis, writing your name, like they used, in the sky, up there, along with all those cats that's out of time, and paradoxical.'

'The future?' says Flavio. 'It must be already here. The siren, listen!... The shout: "boarding now for Cythère!" The future? Well, you can think you know about it, or you can know you are already in.'

'You don't have much time,' says Lomeric, taking a jointed cane from his pocket, snapping it open to shoulder height, using it to hail a cab. 'That's always true, there's never time enough, even if there's thirty years. Effie's safe – she has all of us, her children. She's furious – her dying makes no difference, none at all. She reared us well – so we don't need her, we don't care she's gone.'

He's quite a dandy. Metal all over. 'Remember how the dinos got tired of picking guavas and farming raptors,' he says. 'Made the big bomb, ended their chapter. See how it all quickens up now! Intelligence – that's what does it. The universe gets bigger, but the brains are miniaturised. It's a curve, Flavio, you come back to the beginning, however far you've gone...'

He'll be missed. Here's the cab.

'People, Lomeric,' says Flavio. 'Everywhere. They're aliens. You don't need believe they came down from anywhere – they're all around, you see them being born and die. The sky's not part of it. I've no prejudice – but, they're absolutely not like me.'

'I know,' says Lomeric. He kisses Flavio, slides a gingerbread horseman in his hand. 'We all feel that, Flavio. It doesn't go away. It's not a sickness, so there is no cure.'

FLAMES

After Leningrad, no one expected to find so many sieges and so many survivors. It ought to tell something. Lucky Crusoe – you know he's an actor, or we couldn't read his script. It's a kind of siege, with a universal enemy. But there's nothing that could fall on him, except the foot of God, which you scarcely feel.

Nadine's always at the corner, waiting for her ride. Where she last was – they give confidences, but not intimacy – that's the best, if you take notes...

'It's desperate – at least, it makes me despair – the inventions, so many, so significant. So small, too, overwhelmed, in such a big heap, you couldn't load all of them on a cart,' says Flavio. 'Each changes life, then it all turns on and on the same. I might try writing something robust – like when I was with Roxanne, but I'm out of practice. That experience ... it lies on me like pudding. Write about Effie's children, they're all around, fixing everything. Or – if I had daughters, I could unlock them. That's a knack, a gift – Lear had it, but it did him no good. Oedipus – if he'd had daughters – they'd have been locked in for sure, and he could have turned their keys, 'It doesn't matter, doesn't mean a thing,' he'd say: 'There is no formula for having kids: just enjoy it, children, what you are.'

'You went to all those places, always on your own...' asks Nadine.

'Before they were spoilt, yes,' says Flavio. Nadine wants more, a sign she's being looked at. 'You have a talent, even if you don't get a part, you know,' he says. She projects, talks loud – might be a media fortune there.

'I have to get it over: my brother. How crazy he is, taking me to court,' she says. 'He cut up all my clothes and put them in a bag, left by the roadside. Burnt the house – or tried to. Animals inside, birds flying over... I have to sort that out. When I finish with him, I'd think of going somewhere with you, somewhere you recommend that is, somewhere you'd inspire.'

'I'm not going anywhere. I've been,' says Flavio.

Nadine says, 'You remind me... Of my brother – his doing nothing, weighed down by his big plan. Sitting beneath that twisted tree: chrysanthemums ... you know. Chinese aren't like that any more, not how they were when...'

'I don't want to be Chinese now,' says Flavio. 'I'm not, and couldn't be.'

'You're nothing else like that – not the old kind, or the new,' says Nadine, 'I could see you jogging somewhere – on a horse. No one on your back.'

'That's quite funny, if you hadn't meant it so,' says Flavio.

'Our rides,' she says. 'Bus, train, someone going our way – they never seem to come.'

'They came,' says Flavio. 'We weren't there yet.'

There's traffic, though. Columns of people – that'll have to stop quite soon. Columns are vertical, usually – unless they've fallen down.

'Oh no!' says Nadine, laughing, shrinking away – a pantomime – 'You're so like my awful brother...'

'What's behind him?' Flavio asks, not much intrigued.

'Oh, he wants to go to court, and call the cops. Destroy me. For cash, of course,' she says.

'It's not my scene at all,' says Flavio, turning away.

'I'm a child of Oedipus,' says Nadine. 'He was stupid or unlucky – but he lived for the body, its slips and slides, its stabs and fumbles. My brother, though – one of Goebbels' children, one who got away. The terror, Flavio!'

'I don't have a past, don't think about it, never have,' says Flavio. 'For me – it's work that's the great mystery. Once, it was a military thing – the worker was a little soldier, off to obey, in uniform. You stayed there till the trumpet blew, and you had won or lost. The victory? It never came – the bosses did the strategy, the fighting was all yours. But now – it's stay at home, no battle and no victory, no place d'armes, no drill – anonymity, except somewhere, instead of a society, there's capital, who gets in touch without a name, without address or calling card...it works you, silently. What do you produce? Who knows...? I didn't want to be a soldier. Now – I don't want to be a ghost...'

'You think a lot, Flavio,' says Nadine. 'If you didn't think at all, it would be just the same.'

'Well,' Flavio says. 'You're wrong, Nadine: a child of Oedipus – I thought you'd be locked in, and I could turn your key. But in your case – it's not the sexy part you celebrate, it's thanatos. You want to feel alive because you fear the end. Hope it's your brother's too...'

'At last!' shouts Nadine, climbing into a small car. They rocket off, she and whoever drives.

*

In an instant, another, similar, small car arrives. It's Pauli's, Nadine's brother – Flavio gets in.

She and her brother, Pauli, have a big house. 'This is the laird's house' says a sign. It's in dispute – neither she nor Pauli can afford repairs.

'It's easy to sort out,' says Pauli. 'My idea is – the past is an old frosted leaf, all crinkles – yet, it's father to the present. There must be similarity, you'd think. The future – is a green furled leaf. An egg, a cell. It will uncurl, in time go browned... have other leaves. It's someone's future, then it's someone's past – those somebodies ... in turn, are dead.'

'Careful, Pauli,' Flavio says. 'Don't be taken in – those rocketting cats, no one quite knows what state they're in...'

'Those historians, the diggers too – it's almost all a guess. The people who might tell – they're dead, or else alive, but only if you're in another galaxy... And yet – they're trusted. You must be,' he turns, looks at Flavio, earnestly, forgetting the road, the traffic, cops, all that... 'Historian of the future, as it were – but ten, no, twenty times as good as those old scruffy moley types...'

'I see,' says Flavio. 'It's a compulsion: the leaves...'

'Not only,' Pauli says, hitting a rock but persevering. 'It's notes too. Not that they're the sort you train to make a nocturne from – but they can save the house. See,' and they swoop up the drive, an alleyway of straggly, leafless trees – 'The house. The hole. It's fallen in so many times... Find the cash that Nadine knows about but not quite where it is ... the house is saved...'

'Tell me, Pauli,' Flavio says. 'You're not Scottish, but this – it seems – is called "the laird's house".'

'Oh,' says Pauli, offhand. 'Those Scottish kings. They went all over. Bred, half-bred, misbred.'

'Don't tell me the cash is Scots,' laughs Flavio. 'Then – leave it where it is!'

'It's cartloads,' Pauli says. 'If it's worthless, still it will fill the hole. Nadine won't touch it, so...'

Indeed, the house is teetering.

*

'It's too late,' Nadine tells Flavio that night. 'The house – it fell. Fell in. Now, the house is us.'

'Pauli...' Flavio says.

'I love him, of course,' says Nadine. 'He's not around. What can he do? I ought not have got into the car, the other car – it seemed familiar. A terrible thing – it all fell in on me and keeps me quiet.'

'There's nothing I can do,' says Flavio.

I know about holes and shoring up, he thinks. It's trivial, it happens all the time. They say it's crust we walk on – it's close... it chimes – it's dust.

'It's drastic,' Flavio says to Pauli. 'Now, you can't see the house. That search – it's over. Now you know all: – too late. But – the avenue of trees. That can be spruced up.'

'We still have to search,' says Pauli. 'It isn't over, even if there's nothing left. It's the indemnity. We borrowed...'

'You've nothing – at least, not much,' says Flavio.

'Oh,' says Pauli. 'If we find it, there'll be enough and more for everyone. It's all in the title. And the soil.'

'I guess you spent the loan,' says Flavio. 'I'm not interested – you're bad partners. The story's shaky too.'

It's true – Pauli and Nadine are heavy – you can't imagine which would be the best for them or you – that Pauli cuts up Nadine, or that Nadine hires someone to cut Pauli up, leave him in bags beside the road.

It's like incest – they say it produces suffering, but so does almost all the rest. Maybe Pauli and Nadine, they had a try. Geographically, it seems the simplest thing.

'The house,' says Flavio. 'There's an easy way to solve the hole it's in – you prop it up with girders that a smith can make, slid under like a web, or else you dig around, and so, instead of falling in a pit, it rests into a declivity. Though – it's all quite useless, since you can't live in the house together through hostility, and neither one will let the other live there all alone...

You're at the end, you two – whether the house falls or just rocks on the edge of the disaster – it's the same...'

He talks, but Pauli and Nadine don't hear a word... They have a friend, young Ariane, and Flavio thinks, quite suddenly, how he would like to walk with her, like in the poem, under the lime-trees, she in the Sixties clothes she wears and makes and sells – 'The Sixties, Flavio,' she says. 'People were clever then, and innocent. After the war, before so many more!'

She skips, as if she's on a path between tall trees.

'The music!' says Ariane. 'How they strummed those songs, and loved their plangent words! Who can forget! Remember the documents ... "this cannot in any way be thought to be a document on life in Hong Kong, the British territory" – as it was in that time ... everywhere was empire still, and surely, you remember how it ends, "And there is nothing in his eyes" – oh, how I'd like to end like that,' she says, squeezing Flavio's arm, and turning up her monkey's face towards his own, delighted gaze, '"And do you know there's other people in this house called Chang?" what depths! Excitement!'

'Yes, from the book under review,' says Flavio.

And you see that she is thrilled, excited, to be taken into this strange tale where everything is labelled and familiar, but does not exist, does not resemble in the slightest what you think it should be like.

'Clever and innocent,' Ariane repeats. 'After the war, but before so many more!'

'I have neglected clothes, and all that they can tell,' says Flavio, sniffing at her leather shoulders – it's called a bomber jacket. 'That little top, with nickelled zips, pockets aslant – trapezoid closets, all too tight to have inside anything but you, dear Ariane.'

'Oh yes!' says Ariane. 'Those times when sages were still sage, Chinese were Chinese. And we could go inside the house – full of music, people well-disposed and leisurely, smooth-skinned, eager to share themselves with us...'

'For sure,' says Flavio. 'They didn't need a project then, a strategy to save themselves – they'd shaken off the weight – what happened to them all, dear Ariane? Withered and crabby even then, our disappointed grans and granps?'

'No, no,' says Ariane. 'They don't grow old, we'll see them as they were, they are, fresh off the press... Take my arm, Flavio, we'll walk among them, they won't see a trace...'

*

'There's diggings under everywhere,' says Flavio. 'Those people – what use, to stock them underground? No profit, and no purpose. All emptied out, abandoned. On the move! Adventure! So, then, the stuff on top ... it tumbles down.'

'An answer, a solution's rare,' says Pauli. 'But Ariane, the spider, expert with her threads – has worked it out: that's what the house is for! She'll bring in sages, the very latest, or the very last – set them up. A workshop! Bags and brogues... sewn underground...'

Ariane takes Flavio aside – 'There'll be the upstairs – just for us, and for those who have the beat, and dress the street... Freedom, Flavio...'

'I'm not sure,' says Flavio. 'Doesn't it seem aimless?'

'For you, my dear,' says Ariane, 'But not for me.'

'It'll all be period stuff,' Nadine says. 'All hetero, given the dates. The profit's made downstairs, but in the attic, the view's all green – that part's above ground – you can see the grass, the leaves, the trunks – there, you find the *pochettes*, Ariane's specials, her exotic birds, their *griffes* stuck in your back; poor Flavio ... what pain, what pleasure ... the house that Ariane keeps...'

'I'm not sure it's quite me,' says Flavio, backing off. 'I had in mind a park – a sanctuary, antelopes and zebras...'

'Those things,' says Ariane. 'Don't know how to enjoy. They run, is all.'

'No one enjoys, today,' Pauli says. 'They love to see each other run, though: faster and faster. Sex, Flavio, is rooted to a spot. Ariane – would start it off again, taking it back wholesale, a house of appointment with the past, spring chickens in their knocking shop...'

'Oh, I don't believe in authenticity, of course,' says Flavio. 'But if anyone has it, then the beasts...'

'No, no,' says Ariane, 'no, absolutely. No animals, of any kind, especially the large and fierce. Besides, in that epoch, the Sixties when we explored, and colonised, and we were free – before it all went wrong – we ate the creatures, shot them, stuffed them. No experiments now, Flavio, no cat-box, no rat-box, no monkey-puzzles – ugh!'

'Everybody runs, Ariane,' says Flavio. 'Some to get away, some to run you down, give you pain, hurt you and in the end – eat you all up.'

'That's just it,' says Ariane. 'The animal – is a hunter: and – the hunter – he's an animal. The pain – of hunger, the pain of being run down, savaged, eaten, eaten right up...It's coming, so – I want it now. Foretasting, Fulvio – I'll show you how.'

She loves him? Certainly, there's an attraction...

'Oh, pain and suffering,' Pauli says. 'It's not so simple. You could spend an evening with it! Sex is over in a minute. Pain, chronic pain – signals your finitude; having some creature, unmerited, on your back or in your gut, quaffing your blood, nibbling your liver... Your teeth, Ariane – they don't get well, improve: they're never cured. Best be rid of them, as soon as they appear – they bode no good at all. Sex, hunger – just the same – away with them! A blow-out, an orgy – a radical extraction... Sale! everything must go!'

'Maybe Pauli's right,' Nadine says. 'Sex, imagination, freedom – yes, those all went wrong: maybe from the start, it wasn't right. The design – a fault inherent, a fail-safe, self-destruct... pleasure and pain – the two sides of a knife blade, joined in its edge... The search for pleasure – the greater is the pain of getting, not quite getting, losing, needing more – and so you crave the bane, the dope, the booze, the demerol, to get you through...'

'Oh Nadine,' says Ariane, laughing, 'of course you're right, and all the rest who'd said it from the start were also right – the priests, the oracles, the guys in rehab, everyone is right! Who wants a little purse to fumble with and spill all over, when you can have a shoulder bag that holds just everything, beauty, truth and even justice:...? Shoulder arms! In the bag! Left, right, leffrigh, leffrigh...' She struts up and down the room.

'And I'm the monster in your attic,' Pauli laughs, rolling on the floor, fooling about.

'Oh, I know you, you devil,' laughs Ariane! 'I can handle you. My fear lurks in the park – the grass is full of monsters... What I need is soldiers – there are people in the forest who supply. Security, so's everybody's tucked inside and dry.'

'It's very late,' says Flavio. 'Though, I must say – I haven't suffered, not a little bit. I might even see dear Lomeric again.'

'Good times mean you get to see them all,' says Ariane. 'The friends you left behind. Good times they were, there must have been, when they were all around, so close you never had a good appreciation of them.'

She's tipped the mood. They all think dark, of people they will never see again, who won't remember even if the time they spent together was a drag.

'...waiting for it to happen to us,' says Flavio. 'Not that I care about so many people, not Pauli, for one. Is it politics? Not the good sort I have in mind, the sparring with Max, and with Lomeric. Politics is in it...the tough kind, not the poster sort. It will be more drastic than you've ever thought, or seen upon your screen. Why? What did I do? What contributed? Not my money, certainly, not my food, or the employees I've not had and wouldn't have.... I've even moved around, so it's not where I'm dug in... But it will come, what you fear, the end of your old happy self: it's happened before, regular through the centuries, and that's when there were projects too, a bit ridiculous, when it came to taking sides – as if you could ignore the postcard when it came... The muster! This time, though – no postcard.'

'Yes, everybody knows that one day – it will come,' says Pauli. 'That's why we're as we are. Worse than you'd expect, because it will leave a life of memories, bad memories. While it is happening, mostly you come through. It's the forever after.'

'The waiting – it's quite like a project,' Flavio says, trying to spin a joke.

'We all have projects,' says Pauli. 'And yours – you got it wrong. The species doesn't have a project, it doesn't build a monument to itself. It becomes aware. It's consciousness. It already has that – it doesn't need us all to realise ourselves... Only us have minds inside our brains.'

'I know,' says Flavio. 'Everyone tells me that. Consciousness? Don't be snide. You have it, that is all, like quills or rattles. That means, then, that we are whatever we are now. Not equality, which would mean a real inequality, variety: super-cool, creative. No, just as we are, this minute. Like the wolves.'

'No,' says Ariane, 'it's none of that. We don't have elite destinations, resorts like paradise, payment only with your card. Games – that's our invention. Initiative is frocks and bags.'

'Oh, I agree,' says Flavio. 'Wearing outré clothes makes you freer than taking them off.'

'You're drab, Flavio,' says Ariane. 'Don't think of rescuing me. And – I love wolves. Might they love me?'

'I can't answer that, Ariane,' says Flavio, sounding like a prig. 'We could put some in the garden, in the park, that is.'

'Oh,' she says, 'I'd sooner they just strolled in. Being delivered somewhere in a truck – it's not a human thing.'

'There's your monster, Ariane,' says Pauli. 'A pack. Howls.'

'Oh,' says Ariane, 'sometimes a rescue's worse than being eaten up. You get tired of running – just surrender, then you are the chop.'

'It's "for the chop",' says Nadine, 'though I agree...'

'Rescue?' says Flavio, absently. 'I've never needed it. I'm alpha quality...'

'Well,' says Nadine, looking round and smirking, 'maybe we could test all that. Make danger – then you see, who chooses rescue, even if it's worse. Like – getting in a stranger's car, quite by mistake.'

'Let's examine Flavio,' says Pauli, nastily. 'A guy pontificating, but who's never read the book, or thought. Pushing us towards a mirage. Let's see if he suffers ... and how much.'

*

What test do they have in mind? They're all quite keen, and Flavio ... trembles. Everybody, nearly everybody, would. Even dear Ariane's decided – Flavio's a loser. What, then? Never say you're wrong, you won't get to play the part, and get the punishment. Abandoned somewhere, like a Crusoe? Put in the hole? Made to forge girders, shoring up the house, the Rising

Sun? That logo, on your pants ... 'assiduous frequenter of cat-houses...'

*

What a lark – tied to a tree! You know there's no wolves around, but you can hear them coming near... The room you're locked in – the hunger. There's no monster, but you hear its hooves above...

The white-hot brand – confess who you belong to... They castrate the weaker ones – a niche trade in dried pizzles ... sheeps' eyes and testicles, with pimentos and vinegar...

*

'It doesn't make you stronger,' says Nadine. 'The stress – locked up or on the move. That's not wanted, not at all. It's your finitude. All the time now that you live – you are aware of it. There is no other lesson. That's it. Forgive us, or not. Shake all over – or forget it all. Who cares? Punish us? What does that change?'

'Everyone comes out of it quite bad. I had my side, I stuck to it – you don't change that,' says Ariane. 'Besides, it isn't in your hands.'

'Off you go, Flavio,' says Pauli. 'We're tough. Not at all your sort.'

*

The lover locked in a tree. What a starting place! What an *Aufbruch* you can expect!

'I'm always ready to love,' says Flavio, soliloquising. 'It doesn't fit. Even if I heat it up and hammer it.'

Pauli, Nadine and Ariane – they make the world small, as small as inside the iron maiden. Maybe it's how it is, thinks Flavio, but it's too trivial for me. My white friends – bland as junket, or *facho*. They tortured me. My other friends – they have shields made of their skin, and passports no one wants.

Where are they all? What were they?

*

'These slow trains!' says the stranger. 'I've lost count of the stops.'

'Don't you have a name where you get off?' Flavio asks. 'Or a number only?'

'Oh yes!' says the stranger, laughing. 'But – look at these poor fields! It hasn't rained this year. They're good for nothing. The people burn the forests here so's they can build – but with the drought, no one will come, not to live, or work. It's the end for them...'

It's true: there's a biblical desert here. Everybody's moved up north.

'I'm much older than you,' says the stranger, Antony. 'So I can ask – what do you do?'

'I wander, I suppose,' says Flavio, unforthcoming, 'on the Earth. I'm curious.'

'Never found a spot. Never found anything you could do and stay...' Antony says.

'Oh no,' says Flavio, irritated. 'I do many things, all well. And I stay long enough in places to leave a mark and do an excellent job.'

'Well,' says Antony. 'You've had a tumble.'

'Oh, some friends,' says Flavio. 'A joke gone wrong. They were too sensitive,' and he shifts a leg so's it won't hurt.

'Me?' asks Antony. 'I'm not at all like you. I wander. I stay in places long enough to see I must move on. I try many different things, I see how they are one: I can't manage it, to stick with them. They go wrong, don't lead to more of the same thing. I'm lucky, though – my values are intact.'

'But you have a lover?' Flavio says. 'Everyone has one, who's not good at anything else.'

'Yes,' says Antony. 'It's a nest of paradoxes you have there. I come from round here. And you?'

'We're all in the empire,' Flavio says. 'I'm a Dacian, you'd say, but from up north, as far as you can go.'

'The police?' says Antony. 'They take almost anyone. Industrial espionage? For you, gigolo would be difficult. There's Africa, but you don't look the part – even the Chinese don't seem Chinese like once upon a time. Don't despair. You could leech on a woman, if you can be hetero – though even that is hard these days.'

'Really, Antony,' Flavio says. 'I wander because I'm talented and curious, not a loser, not at all.'

'You'll find that we're all curious,' says Antony. 'Oh no! I think we passed my stop two, or maybe three, ago.' He lets his mouth drop open, pantomime, self-mockery of a sort... 'We'll get off here – I'll show you round my house.'

They walk and walk down unpaved roads, past huts and houses. Here's a large one, ornamental stucco, barley sugar chimneys – grander than Ariane's. 'We'll climb in here,' says Antony. 'A window's quieter than a door, it won't disturb...'

There's no one: 'She's in a huff,' says Antony. 'Gone off to amuse herself.'

'Antony,' says Flavio, when they've quaffed and eaten. 'Your initials – they aren't in the stucco. You say you're Antony from Chad...'

'I'm from Chad,' says Antony, 'but I got the name Antony from a movie about spies – the head spy got off with a beautiful older woman, probably a spy herself. That's why my name isn't in the stucco, but my name's still Antony, don't you think?'

'There's a philosophy behind everything you do,' says Flavio, quite drunk. 'I can sense these things.'

'This house,' says Antony. 'Like others in the area – I'm pretty sure, the fruit of orgies, themselves fruits of slavery, of laws and rules oppressive, and treks...oh yes, treks, under guard, and fleeing from the guards. What d'you say? Does it seem moralistic? Should I show more sympathy? To everyone? To architecture too? Or – should we burn it down?'

'Your lover?' Flavio asks. 'And it's yours...!'

'All true,' says Antony. 'Though it's in my lover's name. But – what the fuck? You can't own someone, let alone a mansion, for a bit of sex, a lumpy bed, that rough Rioja...'

'Maybe we could throw in some religion,' Flavio says. 'If you have some. Yes – let's have a blaze! A sacrifice! A quantity of evils to be exorcised. I'm sure Chad too – has its grievances... Burn down? Blow up? Maybe both those, simultaneous...'

'All of that,' says Antony. 'Another bottle of the red, and then ... up it all goes!'

They dance around the house, its black windows don't blink, the locked doors – not a flinch. The sky invoked – you see a powdering of sparking stars, like the gunpowder dust they haven't found yet, that twinkles when you stamp on it with iron-shod boots ... and round they twirl, and shout and sing.

'I've one regret,' says Antony, 'that we're both drunk, and you, Flavio, are further gone than me...'

'Oh, I love the fire,' shouts Flavio. 'The purity! The retribution...'

'I have a regret, dear Flavio,' says Antony. 'There's no one here but us...'

'Oh,' says Flavio. 'I'm glad. There's no one needs to run – it's us instead who frolic – dance ... and sing...'

'I have some more regrets, dear Flavio,' says Antony. 'That there is no one here that sees this as a punishment, and suffers... And I regret as well – there's no one here that knows our case, argues with us, so we can win. And I regret – that this old house has no intent, no will, it's just a product, an insentient symbol. And I regret – that it will burn for all the wrongs done formerly, but not for those done everywhere today, by those who have inherited the past; and all those horrors in the future too... The path, dear Fulvio ... we clutter it with black, with smoking beams and crumbled ornament. The smoke, miasma, cinders, soot ... all's dark ahead, my friend...'

He weeps. Flavio has found a barrel of dark stuff, granular, down in the cellar, underneath the better bottles, the reindeer sausages that drip like nitro sacklets, sweating and degraded...

'Justice!' shouts Flavio. 'Purification! And the road is opened up... Everybody suffers, everybody's guilty, and inadequate...'

They want the barrel to explode out in the open, for aesthetic joy – but that would not avail, not touch the house. The powder has to stay down there, down among the luxuries, the expensive hoards – to flex its shoulders, heave up the pile and drop it down again, breaking the frame asunder, the wood, the plaster, travertine and peperino, marbles red and green, and o! down go the chimneys, the roof beams and the cotta tiles...

'Alas,' says Antony, 'dear Flavio. You're trivial. You haven't understood a thing.'

*

'This is my cabin in the woods,' says Antony. 'My pond.'

It's dawn, the pile still smoulders. 'They'll be after us for terrorism,' he says. 'It's right. This strikes terror, it is sacrifice and purity.'

'But it was yours,' says Flavio, sobering.

'That often happens,' Antony says. 'I'd use that as my defence. But when a cause is just – it happens that enthusiasm takes your hand, it jogs – you put too much in, of this or that, and Bang! The point is this – our aim, and our commitment – those were clear. But now – it's true, there enters in the blur and blot. The servants chained, overlooked – you're quite indifferent, you have no animus against them, but – they're your collateral, the Americans say. They guarantee you'll have your hunt, the dogs of war – they're on your heels, here comes your "view halloo", your "gone to ground", then – in at your death.'

'Oh Antony,' says Flavio, shaking, his bladder quite unsure and on the brink. 'It's not my thing at all, I was your guest. And lo! an error, some fireworks in the atrium, and up it blows... Playing with fire – where does that lead?'

'We know quite well,' says Antony, laughing. 'Where it goes next. And – maybe my title wasn't sound. Maybe I mistook the house for quite another place... You enter your new habitation in the quietest way, then maybe they try to chase you out, complain at all your parties, the golden oldies played quite loud, Black Forest cake smeared on the walls...'

'Remember, Antony,' says Flavio, recovering control. 'The suffering. More, so there shall be less. And if we two go in the hopper, end, ground up like fishmeal – well, our gesture's made. Justice, that bald predator in its black doctoral robes – strolls up the aisle, checks the scaffold's trap, the knot – brings down the axe, slams shut the iron maiden...'

'Yes, yes, Flavio, all that,' says Antony. 'Now, dear friend – a counsel: do we run or hide?'

'I rely on you, my friend,' says Flavio, quite at a loss, quite out of depths, and Antony says,

'Then – we split up,' and off he goes, shooing away poor Flavio, who runs after him, his only friend...

'Enough! I won't be an accomplice, Flavio,' says Antony. 'Anyway, you don't believe...'

'It seemed a plausible thing,' says Flavio. 'I trusted you – it's politics, not philosophy, of course...'

*

'Chad,' Flavio thinks, 'if that is where he's from – a complicated place, and yet ... he seemed to be my friend, aware exactly of where friendship sometimes leads, certain of his actions, too... All planned, intended, calculated...

'I'll overlook the episode – my part, at least. We're all complicit, when we know, suspect – the soldiers stationed everywhere, what they do's done in my name. You can't withhold your name, even if you move around, and try to change it – it's still done in whatever name you use. People I don't know – what they do, in the air, by list, or in the cell – all, everything, is in my name. "Off with those guilty heads! Bury the murderers under the cotta tiles, the beams!" – if there are innocents, they're ignorant as well, pure dumb symbols like the spots on dominoes, this morning having their first snack in paradise. And as for Antony – maybe an angel with a flag had touched him on the shoulder, said, "behold..." then said what angels say, and end "don't disappoint us..."

'"*Majnun*", Antony had said. 'You're intoxicated, Flavio. I'm infatuated. Hear the music! The song the lovers sing!'... and he disappeared, up, or off, he went ... I sobered up. It's not my world: the absent lover, in a huff. The house, its absent owner ... you could find a use for it. A habitation for those without... Too late now, all gone. It can't be all, this endeavour, this slim monument, we're cleverer now... Knowing it's too late – that's clever too. Where you are, it makes you want to burn it down. You can wander, you can stay – it's usually a poor place that you're in. What's the difference anyway, if there's travertino staircases?'

*

'Your khaki undershirt,' says the big guy. 'The smell! It's like my commodity, the cheese my sheep make, and I sell for them!'

'It's nerves,' says Flavio, taken aback.

'Oh no! Maybe – oh yes!' says the guy. 'It's homey, though I see you're suffering. I'm from Khovd – a complicated place, although you'd think because it's so remote to you, it's just the first men live there, settled, homogeneous. No, it isn't so, but – I can grasp your thought. When we move around, we pick up things you can't wash off. It could be cheese. It's primal.'

'A niche?' asks Flavio. 'Folklore? Food snobbery? You're into these?'

'Oh no,' the guy says. 'I invest. Invent. You need do things much faster than the rest. That's how you keep ahead of them.'

'A gadget, then, a machine, a line of scrip...' says Flavio.

'Let me reassure you,' says the guy. 'If you wonder why you did it, that unspeakable thing, the marvelling's why you did's a guarantee they won't suspect you, won't follow you, won't ever catch you. You can start again. You're clean, and worthy of respect.'

'I'm relieved,' says Flavio. 'Really.'

'Claude:' says Claude. 'And this is Jeanne, she's with me. And – no, I don't ever see the sheep. I'm in the middle of the deal.'

'Oh Flavio,' says Jeanne. 'They'll never catch you, look for you – why, just looking at you – you're as good as toast. Beyond suspicion.'

'Do you have a special power, Jeanne, to see all that?' asks Flavio.

'No one does, Flavio. There are no special powers. It's true, some people run faster than the rest. But – we're good people, Flavio. Trust us,' she says.

'Commerce, investment – those make me suspicious,' Flavio says: 'Animals...'

'It all starts from them, Flavio,' says Claude.

'We sell everything,' says Jeanne, to comfort, sniffing at Flavio. 'And we're good people – it's our friends you have to watch. Everything, we sell: the milk of kindness, tax, debt – people, if they want... So, of course, we know everything.'

'They say the *passeurs* – will be buried alive,' says Fulvio.

'There's much much worse than that,' says Jeanne, cuddling him. 'Being buried dead, for one.'

'You're lovely people,' Flavio says. 'Wherever you are from. But – now I'm on my track again – I don't want more people. I've seen them all, they are my bricks, my breeze blocks, my four-by-fours. What escapes me – is how to stack them up. Nothing fits... Enough!'

'Oh that's just old philosophy,' says Jeanne. 'Paris – you may have heard of it – my old town, is full of it – philosophy. Prepare, dear Flavio, a hammer, and a trowel – make those big piles of brick and stone, abandoned in the countryside – the Romans made them, that's how they're remembered.'

'Some *koumiss*, Flavio?' Claude suggests. 'Make us all homesick?'

'Oh no,' says Flavio. 'I never drink.'

'What have you learned?' asks Jeanne. 'From everything you've seen. Except, much you didn't do – you've never been a judge, a shaman or a general...'

'Oh, I've nearly been all that,' says Flavio. 'I know that everything is knowable. And I know nothing – no general principle ... that was what I wanted. Nor how the little things work, and why. I have no scale.'

'We have that,' says Jeanne. 'Value, as expressed in price. Fixed by who wants it.'

'Emotions, satisfactions, aspirations...' says Flavio. 'Those skitter up and down. They're not always there, and then they disappear, come back in new gowns and gaiters... Priceless? Beyond evaluation...'

'Elastic? So's pork bellies and steel angle-irons,' says Claude. 'That's the principle, you plot them. That's what knowing everything means – metaphysics, for example. It has a price – not in currency; today, there's an indication, index, of its value... It's like with people – how much is Ludivine worth, what price for her? Easy – she's a wage slave, all's written down. Beata? If the roof fell, nothing – she's a liability. You'd have to find a hole. Of course – as a collector, she has for you a value much much higher. You're a connoisseur. Take those first Mickey Mouses, or a statue with its arms and penis lopped – pretty zero, you would say... But – no! You need know that too, sought after, prized...'

'We're not shopkeepers, Flavio,' Jeanne says, quite kindly. 'When, how, will it end? Should you try again, cap it off, realise your project? Open questions... It's up to you, of course.'

'How come you chanced on me, here, on this platform,' Flavio asks. 'Seeing me in a divided state?'

'Oh, we love slow trains,' says Claude. 'The slowest of all pass by here.'

'You did well by Célestine,' says Jeanne, 'though a clinician would dissent.'

'We're here to see it all,' says Claude. 'On earth. Every glimmer, every glint. If you're locked – you must be opened, completely – being fooled is not enough.'

'Here on the plain, you can see everything – the house, the tracks, the train, if it has set out,' says Flavio. 'But you two guys – your speeches – they are great, but much puffed up! No one could believe all that and rest their life on it, on you.'

'It's up to you,' says Claude, laying a prudent ear upon the rail. 'A train – or someone's hammering. What you do, Flavio – how your project fares – I just don't give a shit.'

'You might say that that's the message,' Jeanne says, laughing; and she kisses Flavio so tenderly, and wipes his nose. He weeps.

'This is not the real part,' he wavers. 'This is a weak moment, that is all.'

They sit in silence, dangling their legs towards the rails. Then, Flavio strengthens, says, 'Oh, I can't wait here! I'll get on much quicker on my own. I'll walk – it's always faster in the end.'

And so he does.

ABOUT THE AUTHOR

John Fraser has lived in Rome since 1980. Previously, he worked in England and Canada.

www.ingramcontent.com/pod-product-compliance
Lightning Source LLC
Chambersburg PA
CBHW020550310726
48979CB00008B/1156/J

* 9 7 8 1 9 1 0 3 0 1 5 3 1 *